THOMAS FORD MEMORIAL LIBRARY

3 130 00354 6645

W9-BSH-089

Monster:

The Story of Young Mary Shelley

M. R. Arnold

THOMAS FORD MEMORIAL LIBRARY
800 CHESTNUT
WESTERN SPRINGS, IL 60558

mango
PUBLISHING

Copyright © 2017 M. R. Arnold

Published by Mango Publishing Group, a division of Mango Media Inc.

Cover Design: Georgiana Goodwin

Layout & Design: Morgane Leoni

Mango is an active supporter of authors' rights to free speech and artistic expression in their books. The purpose of copyright is to encourage authors to produce exceptional works that enrich our culture and our open society.

Uploading or distributing photos, scans or any content from this book without prior permission is theft of the author's intellectual property. Please honor the author's work as you would your own. Thank you in advance for respecting our author's rights.

For permission requests, please contact the publisher at:

Mango Publishing Group
2850 Douglas Road, 3rd Floor
Coral Gables, FL 33134 USA

info@mango.bz

For special orders, quantity sales, course adoptions and corporate sales, please email the publisher at sales@mango.bz. For trade and wholesale sales, please contact Ingram Publisher Services at:
customer.service@ingramcontent.com or +1.800.509.4887.

Library of Congress Control Number: 2017951803

M. R. Arnold

Monster: The Story of Young Mary Shelley

ISBN: (paperback) 978-1-63353-651-7 , (ebook) 978-1-63353-652-4

BISAC - FIC014000 FICTION / Historical

Printed in the United States of America

For Linda

Endorsements

"M. R. Arnold has managed an extraordinary feat of fiction: channeling Mary Shelley so authentically in this richly researched, vividly executed rendering of the story behind the woman who gave the world *Frankenstein*, you could almost believe she had written this book herself."

—Jordan Rosenfeld, author of *Women in Red and Forged in Grace*

"*Monster* is a vivid, absorbing history, full of insight and compassion for the founder of science fiction, Mary Shelley. Like her Dr. Frankenstein, she created a monster... from Wollstonecraft to Lovecraft to Starcraft."

—Leonard Carpenter, author of the *Conan series and Lusitania Lost*

"Engaging from the very first page, *Monster* will pull you deeply into the life of the young Mary Shelly, a life both triumphant and tragic. Expertly researched and brilliantly written, this is one true story that will haunt you forever."

—Susan Tuttle, award-winning mystery author of *Proof of Identity* and author of the *Write It Right* series

Acknowledgements

Thanks are most certainly due to some wonderful people.

Susan Tuttle, who taught me how to write fiction, and the members of her Wednesday Morning and Afternoon classes for putting up with many scenes-in-progress.

Luanne Fose, for listening to me. You encouraged me to keep going.

Deanna Richards, for buying me breakfast. There were days when that was about all I had to eat. It is not too much to say your encouragement kept me alive.

Members of NightWriters, the premier writing club on the California Central Coast. They are the most supportive bunch of people an aspiring writer can know.

Harrison (not Ford) Grumman, who let me bend the ears of his company one night while I told this story out loud for the first time. Their feedback helped.

The Reverend Doctor Dale Vanderstelt, master story teller. The one about a monster in your lake appears here, nearly unchanged.

To my family for letting me work this out, especially my granddaughter Anna who has decided she wants to be a writer someday.

Jordan Rosenfeld, editor. You suffered through an early draft and made my work sing.

And especially Brenda Knight, who looked over my pitch letter and said, "Send me the manuscript." She put me in touch with Team Mango, who brought my book to print.

Author's Note

About a decade ago, I was working on my first attempt at a novel when I asked, "Where does science fiction come from?" On that day, I began this book.

A brief review of Wikipedia led me to understand that more than four thousand years ago, the Sumerians were inventing fantastical plots and characters. Four hundred years ago, Shakespeare had a Mad Scientist, but it was the fiction of the late seventeenth through the nineteenth centuries dealing with the role of science and humanity that is most often cited as the spawning ground of the genre.

One work stood out to me: *Frankenstein* by Mary Shelley. Among the many scholars and writers, Brian Aldiss (multiple winner of international writing awards) called it, "The first seminal work to which the label science fiction can be logically attached." When I learned the key ideas behind *Frankenstein* were the product of a teenaged girl, I knew I was hooked. I spent years of research and writing to find my answer.

As my research deepened, I started to feel like a detective who gradually begins to suspect that the femme fatale is playing him. It seemed, at first, like a straight-forward story—a college history paper. But when I pushed a little further, I began to suspect much of the information surrounding Mary Shelley was missing, censored: by herself, by her family, or by people with their own axes to grind. How terribly censored this woman's life has been, and continues to be, provides focus for my website and conference talks.

What I found as I researched called for a new perspective. Again and again I had to remind myself she lived in the Regency Period, not the Victorian. My rebellious years were spent in the Midwest: I was a teenager in the sixties, and I went to college in the seventies. It has been a while since such things as free love and alternative governments were general conversation, but for the enlightened philosophers, this time must have been like San Francisco's Haight-Ashbury neighborhood in the sixties.

As I continued to dig, I found even the most respected historians can present contradicting information. My background as a journalist and an academic researcher proved invaluable in choosing to include or discard information.

How bad were her very young years? They were like fairy tale stuff where the mother dies, the evil stepmother appears, the stepsister forces her to submit to her plans for the handsome prince. Which was bad enough, but then the story got very dark. I learned that if you look too deep, you'll hit muck. In short, the historical record is rife with real or strongly implied material for the prude to condemn.

When I was at the point of asking myself whether I wanted to go on, I started to wonder what it would be like to know these people. I kept wanting to hear what my characters were saying. I found Mary Shelley's writings to be alive with the type of detail needed to understand her and others close to her. Her journals and memoirs are so rich in her reactions to people and places, I felt I knew what she was thinking. These guided me in recreating the things that might have been said or thought in private moments.

What emerged was a serious, studious young person, but I wanted to know what made her smile, and that is where research failed me. It seemed no one had recorded an instance describing the sound of her laugh. In order to know her better, I decided to change my intended biography into a novel. I invented scenes that advanced the plot and expanded on individual personalities, but did not affect the main facts of her life. I gave her room to laugh.

At its heart, this story is about a young woman learning to write what she called her "little book." It was her first attempt to publish fiction, which she did, and with a London publishing house at that. Her book has never been out of print in the two hundred years since it was published. And she did it by the time she was twenty-one.

What I never saw coming was how much her story would affect me. I hope my readers will know her as a very young person doing her best to navigate an immensely complicated life.

As John Greenleaf Whittier writes,

> *For of all sad words of tongue or pen,*
> *The saddest are these: "It might have been!"*

Chapter One

I Begin

People often ask me how I, when still a young girl, came to think of, and to dilate upon, so very hideous an idea as Frankenstein's monster.

A dreary day at the end of the year of my fourth decade: as good as any for considering my actions and thoughts. The cause for my introspection? A third edition of my little book is to be published, and I have been asked to write a foreword for it.

The fire in my room burns low. Blue coal fire weaving toward the flue distracts me with its beauty. Its crackles echo the rain outside lashing against my windows, where I see the final leaves of autumn blow by in twisting flight. I sigh, enjoying the sensation of breath expanding my lungs, and, sitting in the worn rocker made of good English oak, I look down at my hands as the wan winter light falls soft on the thinning skin. Cold settling about my shoulders defeats my shawl.

Place me astraddle the dying of the Enlightenment and the birth of the Romantic Periods: a time of bloodshed when kingdoms fell and democracies rose, a time when French terror resulted in an unbridled ambition that nearly burned down all of Europe. In Britain, a nine-year regency bridges the insanity of one king and the coronation of another. Those years saw a hero named Wellington defeat the Emperor of France, saving Europe from the yoke of his reign.

A time of confusion and upheaval? Sans doute, but I remember it as a time when I was a part of a movement where we were sure the wisdom of thought had, at last, defeated all authority when all men would be educated so as to be responsible. We knew our minds would guide the societal structure of Britain and the world from darkness to light, resulting in refinement and cultural achievement. My father and mother were at the center of great thoughts. They called my father the Great Anarchist. My mother penned the Rights of Woman, *a companion to the American* Rights of Man. *My parents championed the idea of non-secular institutions from monarchy to marriage.*

I was married, and though I ought not be called a reluctant wife, I am inclined to think of the state of marriage as superfluous. The principle of free love, that is, to love without need of the approval of church or state, is dear to me. I am a mother who took joy in her children, though I have lost children also, and I grieve them. An authoress. No reluctance in that. But of all the subjects I could have chosen, that of my little book was as great a surprise to me as to anyone. Say rather it chose me, or say I had no choice.

Often I find I must remind people my book is not truth, but fiction. Long ago, a teacher, a Scot and one I should have loved better, gave me to know that while bald history presents a flat map with markings for hills, valleys, and fields, fiction imagines those bare lands as sparkling blue rivers, verdant grass-covered alpine meadows, and dusty roads winding through forests, letting us hear birds as we walk beneath the boughs. I've tried to live my life searching for what is true, occasionally finding it revealed by flashes of insight as a midnight thunderstorm lit by lightning.

If you are to understand me, you must hear of my mother who died when I was but days old. Though I learned of her through her published works, it was not until I read her journals and handbooks that I came to know, and love, her. Often do I contemplate what she must have endured to live as an independent woman, to think, to soar among the heights of philosophy and so encourage other women to live for themselves however they would choose. That idea was her gift to me.

Although his love for my mother was great enough to take both of her children to raise as best he knew how, Father, who knew so very many things, found the raising of two small girls surpassed his wisdom. And so, the man set about finding a replacement wife the way he approached most things: with his mind rather than his heart.

What he found suited his method. In her he saw a mother and a teacher, but to me she was a liar and a harridan. My stepmother was the reason for my lack of pleasant memories associated with our home. She arrived in my house when I was three years old and Fanny was six.

My fingers trace the letters on my mother's tombstone. "M-A-R-Y. That's me!" I cry as the letters make sense!

"She's but three." Father's voice caresses me. "Her mother was brilliant, also."

"Your daughter is growing to be a beauty," murmurs Louisa. "Remarkable eyes. Gray, I think, but with more than a touch of green to them." As my governess and my father walk home with me and my sister between them, we escape the shadow of a building and a slanting radiance of early morning catches me. "Oh sir, look at your daughter's hair. How metallic it shines in the sunlight!"

"Metallic? Hardly a description for my little girl."

"But it is. Fine spun copper and gold, I'd call it."

His head turns to the side as though something pains him. "She reminds me of her mother in many ways."

Another day and my father's voice echoes from the doorway. "There you are, Pretty Mary." And I turn to see him.

I would call him...imposing. A John Bull of a man of scarcely fifty years, more well-favored in his appearance than not (though he does have a large nose) but without the girth associated with most men of substance. Bald on top and dignified gray to either side. No need to mention that he enjoys the good repute of an elite intellectual community. To his detractors, Father is thought to be a *difficult* man, one tactless in voicing his opinions. Yet as I know him, he is one who places a high value on exactness and the importance of speaking truth, blunt speech or no.

At my smile, he enters the room and sits on the bed, patting his lap for me to come to him. I jump onto the bed, slide into his embrace, and kiss him.

How stiffly he returns my kiss. *Have I done something wrong?*

"What is it, Father?"

"I cannot hide a thing from you, can I?"

With my ear against his immaculate white shirt, I hear his voice rumble deep in his chest. "I've found you a mother! You've no need for a governess any longer, for your new mother is a teacher, one who will fill your mind and our home with her wit and thoughts."

"And where will Louisa go?" My voice trembles.

"Whither she will, as she must. You must not dwell upon a servant, Mary, for you have better now."

The woman sits in one of the chairs with red velvet cushions in the great room where Father holds salons. Short and stout with a round florid face, she's smiling as though it is a thing seldom done.

"Mary, Fanny, this is your new mother," Father says, holding our hands as he leads us to her.

Fanny's shy, but I say, "Welcome to our home, Mistress."

She blinks. "My home, Mary." She puts her hand on my shoulder. "Even as you are now mine."

"Kiss your mother." My father gently tugs me toward her. I falter two steps and put my face up. She lowers her cheek to me, I purse my lips and, feather light, touch them to hers.

I believe, for my part, I go to her full of good will and welcome, but I feel her flinch as my lips touch her cheek. Fan pecks at her, too. *There, that's done.*

Father says, "Now you two, kiss your new brother and sister."

The girl is in a white dress with lace edging at the neck, wrists, and hem and a pair of tiny black pumps. We seem to be of an age, or she is only slightly younger. Jane, for that is her name, bends slightly toward me that we might exchange a kiss of welcome. As she embraces me, she hisses, "You'd better be friends with me."

With my heart hammering, I turn to the boy. His name is Charlie. Older than me, dressed in yellow and busily picking his nose. He presses my lips with his, hard and long.

"Ah, look, Godwin," the woman says. "We witness a budding love between siblings." She grasps my chin and forces me to look at her. "Mary, you are fortunate, indeed to have such a brother and a new sister who will help me mold you."

Mary Jane Clairmont, a woman of modest achievement, a failed schoolmistress. She should have been gratified at the acclaim that would attach to her because of him. All of which might make a woman assure herself of the well-being of his progeny, yet she makes it plain my sister and I are beings to be suffered until we are wed and out of the house. What do I know of her reluctance to accept a marriage with so cold and indifferent a man as many perceived my father to be?

Her own children, however, are another story. I forget from what source I learned it, but her eldest child, Charles, and her daughter, Jane, were born out of wedlock. My stepmother had expediently, although ex post facto, altered their circumstances: in short, she clept the three of them with Clairmont's last name despite being a cast-off woman with two bastards. Having appropriated the name of the man who fathered her children, she pretended to be a model of motherhood in the same way she mimed the role of a caring human being. Other suitors, upon discovering her character, counted themselves fortunate to have fled.

In the interests of complete disclosure, I should admit I was spared a similar status by a matter of days. Despite his principled belief against marriage, when my mother lay dying after birthing me, the great love my father had for her prompted their marriage, thus ensuring the world knew she was cherished.

———————————————⋄———————————————

At a salon when I have but ten years of age, a time before I am thought fit to attend learned gatherings, I put into action my intention to secret myself behind the sofa and listen to the speakers. Unfortunately, I make the mistake of telling Jane.

"Let me come with you, Mary, or I'll cry."

Damn her. Jane designs her crying for the effect it has in getting her way. I grudgingly admit she's good at it, but the speaker this night is a special friend to Father, one seldom seen for many years. "Then hush yourself and listen," I tell her. "We'll steal into our hiding place as the guests arrive and wait until Mr. Coleridge reads."

With its ivory-colored plaster sheathing the walls and high ceiling reflecting light from lamps and candles, the great room is where adults meet to exchange ideas for entertainment. A place where men, in coats of black and blue and green with pantaloons of buff or yellow or white, flirt with ladies in long columnar dresses of white who flaunt bejeweled necks and ears. Tables covered with linen and supporting food and drink line the side nearest the kitchens. Overstuffed wide couches and chairs face each other, leaving a space for presenters to stand. Before our guests arrive, I pick a crevasse between one of these couches and the wall for my hiding space.

In the event, however, from the moment we creep under the couch, Jane threatens to expose us. "Shhh, Ninny!" I whisper. *The girl can make a racket in a feather loft.* Still, all proceeds according to my plan.

Dust tickles my nose and dries my mouth and throat as we wait, and wait, and wait. At last I peek under the couch. I know Father's shoes, with their polished toes and scuffed heels, as he rises to introduce our guest.

"We are most pleased this night to welcome Mr. Samuel Coleridge, lately returned to us from his Majesty's service in Malta.

"His thesis is that it is essential to the author's art to craft a work of vivid detail. He says through the use of this skill, an audience becomes so involved in the story, they forget themselves in the created events. Terming the effect 'the suspension of disbelief,' he cites it as a way for listeners or readers to better appreciate the message of the work.

"I invite you to listen to this poem and judge for yourselves the effectiveness of his words as the author reads."

Mr. Coleridge steps to the center of the room, though all I can see are his shoes and the striped hems of his pants, and begins to read:

> It is an ancient Mariner,
>
> And he stoppeth one of three.
>
> 'By thy long grey beard and glittering eye,
>
> Now wherefore stopp'st thou me?

Such is his skill, I am soon lost in the story, the meter, and the rhyme, but when he says, "The Albatross about my neck was hung..." idiot Jane giggles.

"Out!" My father summons us. "Now!"

As we creep from behind the corner of the couch, I look up to the poet. Contemporaries like my father call him a giant among dwarves, but he does not appear to be colossal to me: a bit taller than the average man, but no Goliath.

We stand in front of the assembly awaiting our shaming when a miracle occurs. Mr. Coleridge puts his hand on my father's arm and says, "I remember well my time spent in a school for the poor and the difficulties I endured while I thirsted after poetry. If these young ears so wish to listen that they secret themselves in a most uncomfortable location, pray you allow them to remain."

"Let them sit in front of me, William." Jane's mother simulates the ideal of motherhood for the assembled company. "They shall be silent." Then, leaning forward and whispering so only I can hear, she intones, "Or you shall be whipped."

But she has no cause as I am rapt in the story and never budge until it is done.

Mr. Coleridge takes up from where we interrupted. His words spin me into a world rounded with thirst where all the men onboard the mariner's ship have died, where the very planks of the ship shrink for lack of water, all of it his fault, his fault, his most grievous fault. But wait, the mariner is saved! Salvation and rain fall upon him, and the dead albatross drops from his neck. He blesses the denizens of the ocean who have plagued him, and angels inhabit the bones of his fellows to steer the ship homeward. There he discovers he is under a compulsion to tell a man about to attend a wedding not to take the presence of God lightly, but to say his prayers with a willing heart.

So moved by the poem was I that I thought of renouncing my father's atheism and believing instead in the Christian myth; such was the suspension of disbelief Mr. Coleridge wrought in me. But now the Rime is done and the poet steps to where I sit and says, "By your face, I see my words have found their mark."

"Yes, sir. I wish I too might be a sadder and wiser person, so I could write as well as you that my words might find other hearts."

Father is both flattered and impressed by my behavior and from that time forth I am allowed to partake of the salon's feast of ideas that flows most bounteously from the likes of Charles and Mary Lamb of Wordsworth and many others.

Climbing into my bed and kneeling upon my covers, I kick off my shoes, pull my legs up, and slide back, propping my shoulders onto my pillows so their lace shams tickle my cheek as I turn to gather my writing instruments. I lean my diary against my knees before I check my inkwell to be sure it is safely anchored that I do not stain the sheets. Ready at last, I stroke my quill over my lips and think.

Father says each time I write I must know what message I wish to impart, and so I cast my mind in search of a theme. In my stillness, I listen to the London sounds streaming in my window on the breeze.

Perhaps I shall write of where I live. London's Polygon forms a cultural center for the world, and my father's house occupies a prominent place in it. Listening to the music of the city, I am aware of the background theme of commerce. The greatest city on earth rumbles with thousands of carts, wagons, and drays and the shouts of merchants. In the street below I hear horse hooves clopping on the stones.

I close my eyes. Some are single mounts and riders. Do the horses of men who sit astraddle and those of ladies with their knees hooked over the pommel sound differently? Horses of the wealthy step with precise gaits clipping the pavement while tired, laden draft beasts wanting the comfort of their stalls plod to another rhythm. Wheeled traffic adds a counterpoint, with carts and wagons creaking and swaying under their loads. Carriages rattle, dogs run barking to nip at the heels of the horses, and a peddler sings of tin pots at the corner. A vegetable-seller cries his wares at our stoop, urging Cook to come out and see.

At some remove, a woman shouts. She's too distant for me to hear her words, but I can tell she wails in anger. There, that is of interest. At whom, I wonder: a less-than-faithful suitor? Or is she a maid dismissed for poor service now sensing the years of life as a drab that lie ahead?

My father praises me for using my senses. "If you would be a philosopher, you must learn to write, and daily practice is the best way to become proficient at communicating your thoughts. Remember, your mother was a powerful writer."

But what is it that makes one a writer? I stroke my lips with the feather of my quill again. *Ah!* Having found my theme for the day, my eyes open and I smile. I bend to my pages, wishing to be as valued for my work as my mother had been.

More than writing occurs upstairs.

My trembling breath vibrates the air within my wardrobe. I push the door ajar, touching my fingertips to the wood and tracing the grain. My eye pressed against the crack can discern the doorway to my room and a piece of the hallway beyond.

Is that a stealthy step? Holding my breath, I pull back instinctively from the chink in the wardrobe door.

He might be in the hallway.

"Mary?"

It's Jane! I reach for the door. But, wait! Charles tricked me one time by making her call out to get me to reveal my hiding place.

"Mary," her voice shakes. "Where are you?"

I push forward on the door gently until I can see the room again through the crack. Soft stocking-covered steps sound in the hall, but hold! There is another set.

They pause, a lower voice rumbles indiscernible words, and knowing that, I guess the rest. Jane is caught! At last, as the steps move off, I draw another shaking breath.

"Mary?" Little William wails. "Maaarry!" Only four, he has been placed in our care. "MAARRYY!"

Emerging from the safety of my wardrobe, I stand motionless in the center of my room. "Hush, Billy," I whisper, hoping I am quiet enough not to be heard by Charlie. "I'm coming."

Tiptoeing to the door, I check that the hall is empty and run to Billy's room.

"Tipstaff!" Charles crows from behind the door. "You're mine!" His hand tightens on my shoulder.

"Ow!" I spin out of his grasp. "Let off!"

"Then do as you ought."

I glance at Jane. Her face is alight with naughty anticipation. She's wearing only her stockings and garters.

"Yes, Mary," she says quietly. "Must take off your dress."

I'm more chagrined at being caught than angry or mortified. I untie the thin blue ribbon that circles me just below my budding bosom and slide the smooth white fabric over my head. Turning to face Charlie, I say, "Will you have my stockings as well?"

"They're not in the way," he says, stroking my nipple with his knuckles.

The last few times we have played this game, the penalty for losing has progressed from giving him a kiss to more explicit defaults. This time, the price of his triumph is to allow him to touch my nether region. Charles' version of hide and seek is not one I can afford to lose many more times.

"Stand you here on one side of me and Jane on the other. Good, that is exactly as I would wish."

Jane reaches over to clasp my hand.

"Open your legs," Charlie smirks. I close my eyes and do as I am bid.

His hand is warm, cupping my sex for a few seconds. Then he begins rubbing me in a circular motion. I hear Jane give a tiny gasp. I feel a finger tracing my furrow and lower, exploring the folds of flesh.

It is not...objectionable.

"OH, MY MERCIFUL HEAVENS!"

My stepmother in the doorway swings her big, red face from her daughter to her son. Jane, predictably, begins to cry. "Hush Jane," Stepmother snaps. "You, at least, have done nothing wrong."

But then Stepmother focuses her medusa's gaze on me.

"FILTHY, FILTHY LITTLE GIRL!!! Your father shall hear of this, dirty miss. How dare you?"

She digs her nails into the skin of the back of my neck, and, so pinioned, she marches me downstairs to my father's study.

"I'll harbor no bastards beneath this roof, William," she intones, propelling me into the room through the expedient of her claw.

As an opening line it does not bode well, but I am past caring. My anger flares. It is one thing to be embarrassed in my actions, another to be humiliated for her sport.

I spin around. "And do you believe your perfect son capable of inserting offspring into me with only his finger?"

"You do something with her," she screams at my father, as she batters me to the carpet with her fist. "For by the Lord God, I cannot!" She slams the door as she leaves.

Light yellow walls with dark, brown wood molding where the walls meet with the ceiling and floor surround his library, with his massive oaken desk set in the center. I notice cracks in the plaster. They've spidered higher on the walls in the past year and grown wider until I can count the laths through the holes. Flakes of plaster speckle the floor.

"Ah." He sighs and reaches for the tumbler of whisky that is to be found more and more often upon his desk these days. "Little Mary. What did you do?"

"It was but a game." My voice shakes, my body begins to tremble with reaction to what my stepmother did. I'm frightened, and angry, and hurt, and I cannot help myself. My tremors turn to uncontrollable shaking.

"Here," he says, opening his arms to me. Though I can barely control my legs, I step to him. He lifts me onto his lap and wraps me in his coat, and I bury my head into his chest and heave my sorrow out. He holds and caresses me until I grow calm. Some little time later, I am still and my breathing slows. He lifts me to carry me upstairs to my room and, knowing I am loved, at least by my father if by no other in this house, I dress for supper.

As my father viewed my progress toward adulthood, he sensed my lack of education in everything but the philosophy he and my true-mother espoused, and he began to seek a tutor for me that I might not remain narrowly focused.

Chapter Two

Education

My presence in my home became an issue. An education involving boarding school became a solution.

No matter how loved children are—or despised, depending upon the parent's disposition—they must leave home someday. For the parents, the problem of when and how to relieve oneself of offspring breaks down thusly: where may I send them, with whom may I entrust them, and how little can we pay? A balancing act where which of these criteria is foremost depends upon the child to be disposed.

That I should depart became a goal of my stepmother. Her concern was for expediency and economy. Expediency in that she could not shed herself of me soon enough were I to depart immediately, and economy in that the family should not bear any more than nominal expense to be rid of me.

I should, in charity, mention one other consideration related to social convention: I must depart in such a way that no breath of scandal touches her. It simply would not do, for example, were it known she sold me to slavers. Her attempt to make me worthy of at least a man of business, rather than a plaything of a patron, showed worth only in its desire that the gossip neither speak of me as a shopgirl nor a whore, but just barely. I did overhear her say, as though considering, "I have seen younger drabs on the docks."

Education encompassed a broad range of subjects to Father: he kept a house where the politically adept were always welcome as he sought their thoughts on the subject of what I might profit by through study. In 1809 one of the Founding Fathers of the American nation stayed with us for a time.

My father, in preparation for seeking a place for my sister and me, inventories his children with the same unflinching realism that causes others to label him difficult. As I read his journal, I see he'll never understand the importance of kindness or discretion in delivering the truth.

> *Fanny, the eldest, is of a quiet, modest, un-showy disposition,*
> *somewhat given to indolence, which is her greatest fault, but*
> *sober, observing, peculiarly clear and distinct in the faculty of*
> *memory, and disposed to exercise her own thoughts and follow*
> *her own judgment. Fanny is by no means handsome, but in*
> *general prepossessing.*

My character is cataloged as well.

> My own daughter [Mary] is considerably superior in capacity to
> the one her mother had before (Fanny), and my daughter is the
> reverse of her (Fanny) in many particulars. She is singularly bold,
> somewhat imperious, and active of mind. Her desire for knowledge
> is great, and her perseverance in everything she undertakes is
> almost invincible. My own daughter is, I believe, very pretty.

I am certain at least one man, other than Father, finds me interesting. An American, Aaron Burr, finding himself in some political distress, came for a visit. I think him well made, of handsome parts, but not particularly tall, perhaps a hand's width above my own height, and I am reckoned short even for a woman. He has a high forehead, his hair is both dark and long, worn in a club and tied with a dark ribbon. A straight nose and two large eyes of deep brown dominate his face, yet when he smiles the corners of his eyes crinkle with pleasure and he assumes an expression that shows joy lights his life more than sorrow. He impresses me as one of those determined men who, though they face obstacles, seek to overcome them, never offering an excuse when action is required. By repute, he is said to have been an officer in their revolution and no less than Vice President of their United States with a reputation of an interesting, chequered life.

We three sisters, Fanny, Jane, and me, he calls Goddesses. "For you are of a set and each as beautiful as the other." Blatant flattery, but effective nay-the-less in making us blush with pleasure. We agree to think him brave when we learn he killed a political rival in a duel. Speaking with him at dinner the first night, I find him as brilliant as he is patient.

I sit in my place farther down table than the adults. We are using the silver service tonight, I note. My father, as is his wont, compliments our guest, in this case for pretty comments he made concerning my mother. Mr. Burr responds, "I have a portrait of Mary Wollstonecraft over my mantle. Thank you, Mr. Godwin. I do know the writings of your late wife. My own wife introduced me to her remarkable work."

When he pauses from holding forth on the topic of equality found in my mother's writings, I ask a question of him about American philosophy.

"What you say is in keeping with that peculiar manifesto your government delivered to ours in '76, which asserted not only that the original state of men is one of equality but went on to declare men endowed with rights, ah," I pause to take a sip of water, "the proper word is 'unalienable' rather than 'inalienable,' which agrees well with the writings of both my father and my true-mother, but..." I do not wish to offend by employing the bluntness I've learned from Father.

"Go on." He smiles. He seems genuinely interested.

I pause to judge my words before I speak. "Why did your countrymen require the justification of a creator? Was this pandering to the superstitious among your people, or were you attempting to threaten those of my nation by positing Americans as enjoying the protection of a logically impossible being? Do you suppose, having bestowed the largess of equality upon the American people, this god would take umbrage toward any who would threaten his work and so rise to their defense?"

His eyebrows rise. "Perhaps it was hyperbole, perhaps a mixture of philosophy and faith. Pass the salt, if you would," he answers, deftly deflecting my question.

"Mary," my father says slowly, "do be kind to our guest, for he is an exile from his land, and, as he says, his wife is a most devoted follower of your mother's philosophy."

"From his voice as he speaks of her, I think he is much in love with his wife. He did say she told him she thought herself an advocate of my true-mother." I glance to my stepmother. As our eyes meet I smile. "They must have spoken on many occasions of the equality between the genders. Did you note he told me he sees the mirror of my true-mother's intellect within me? I think he could not have said a better thing to me. Fear not, Father. I shall be kind, but he has a mind I would know."

At any gait, I am not averse to his consideration any more than to that of any well-spoken, well-educated, and reasonably clean man. I believe he thinks me as interesting beyond my years, and he gives evidence of a desire for my company. He particularly desires me to sit near him during the evening readings by our other guests, soliciting my reactions to their material. I am sure he thinks himself a teacher, which interests me.

One morning after reviewing with us my mother's philosophy regarding education, he proposes the three of us sisters visit a school in London, saying, "I would know your thoughts about a new form of education purporting to improve society. It is called a Lancastrian school."

We enter a classroom arranged in tiers. Fanny says, "It appears to be an amphitheater, allowing the students to view the teacher without impediment. An arrangement like this ought to provide focus."

A few minutes later, Jane says, "I think the students are learning various forms of writing. Those in the lowest seats are forming sentences and paragraphs. Those above them are practicing essay. And again above, I think are learning the fictive voice. At the ultimate remove upward, poetry."

After some time I say, "Would it not be more likely to effect improvement of our culture if you could double the number of educated people leading us?"

He pauses and looks closely at me. "How would you bring this miracle of doubling attendance about without splitting these students in two?"

"Pray tell, where are the young women?"

I have seen other adults favor me with the look he gives me, though I should be used to it by now. Though he whispers to himself, I hear him say, "She has so few years." Then he raises his voice and turns to me. "Your pardon, Mary, I had forgotten who your mother was. You are surely her daughter."

I much cherish that observation. I also enjoy that he notices things about me other than my intellect. Oft-times, I note his gaze sweeps from my eyes to my mouth, and lower. One night during a salon I overhear him say he thinks me... "pretty." I weigh scant six stone of awkward arms and legs, but this man said I was... "pretty"? Well, that will be thought upon.

I become conscious of the attention of men from that time forth.

Mr. Burr's assertions regarding equality notwithstanding, there are inequalities that draw my attention. I am aware of how quickly the fortunes of my father are waning.

"Never forget this," Father says. "The remuneration a person receives for his or her efforts is dependent upon the opinion of society rather than the difficulty of a task. With philosophers, a different scale of relative worth is ordained, but the results are similar. A few speak truth, but in the present moment, because our nation must battle with the French, criticism of the ruling class is seen as a threat. The public perceiving the events that occurred in America and France has developed a causative relationship between espousing the ideal of human equality and the event of war.

"And so, my little dear, although I but speak the truth about the ways aristocratic privilege damages our culture," he says, holding my hand, "the public sees the lords as their salvation and disparages the value of thought. In short, through neither ability nor fault we shall be destitute."

"Is this enough that Stepmother should seek to put me out to earn money through industry?"

I see a trace of guilt cross his face. "It is not. I could wish for a better school for you than one teaching domesticity."

"But can one be found, Father, within our means?"

He hunches his shoulders. "I hope so."

One day will serve as a model for all the days that now fill our house. Clutching my arm, Stepmother throws open the door to my father's study and says, "This girl responded to me with a most impertinent reply."

My father's voice is mild. "Were you, Mary, perhaps less than clear to your mother? Did you fail to make effort to understand and be understood?"

"Father," I say, "not only was I perfect in my apprehension of her desires, I was precise in my speech."

"And what did you say?"

"I said, 'No.'"

Stepmother bares her teeth, flings me toward the hallway, and slams the door. I listen to her damn the state of our family in general and me in particular while standing outside. Her voice would be clear to those living in Cornwall.

"I shall be heard, William Godwin. You will attend when I say that girl shall no longer continue to pollute my house, my children, or my husband!"

Through the storm, my father never loses his temper or raises his voice. I lean forward to know his response.

"I presume you mean Mary and not Fanny?"

"Who else be the author of such havoc?"

"Who else but the youngest daughter of my first wife?"

To remind her of a relationship which haunts every aspect of their lives is so eloquent a blow it would have gone home against the rhinoceros. However, my stepmother is made of sterner stuff. I hear the woman thunder evidence of my deficiency.

"O, how the ungrateful child's tongue is sharper than a serpent's tooth, William, and you would know it was you less besotted of her."

How does the woman create a sibilance conveying such filth? But Father is not without weapons of his own.

"I have, and continue to advocate, the philosophy and the methodology of child rearing espoused by my late wife. A child spared corporal punishment but raised in reason will surely become a superior adult, while a child who is the object of scorn will display contempt for others throughout his, or her, life. This will, if not today, then in the future, be evident."

Her footsteps advancing toward the door and the rattle of the knob as she lays her hand upon it give me time to scuttle behind a convenient chair before she delivers her parting shot.

"Didn't harm me to feel the rod. Not before the Earth should pass away will that one achieve reason! Hear me, it is your overly affectionate behavior toward her that is at fault! If you will not grasp this nettle, I shall be forced to protect my home. Fair warning, William, for the sake of your soul, you must be done with that girl."

With that, she exits, slamming the door. I watch the breadth of her back as she departs like a leviathan slipping beneath the waves.

Say on as you will, harridan. My father will no more be done with me than I shall be done with my father.

It was a near thing which might occur first: the discovery of a school or open war between my stepmother and me.

Chapter Three

Homeleaving

Life is a necklace where stones become years slipping through your fingers as you seek to catch and slow their course. Whether the journey of time be slow or fast, none may stay the passage. Yet there are those moments when time becomes rapids and things of import blur indistinct in our memory.

I hardly remember meeting Percy.

A new literary light burns bright in the universe of Father's acquaintance: a demigod who styles himself Percy Bysshe Shelley.

We are warned to dress for dinner this night and so we arrive late at table. "If our guests arrive before us, we'll make a better entrance," Jane tells me.

As I take in the table, I see the comet speaking some witticism to Father. I'm surprised, I confess, for all the esteem in which I've been told Father places him, I'd say he does not yet have twenty years. *How young is he?* Taller than most men, emaciated, and slightly built, with thin wrists unhidden by the frilled cuffs that escape from his jacket, his affectation of dress fair shouts his occupation. Flowing. *There's a word saying much with little.* His blouse, of such a white a nun's wimple would not compare, has the wide, full sleeves affected by artists and a ruffled neck that drapes from loosened ties. His trousers, tight cut, the better to display his considerable prowess as a man, *not that I notice*, are black as a priest's cassock. His features are either aesthetic or effeminate depending, I suppose, upon the prejudice of the individual describing him. Aesthetic, I decide. His color, visible above the deep V of his shirt, is fair to the point of womanly, and his hair cascades in curls to his shoulders. His face is finely chiseled of the palest marble, yet the perfect Cupid's bow of his lips purse as though seeking kisses.

Again, not that I notice.

I sit between Fanny and Jane thinking we make a formidable trio of color and shape. The poet sits on Father's right with a rather pretty young woman who must be close to our age. Shelley's comely wife Harriet, a *mouse where he deserves a lioness,* sits reserved and all but silent, nay-the-less she casts her presence over the young Prometheus. Often she simply sighs in such a fashion as to retrieve Percy from whence a particular flight of fancy leads him, and as often do I note his displeasure at being so leashed.

Father raises a glass and says, "I am most pleased to present to you the author of *The Necessity of Atheism,* Mr. Shelley." I take a sip of wine. Father clears his throat and says, "It is Oxford's shame to have lost such a mind, and our fortune."

Fanny spoke to me of the debt father owes this man. According to her, this scion of the house of Shelley freely bestows sums as vast as his purse will stretch.

Shelley rises to accept the toast. In a light but well moderated voice he says, "Allow me to express my pleasure at being here with my most honored host, whose work sheds light upon the role of government and governed. As for Oxford, the dons made it clear to me my studies lessened their own repute." He reaches for his glass. "In short, they rusticated me." Lifting his glass before he drinks, he looks directly to me and his eyes, the very shade of the sea after a storm, go wide.

I am lost.

I quite quickly lift my own glass to disguise my traitorous, blushing countenance.

Fanny leans toward me and whispers, "I find myself falling 'neath the spell of him."

"You have my sympathy," murmurs Jane, fanning her face with her hand.

I whisper, "Have a care, sister. You, too, may fall 'neath his spell." I wonder how it would be to fall 'neath him.

"The natural world has influenced my politics," he continues. "I seek to establish a theory of natural, peaceful revolution. It is natural for people to change their state from tyranny to the anarchy much lauded by Mr. Jefferson of the colonies. Ah," he amends, "I mean our late colonies. Though the American States were born of battle, I say each man, or woman," he makes eye contact with me and my heart misses a beat, "assumes responsibility for the state of the world. Revolution, slow and sure, be a necessary, natural consequence of well educated, virtuous humanity."

We applaud him politely, but that night at salon, I learn how radical his politics can be. He chooses to read what he calls an early draft of a poem, but before he reads, he delivers a prologue upon his intentions. "I desire my years should be more useful than illustrious. I feel my life a fervent call to my fellow-creatures that they love and serve each other. This be the noblest work that life and time permits me. It is in this spirit I am composing my present work." He begins,

> Nature rejects the Monarch, not the man;
> The subject, not the citizen; for kings
> And subjects, mutual foes, forever play
> A losing game into each other's hands,
> Whose stakes are vice and misery.

"No wonder he has father's attention," Jane whispers. "He's political."

"More than that, surely. The man's an altruist," I murmur in response. "He will find audience among the romantic."

In these days of the war in Europe, it is easier to look forward to the sort of millennium of freedom and brotherhood he envisions as the proper state of mankind than to look to the present reign of prejudice, ignorance, and spite. He makes me think those men timid who toil toward wisdom through decades of contemplation. I resolve to honor those who act to bring about a change in our culture. Especially through their writings.

While I pay attention to him the rest of the night, noting who he cultivates and how he directs his attentions, I find I am not alone in my perception of an unmistakable animal virility.

Jane, with her usual tact, says, "He's a great, throbbing male."

I pity his wife for, with prescient sight, I know Percy Shelley will have any woman he wishes. Here, palpable and cognizant, youth ascendant and rampant stands poised in my company. I feel the winds of profound change blow through my heart.

My continuing education and my residence in London continue to be a problem, but then, my father discovers a solution to the problem, one that will expand my horizons to the stars and set my mind free to follow beyond the limits of dreams.

"Mary?"

I look up to find Father at my door, a surprise for he seldom visits my room. As he is smiling, I put down my journal and slide off the bed. "Come in, Father, please?"

He crosses the floor between us practically bouncing, sweeps me up into his arms and kisses me thoroughly until at last he pulls away and says, "Pretty Mary, I have found a tutor for you."

"Wh-w-what? W-w? Who?" I never stammer.

"During the salon of Friday past when Mr. David Booth, ah, do you remember him?" He puts me down.

"I think so. Is his wife Margaret, and does she have dark auburn hair?"

"Even so! And as bright a woman as I hope you will be. But the import is this: Mr. Booth introduced me to his father-in-law, Mr. William Baxter, the natural philosopher from Dundee who writes so eloquently upon the flora of Scotland. He has raised five daughters, five, think of that, and tutored them well."

I think a moment. "Margaret is exceptionally well spoken, Father. If the rest of his brood be so well raised, I would think him a great teacher, and one in keeping with my mother's theory regarding the importance of teaching women."

"Just so! Even so! Anthony Carlisle was at my elbow when we met and approached us saying he had read a monograph Baxter had written upon botany. Baxter blinked and said he knew Carlisle's experiment using electricity to separate water to its constituent components. We stood near the buffet, there was a chafing dish emitting the savory odor of bacon and pâté..." His eyes get a far-off look as he tries to recall the supper.

"Father." I smile as he is especially dear to me when his mind takes him from his subject. "As you are a political thinker, why has natural philosophy excited you?"

"Ah. Baxter. He teaches a wide range of subject matter using logical methods even as I do. He says natural philosophy is a subject as fit for study as any, for it seeks to understand the workings of the world. In his words, 'The great navigator, Cook, before he was killed by the aborigines, did a great service to us all through his three voyages of discovery.'" He turns to me with a radiant smile. "Oh, my Pretty Mary, here be a teacher worthy of you."

I take his hand. "Are you determined to send me away from you and to him?"

"For a better place away, would you not leave me for a time?"

"What assurance do you have he might welcome me?"

He waves away my concerns. "He is a philosopher above all else, and philosophers must teach acute minds. As you are acute, he will welcome you as a student." He smiles. "You leave for Dundee on tomorrow's tide."

"Father!" While I am reconciled to my father being one of those for whom logic overrides emotional response, still, "I'll need time to adjust my thinking to this situation."

"Will arranging your thoughts modify events? I've acted as events dictated. This elegant solution to our dilemma arrived in the post this morning as a letter from Baxter that spoke of education and the need for students and teachers to delve into a variety of subjects. With his letter still in my hand, I determined to send you to him. Since that time, I have arranged your passage on a ship bound for Dundee and came here to your room to tell you of your great fortune."

A thought occurs to me. "Have you informed him of your decision?"

He shrugs. "I shall."

"Does Stepmother know?"

He shakes his head. "I shall inform her after you've sailed. She's away for a visit and will not return until you've gone. Now, tell me you're happy to be going, and give me a kiss." Maddening man. But I, knowing I was cherished and about to advance upon a great adventure, came to him gladly.

So eloquent was this solution, my father determined he would send his daughter, of almost fourteen years, on a ship, alone, to Scotland to be tutored by a man he had known for a week.

Aye, that much.

Chapter Four

"Is she dead, then?"

Six years earlier, Nelson destroyed the French fleet at Trafalgar. England has ruled the seas since, so I had no fear on that score, but a fate worse than capture overcame me. I am one who cannot venture in ships without getting sea sick. As the sea was rough, I tossed about my cabin while copiously voiding myself for the duration of my voyage north.

Still, though I scarce knew it, here in the North, with these people and at this time, my life began.

"A-hem?"

I awake lying in a soft, clean bed. Peeking through slits in my eyes I see a girl near my own age dressed all in white. Her auburn hair with its deep red glints forms a nimbus of curls around her head, so tangled it hints she may have been out-of-doors already this day.

In a quiet, soft burr she asks, "Are y' woke?"

Although my curiosity about the place I have paid so much to reach is piqued, I think I am, decidedly, not in the mood for company. Not to move, not to open my eyes, not to answer seems the best course. I hear the door close.

When I am quite sure she is gone, I sit up and survey my room. This chamber is roughly ten feet in height, fifteen in length and twelve in width, with walls of heavy wood, bright with oil and smelling of oils. Corner supports evoke Corinthian columns and capitals, and a wide crown molding carved with repeating knots bounds the room. Five panels comprise each wall, with chair rails surmounting carved wainscoting. Thick rugs provide a resilient surface for walking and warmth.

I discern I am both clean and clad from neck to toe in a white nightdress of the finest linen. I slide from the bed to explore. A window, the only one in the room, draws my attention. Before my eyes lies anti-London. Wide lawns run down to a stream an hundred yards from the house. A forest, unbroken by other habitation, stretches from horizon to horizon, and hillsides rise in the distance.

The lord of this manor must be well-to-do indeed.

Hunger overcomes my desire to remain aloof. There is an ewer of water that sits atop the dresser in the room, and I drink. Within a wardrobe I find my clothing neatly hanging. *My third-best dress will do,* I think, shrugging into the soft folds of dark blue. I brush my hair and descend.

When I discover him, Baxter, for this must surely be him, is seated at a large and heavy oak table in the center of a room. From the books and paper upon it, I see it serves as his desk.

He rises when he sees me, and I think him a fit man with dark hair combed forward in the manner of Napoleon or Caesar, with his face clean-shaven. More importantly, it is a kind face with large and dark eyes, a straight nose, and a pointed chin. My first thought is that he is not as old as I imagined. My second is that his eyes show he has suffered some tragedy in his life.

The coat he wears is of deep green with wide lapels, atop a waistcoat and white shirt with a matching cloth around his neck. Buff-colored pants, stockings, and a pair of heavy black shoes with silver buckles completes him cap-à-pie.

"I'm most pleased y've recovered well enough to sit we' me, Mary," he says softly. His pronounced brogue is barely understandable to me. "I am aware your seasickness was extreme. 'Tis a tribute to your youth and stamina that you are able to walk aboot m' home only a day since your arrival."

I pause for, on the whole, I think him handsome. Having introduced myself and assured him I am well, I point out his malfeasances in a rationally ordered list with, the leaving of a guest to famish last.

This does not solicit the expected response.

"Weel," he says, "I will first note, having raised five daughters, two still at home, and three sons, my capacity for ingratitude approaches the infinite, but let me attempt enlisting your cooperation nae-the-less.

"Should we begin your education at the beginning, I must know what is it that you know, Wee Mary." Just then a great clock in the hall chimes the eleventh hour. Two girls enter the study carrying notebooks, pens, and inkwells and smile toward me as they seat themselves at the table in the room's center.

"Welcome to our home," the younger of the two girls says, nodding to me. I recognize her as the one who looked in on me earlier. "I am Isobel." She smiles shyly at me and I note a spray of freckles across her nose. "I have fifteen years, and I would we were friends."

I nod in return to her and look to the other.

"Y' may clep me Christine though my given name is Christian." she says with a lift of her chin. She's an arresting tall beauty with red hair falling in soft waves below her shoulders. "Seventeen."

I straighten a little in surprise. *She seems a woman rather than a girl.* I might expect one of such advanced years to be married.

By the way they take seats at the table and open their journals; they indicate their readiness for lessons rather than food. Baxter turns to me. "Sit y' doon." He opens a cabinet and takes out another set of writing instruments and a notebook, which he places on his desk next to Isobel. "Do y' ken the etymology of the word 'philosophy'?"

Does he think my head as empty as my stomach? I would have him know me as one descended from great thinkers. Walking around his table to take the seat allows me time to parse his sentence that I might decipher his question and form a reply to impress him. I use the tone of voice one uses when speaking to idiots.

"The simplest answer to that, and therefore an answer whose meaning is least likely to go astray, would be that the word derives from the Greek 'Philosophia,' a love of wisdom. I read the entire of my mother's works by the time I was ten, and it took me only a year longer to digest the work of my father." *That should teach him not to ask foolish questions of me.*

His face betrays none of the surprise other adults show when I offer an example of my acuity. I look to his daughters and see carefully neutral expressions.

Perhaps a bit more is called for.

"Herakleides Pontikos, whose mentor was Aristotle, attributes the word Philosophy to Pythagoras and differentiates Philosophers from Sophists on the basis of pecuniary exchange. Philosophers exchange information without demand of monetary reward, thinking knowledge to be a reward in and of itself. A Sophist, however, seeks a living wage from those who would pay for information." I tilt my head and smile.

That should do.

It does not.

Mr. Baxter glances at me from his seat. "And what is the proper study for a philosopher?"

Well then.

"There are six: Reason, Existence, Knowledge, Mind, Values, and Reality." To this list, I add my opinion, sensing his next question. "Of these, it seems to me that Reason is the greatest."

"And as a natural philosopher who studies the earth and that which walks upon it, or swims within it, or flies above it, or more to the point, the planet and that which grows upon it, where would you say lies my prime interest in these six areas of study?"

"I would essay you are most concerned with knowledge. You would be one who creates taxonomies or catalogues." I sniff. "These have something akin to the occupation of a librarian, one who brings order to books: one for the birds, one for fish, and one for animals. These organisms already exist and you have but to name them and so avoid the necessity to discover anything new."

"Weel then young Mercury, let us begin with that."

"I'd rather not." And with that, I march off to my room where I intend to read quietly, awaiting the dinner hour.

A soft tap on the door intrudes on me.

"Come."

Isobel enters and says, "Father asked I check on y' to see whether or no y' are well."

"I am indisposed." I mutter as I push back from where I sit on the bed and shift my shoulders deeper into the pillows.

"As well y' might be." She says seriously. "D' y' mind how y' came to us?"

I blink and peer toward the window. "In truth, I remember little of the last week."

She looks upon me with concern and says, "Understandable. Would y' hear of your arrival to Ellengowan?"

I turn to her and say, "That would be most appreciated. But what is the word you just used?"

"Ellengowan? 'Tis the name of our home. Well, this one. We've another near the banks of the Tay we call the Cottage. We move there every year to take advantage of the summer. Soon, y'll repair there in our compn'y."

"Could you speak to my arrival then? I find myself a stranger in a strange land."

Her smile broadens. "So spake Moses to Zipporah in Exodus 2 and 22. Weel then," she plumps down on the edge of the bed, "list ye to th' tale."

She lifts some pages from a pocket in her dress. "I ought to begin with this letter which is from your father." She passes it to me saying, "As it traveled by post-chaise, it reached us almost a day before you, his daughter, did."

I hold the pages gingerly knowing what my father is capable of saying to others about me, and dreading the effect he may have had on them.

It reads:

> *My Dear Mr. Baxter:*
>
> *I have shipped off to you by yesterday's packet, the Osnaburgh, Captain Wishart, my only daughter. She is four months short of fourteen years of age.*
>
> *I attended her to the wharf, and remained an hour on board, till the vessel got underway. I could not help feeling a thousand anxieties in parting with her, for the first time, for so great a distance, and these anxieties were increased by the manner of sending her, on board a ship, with not a single face around her that she had ever seen till that morning.*
>
> *I daresay she will arrive more dead than alive, as she is extremely subject to seasickness, and the voyage will, not improbably, last nearly a week.*
>
> *I am quite confounded to think what trouble I may be bringing on you and your family, and to what degree I may be said to have taken you in upon so slight acquaintance.*
>
> *The old proverb says, 'He is a wise father who knows his own child,' and I feel the justness of the apothegm on the present occasion.*
>
> *I believe she has nothing of what is commonly called vices, and that she has considerable talent. It is my desire you will consider the first two or three weeks as a trial, how far you can ensure*

*her, or, more fairly and impartially speaking, how far her habits
and conceptions may put your family very unreasonably out of
their way; I expect that you will not, for a moment, hesitate to
inform me if such should be the case.*

I am not so insensible of my behavior toward this household thus far that my conscience twinges at the justice of my father's words; however, I have been sore used. *They might adjust for a guest.*

*I am anxious that she should be brought up like a philosopher,
even like a cynic. It will add greatly to the strength and worth
of her character.*

*You ought be aware that she comes to the seaside for the purpose
of bathing. I should wish that you would inquire now and then
into the regularity of that. She will want some treatment for a
weakness in her arm, but should not require a professional man
to look after her while she is with you. In all other respects she
has admirable health, has an excellent appetite, and is capable
of enduring fatigue.*

I am, my dear sir, with great regard, yours,

—William Godwin.

"There is nothing wrong with my arm," I mutter, not looking at her. I feigned the injury. It had been expedient to invent an infirmity and tell my stepmother I could not write so I might thus escape her importuning for matter to print.

Isobel nods to indicate she has heard me and continues the story. "Upon receiving the letter, my father told us from what he could recall of your father, this was not such a negative assessment as it would have been from another. Rather he thought it was your father's idea of an honest accounting of his daughter, and we must await your arrival and make our own judgments. And so we shall, but your arrival was not...fortuitous." She shrugs.

"'Twas midday when a coach, wheels crunching on the gravel drive, rolled up to our door. A tall woman was seated next to the driver rather than inside as we might expect. She appeared a lady, dressed quite well, all in grey. As the conveyance rocked to a halt, she looked down from her perch to my father, saying, 'I am Mrs. Nelson of Great St. Helen's, London. Are you Mr. Baxter?'

"My father allowed the truth of this, and she said, 'Mr. Godwin, who, I was assured, was known to you, secured a promise from me even as we stood upon the deck of the Osnaburgh that I should look after his daughter during the voyage and make sure she arrived safely. Had I known what that would entail, I would have refused. I hereby impart my charge to you as soon as you are able to remove her from the coach.'

"'Is there some reason she is incapable of alighting on her own?' father asked.

"'She became seasick before we left the confines of the Thames,' Mrs. Nelson said, her shudder indicating evident loathing at the memory, 'and remained so without the slightest improvement the entire seven days we traveled the Channel, into the North Sea, up the Firth and to the docks here in Dundee, so long a voyage being required by contrary winds and boisterous seas. In short, she remained in her cabin, ill, for the duration. I was able to change the bucket in her cabin twice a day until it was thought there was little other filth she could produce.

"'I wish it known,' she said, as though in her defense, 'I am not insensible to her condition, but the best I could do without becoming ill myself was to have two of the sailors sluice her down with tubs of water as we traveled up the Tay to the docks. The expedient of this simple rinsing of the muck clinging to her brought about great enhancement in her apparent condition. So improved was she, we were able to go below to remove her from the view of the sailors and change her clothing. It was thought she might keep down a small bowl of gruel further thinned with water as we docked.

"'However,' the lady said, 'in a most unfortunate coincidence the rolling coach simulated the motion of the ship from the docks to your home, causing such renewal of her *mal de mer* symptoms, thus negating previous attempts at improvement in either her condition or appearance.'"

Isobel shakes her head saying, "The woman never faltered in her direct gaze toward my father and did in no wise appear embarrassed at delivering you in such a state as she described, saying, 'I fled to my present seat and listened to the continuous sounds of distress from the quay to your door.'

"Father nodded to her, letting her interpret his action as she would, either gratitude for her aid, sympathy that she had been sore used, or acknowledgement of the character she showed in continuing care of so difficult a charge," Isobel said in confidence.

"Stepping around the horses to the door of the carriage, I grasped the handle and opened it. And, Mary," she says shaking her head, "'Twas as though a miasma redolent of the seventh level of hell flooded the roadway from the interior of the carriage.

"'Och, fie Daddy,' I said, clapping a handkerchief to my nose as I attempted to peer into the coach. 'Is she dead, then?'"

Isobel leans toward me, smiling as though she would deliver joyous information of great import, and chirps, "Y' dinna die! Indeed, here you are, and so m' father wishes discourse with y'."

"But I do not wish 'discourse,'" I lade the word with sarcasm, "with him. I would 'discourse' with my dreams and say I gain more for it."

"Och!" Her voice was soft. "Weell, you'll learn better, for y' are intelligent." Her mouth quirks. "At least by repute."

Isobel's eyes find mine. She takes a breath. Her mouth softens, and she says. "D'y ken we've both lost our mothers? I'd have y' for a friend for no other reason, Wee Mary." And with that, she quickly hugs me and leaves.

Well, there's matter a plenty to think upon.

Mr. Baxter requires I orient myself to my surroundings during the following weeks through the expedient of long rambles with Isobel and Christine. I find their constant chatter as informative as it is felicitous.

"Dundee is an ancient place," says Christine in a clearer burr than Isobel's way of speaking. I look at her in the morning light. She is tall. Her rich dark auburn hair is swept up into a bun. As she stands erect, I notice how thin she is. I'd call her regal. In contrast to Isobel, no freckles dot her nose or cheeks. "The people named it for the fort, the Dun, and the fires, the Dèagh that crowned the dominating hill near its center." She thinks a moment. "But there are several stories of the name's origin." She wags her head to the side acknowledging the existence of other opinions while implying a lesser value of them. "None know the truth. The city lies in a broad shallow valley ringed by low mountains whose inward sides slope gradually to form a wooded bowl broken by the River Tay."

Isobel uses her hands to illustrate when she says, "These low hills show sheer and barren slopes tha' face the town creatin' a natural palisade, as though the verra bones of the earth protect us. They make a braw show when covered with snow in the winter."

So great is the difference between London and Dundee, I gaze upon this landscape with awe, thinking what the girls call hills are the highest of mountains.

"Now look y' to the east," Christine calls to me from where she stands atop an outcrop of rock and points to her right. "See? There lies the North Sea that carried the Vikings to Britain on their earliest raids."

Little by little I absorb these lessons and come to thrill in the method by which the Baxters impart them. No fact is left in isolation but always paired with another, thus giving a context for each piece of information.

For instance, strolling the quays and docks along the Tay, I learn Dundee's wealth derives from two main sources: linen and whale oil. Famed more than a century for its whaling industry, the city reeks of oil and the flensing of whale bone done by armies of knife-wielding women upon the shores. The waste leaves a stink that infests the city when the wind is out of the south.

"Might we seek out men who can tell us of the northern seas?"

Christine looks askance, "Enhanced to entertain us, no doubt," but Isobel's smile hints of her anticipation of a good story or two.

One man, a huge specimen dressed in varying shades of blue and sporting a gold ring in one ear, claims to be a harpooner. The three of us stand in a line in front of him. He runs his marksman's eye over Christine and, flicking his tongue over his lips, he says, "Little misses, I have battled leviathans amid towering mountains of ice, seeking the lives of devil fish and their oil." With that he launches into a story of a voyage to the far north and of a hunt and kill that features monsters bent upon his destruction with himself armed only with his courage and a knife.

Another, a helmsman with hands as large as plates and skin cracked and brown from the weather, tells me of seeking ways through shifting channels in the ice as it groans and cracks. "Sure, did I not live the terrors of knowing how the ice-bounded open water might crush my ship and I would sleep in the arms of Davy evermore?"

So engrossed in his story am I, I am sure my eyes and mouth are as round as the portholes lining his ship.

Many and many of these accounts I commit to my journals at night. As I listen to their tales, I realize I am learning a lesson about crafting a story. *I must remember, every story needs danger.*

In my heart, I began to use the word "home" when I thought of Dundee, but sometimes, wisdom comes at the price of great pain, and I wondered what price I would pay.

Chapter Five

Another Set of Lessons

My time in Dundee molded me in ways both overt and subtle. The people of the town colored my days with their stories, while at night the staff within the house surprised me with their forward, democratic mien, yet they carried out their allotted tasks with ability and such pride I became aware of the advantages found in working with people rather than ordering them to labor for me.

Isobel and Christine became as sisters to me. Their father? As Isobel would say, "Aye, th' mon's a coil." To me, he was a careful teacher who so cherished learning; his life became a lesson in the enjoyment of change and growth.

As Mr. Baxter requires, I write out ancient tomes of philosophy as syllogisms to test the truth of Aristotle, Plato, and Socrates. Logic and epistemology are my twin guiding stars, my Castor and Pollux, but it is the fields that round Dundee upon which I batten and run riot with nets and cages o'er the hills and meadows of the lowlands.

As the summer arrives, we shift our lodging to the Cottage: thick white walls, an interior all of wood shining with care, and a loft upstairs where all three of us girls share a room with walls that slope inward under a thick thatch roof.

Days become weeks of wondrous freedom spent tramping the hillsides around Dundee, getting filthy while gathering specimens. We eat what we can find afield or what Cook has packed for us to carry and cool ourselves in the streams of this natural philosopher's dream.

Mr. Baxter requires of us this day that we secure frogs for a lesson in dissection, and though I am eager to "Peer within froggie's guts!" as Isobel puts it, on this hot day the bloom of enthusiasm is fast wearing off the thistle of reality.

Women wear skirts. Female naturalists, as I suppose we be, wear wide skirts of tan, closely twilled linen that is thick and heavy but falls in graceful folds to our ankles. I feel it an impractical outfit when so much better a solution lay at hand.

"You'd think we could wear trousers." Logic defeated. A broad brimmed hat, a blouse of white linen with a neck cloth, a jacket of the same stuff as the skirt, and a pair of thick green cotton stockings worn with boots complete my ensemble, and at this moment, I hate every stitch. But Christine takes a path toward a wood and soon we enter the shade beneath the cool boughs.

"Hist!" Isobel freezes, intent upon some treasure beneath the bracken covering the ground between the boughs. We stand motionless as statues in the gloaming. I hear a mosquito whine about my ear and I feel its sting on my cheek.

I slap it.

"Fie, on y'!" Isobel turns in fury. "A moment more and we'd have a bonny boonie!"

Her pronunciation of "bunny" along with the scowl on her shining face is too much. I fall to the forest floor in a paroxysm of laughter.

"Gone daft, y' are." Disgust on her face wars with a smile twitching the corner of her mouth.

I can't help myself. My sides ache, I've no breath, and yet I cannot get my body under the control of my mind. She shrugs at her sister, says, "Wha' can be done wi' the insane?" and plumps down next to me, pointedly waiting for me to finish.

"Y', y'," I wheeze, "you said, 'Goondeft,' you did!"

"I dinna iver."

"And you called it a 'boonie!'"

"No' a whit!"

Her flat statement of denial sends me off into gales of laughter again. When I run down she lifts her chin.

"'Tis y'r London accen' which is weirrd." And making a circle of her finger and thumb, she places it over one eye. "Pip, pip, cheerio!"

"The Scot accent is stupid," I return fire. "'Och, Y'r tartan is oopside doon'."

She huffs and plants her fists on her hips. "Weeell if y'r goin' t be insultin'!"

Christine calls halt to our fight. "There's a stream that way where we might cool your brains."

Moments later by the water, she reaches up to pull the pin from her hat and releases her glorious auburn hair to fall to her waist. Sunlight through the leaves dapples her skin with shifting shadow. I hope when I am her age, I might be as beautiful.

After we've rinsed them free of perspiration, our clothing drapes upon some bushes in the glade to dry, a reassuring indication of how long we'll be here. I'm seated upon a green slippery stone, cool at last. My legs stretch in the water and my body, propped up on my arms, stretched out behind me.

"Wee Mary?" Christine seems thoughtful. "When y' noted Isobel's accent, some of what m' father said concernin' the art of writin' comes to mind."

I quirk an eyebrow to her. "Go on."

"It made me remember of a problem Father mentioned. He said, 'D'y' not see how y' may separate characters in the minds of those who read y'r work by imitation of the way they speak?'"

"Och, there's wisdom," Isobel breaths. "And use it I shall!"

"Thanks, it's a most skilled method." The Baxters' encouragement for me to capture my fantasies, no matter how foolish, on my pages is making my skill at writing grow.

My imagination and my gaze rove through the green of the shadows. I tune my ears to the music of the stream as the noisy cascade falls through a rocky trough to the pool where Isobel and Christine, immersed to their freckled shoulders and clothed only in crimson hair that streams behind them, paddle about. I picture the three of us as elementals. We three be naked Naiads alive within a myth of pastoral perfection.

"Come, join me, Mary!" Isobel calls.

"Nay. I cannot swim."

Christine blinks in surprise. "But y' said you enjoy bathing in the ocean. How is it that you canna swim?"

"One does not need to swim to bob upon the waves."

"Come t' me," Isobel says, holding out her arms. I ease into the water, but I thrash back to shallow water when my feet do not touch bottom.

"O' whist, idjit!" Isobel says, averting her face from the cascades of water my splashing sends. She comes closer. "Here, hold on to me."

And so I begin another lesson, entitled "Swimming."

"Now watch Christine."

Christy slowly and with deliberation moves her hands, scooping the water down and back, and kicks her legs near the surface so I can see how she supports herself.

"Now, lie you across my arms. Shush fool, I'll not let y' drown. Do you imitate her."

Within that very hour, I span the pool kicking and puffing and frantically churning my arms until my feet stand upon the leafy bottom.

"Braw Mary!" Isobel crows. "Y' did it!"

"I have done!" Courageous and rampant, I stand upon the farthest bank in a heroic pose, my legs spread and my arms folded. "Like Alexander the Great, swimming the Hellespont lies within my ability."

"Have care, Wee Mary," Christine says, smiling. "Does not the Bible say, 'Pride goeth before a fall'?"

I stand above the newly conquered riffles and whisper, "Confidence goes hand-in-hand with achievement."

On that day, I embrace nature and all that encompasses the natural world with a need found deep within me. I disparage London's male stone and corners, straight lines and harsh shadows. I care not for the allure of manly strivings that result in a city's pervading stink of manure, cess, and smoke. My love of regularity gives way without a struggle for a newly appreciated feminine woodland world of curve, shadings, and breezes scented by herb and flower…

"FROGGIE!" Isobel screeches and dives.

We return to the Cottage triumphant, six large frogs in our cages. As soon as Mr. Baxter examines our catch and pronounces them "adequate," he leads us outside to a small wooden building well away from the house—his dissection laboratory. A tang reaches my nose as we enter.

"Formaldehyde," Christine says, touching her nose with one hand while indicating a bottle of fluid with the other. "'Tis responsible for the reek. Have a care not to let it touch your skin for long but rinse it off with water as soon as y' may."

She shows me how to "pith" a frog by deftly inserting a steel needle into its brain, explaining that the animal will neither feel pain nor jerk about at what we do to it, but will continue to live for a time in a state of mindless paralysis, allowing us to view the processes of its organs. We pin our subjects to a dissecting tray lined with black wax, and amphibian secrets soon lie open to my inquisition. This day, I behold a beating heart. I pore over the workings of lungs, heart, and gastronomy. But then Mr. Baxter proposes a different experiment.

He indicates a machine resting upon our table saying, "Y' may examine it. This devise generates electricity." I look to see a handle connecting to an armature strung with wires and held between the poles of six black iron U-shaped magnets. Isobel thinks it great sport when she has me hold the wires while she cranks furiously and I drop them suddenly.

"So, y' might be certain wha' the machine produces, although unseen, is efficacious."

Fingers all a-tingle, I nod to Mr. Baxter to indicate I am through with my perusal of the machine.

"And now I apply the Galvanic Fluid…"

The frog jerks.

"OH!"

"Dinna scream, Wee Mary," hisses Isobel. "'Tis irritatin'."

"I most certainly did not scream…OH!" I scream. "He moves again!"

"Galvanni's stimulation by the electricity causes the muscles of animals to react," Mr. Baxter tells me. "More?"

"Please." I lean closer.

He touches the probes to the legs of the creature. "Turn the crank on the generator, when you are ready." Knowing what is to occur makes my breath quicken and my lips part.

"There! He moves," I say. "Have you returned life to him?" I think of sewing him up and releasing him to his pool.

"There are those who hold that, should an application of electricity be induced with proper method, and for sufficient duration, and of adequate strength, re-animation of the dead is possible." Here, Baxter shakes his head. "But to what sort of life? What nightmares inhabit the dead? No, such re-animation should ne'er be tried."

"Does that mean it will never be attempted?"

His eyebrows rise at the thought. "I canna say whether or no it ha' been. But to measure what lies between the worlds of life and death ought be encompassed by the proper study of ethic." He lifts his head and looks into the distance and, placing his hand upon his chin, murmurs, "Perhaps when we've time we'll speak of ethos and ethic. As to the re-animation of the dead and why I doubt the outcome of such experiment, have y' heard of the experiments of Giovanni Aldini?"

I shake my head.

He snorts. "Knowin' your father as I do, 'tis a surprise to me y' hae not. Aldini was a theatrical charlatan whose reputation was of fleeting moment. Galvani was his uncle. He did show to his nephew the secrets of his research, and the boy, for a boy's wisdom was all he possessed, believed there was money to be made by presenting half-truths cloaked as science to the public." Baxter swept his hand as though to brush away trash. "He would take the corpses of animals and apply his Uncle's electrical stimulation, causing the poor beasties to jerk about to the gasps of the crowd eager to pay for the sight."

He stops, his consternation plain in what I presume is a silent debate over what he should say to me.

"That was far from the worst, wasn't it?" I say with all the calm I can muster for, by premonition or deduction, I think I know the answer. "He used people for his demonstrations, did he not?"

Baxter lowers his head and utters one word compassing a world of disgust: "Aye."

Again I wait while he thinks, and Isobel's hand slips into mine. When I look to her she silently touches her finger to her lips.

At last Baxter says, "'Twas in London Town. Y' would have been a tiny colleen of six years. Be thankful that…" he hesitates, "…that your father dinna carry you down to Newgate Prison for the show." Baxter sighs and says, "Aldini cozened prison officials into allowing him to demonstrate his 'Principal of Animal Electricity' on the body of a hanged murderer." He turns a fierce face to me and lifts a finger to make a point. I hold my breath, squeezing Isobel's hand. "N' matter what the criminal done, he is a mon and dinna deserve t' be played upon." In times of stress, his burr becomes acute. "There be lines of decency tha' mus' no be crossed.

"Accordin' to firsthand accounts, Aldini caused the body of the criminal to be placed upon a plank tilted for viewing and applied his electrodes here, and there, about the corpse. An eye opened toward the audience, the jaw opened and shut. But he was na' satisfied. When he touched a probe to the corps' anus, the dead man's body convulsed and fearsome noise emitted from his mouth. The audience was shocked to silence.

"Such dramatic Jonnies are always wi' us, and a bane upon a life based on reason, d'ye see?"

———————○———————▶———————○———————

Baxter did something then he had never done before. He laid a hand upon my cheek and, looking into my eyes with all the force inside him, said, "'Tis the cause of science that is most noble of any. For an hundred years, science has labored beneath superstition to delve the mysteries of the World.' Tis why charlatans must ne're be tolerated."

Chapter Six

"Does the world spin differently for women?"

View that which we know, that which we trust, through another set of preconceptions, and it's as though you see while standing on your head. All wrong and all right reversed and shifted. At first what you believe is so, is not. Then what you had not previously considered becomes apparent and, eventually, familiar, and you accept that which was strange, as normal.

While living with the Baxters, I learned another way to measure the year—an alternate reality or one atavistic where emotion, rather than logic, may be used as a tool. In that world, the subjective is real.

Might it be where fiction comes from?

Scots use a phrase as curious as it is apt to describe the year. They call the turning of the seasons the Wheel of Shadow and Light. To the people of Dundee, this phrase describes the soft grey short nights and long days of summer that warm their sheltered valleys followed by the black cold of far northern winter.

Hitherto, logic and reason were my Alpha and Omega. Now these became but two letters in an expanding alphabet.

"Ah, Wee Mary, there y' are in the wrong of it," Christine says.

"I do not see it." Folding my arms, I say, "Reason and rationality, these separate us from the beasts, these lift us above petty emotions, above the tyranny of Theology."

"Och."

So small a sound to hold such a world of meaning, but within that sound Christine gives me to know there is so little in my philosophy, she finds herself at a loss to know where to begin. But, being the child of a teacher, she knows she must try. So, hesitantly at first, she says, "Ye ken a time when myth as explanation of the worrld has passed, but have you asked wha' replaces it? We Scots are as enlightened as any. We are known for putting an emphasis on knowledge based upon what we can verify with our senses. We say, 'I'll believe in nothing I cannot know through seeing, hearing, touching, tasting, or what we scent.'"

When I would speak, she raises her hand to still my tongue. "But, I tell y', we Baxters place a value on that which our emotions detect as well. Has y'r heart ne're thrilled to something beyond your ability to touch? Can y' tell me feelings are nae real?"

I had not given thought to this. "Do you mean, love?"

"Ah, see Isobel?" Christian's soft smile caresses me. "I said she was bright."

According to the catechism of the Baxter family, in the rest of the world what is known as woman's wisdom is traditionally discounted to favor a male view. Equality between the genders forms another theme of my ongoing education, one that continues growing familiar with use. I think this easier for me to digest than it would be for most people. I know well what my mother wrote upon the subject.

According to Baxter and his children, although even in this enlightened age, though women might be spoken of as equal, men have altered the importance of women in favor of themselves. This was another of my mother's more trenchant observations.

Christine leans forward and takes my hands. "Here is what you need to know, Mary. Men's ways have nae always been foremost. Once there was a people, the Druids, who taught of a life centered upon the woman with men payin' respect to us for our place in the world." She nods her head. "Only proper. What woman does not appreciate the admiration of a man who she loves? Is it not like this in your mother's book? Do women not have an equal place in the world, a place alongside, rather than under men? Father asks that you think upon this awhile."

The more I turn these days over in my mind, the more it seems only logical that there should be women's values separate from those of men, and once I admit to multiple sets of ethics, I must concede they are equal.

When I arrived in Dundee, I thought I knew so much. Now, I understand I have so very much to learn.

A rare sunny afternoon lets us sit beneath the pines that grow on the edge of the Baxters' grounds. We may sit or recline on a soft carpet of fallen brown needles, where it's relatively dry beneath their branches. The sun's warmth on the earth gives off a loamy smell, and the fitful breezes sighing through pine boughs soothe with a whispering concert.

Mr. Baxter encourages us to write wherever we want. Some days we troop to the top of the hills surrounding Dundee, some days we find ourselves a spot on the banks of the Tay. When showers keep us in the house, he has us do exercises in building settings or descriptions of a character, a plot, or a scene. Any number of other aspects of writing form our lessons. Applying them, however, is left to us.

Christy recalls me to our lessons. "As your writing advances, so must your knowledge of more advanced technique. Attend me: I believe you should consider the rope. All of a piece from end to end. Each bit depends on what came before and each piece connects to what comes next.

"Think of the plot of a story as a rope. Y' begin at the beginning, by crafting a heroine," she shrugs, "or hero, and placing this worthy in some peril. Proceed with the plot to introduce other characters who might, or might not, assist in navigating problems to a climax where these perils are solved, and thence, shortly to the far end where you leave us gasping in your brilliance.

"But consider this: as y' can weave one rope atop the other, so too with plots. The reader can connect one story with another until the two become one. Begin with an introduction of your special character and let us know some danger exists, but then welcome another plot with another character. Here be a braw opportunity to bring us to know of a villain. What did the evil one do, say, feel, see? Now let us know the two stories are indeed one, connected by place or circumstance. And first write of one, weave it with the second, then the first, and so on."

"Oh, that is good."

Many days later, as I begin to master these forms, I think, *Here in this strange place, these people are teaching me ways to let my fancies take wing.*

Again, I wake to the sound of rain. Pushing off my covers, I pad to the window and look out on a grey and cheerless day.

A soft knock on my door. "Mary," Isobel's voice through the wood. "Are y' wake?"

I skip across the room and throw open the door. "Indeed I am! What o' th' clock?"

"Near eight! We thought you would sleep away the day." She's holding a tray in her hands.

"Swear, I would not! Is that breakfast I smell by chance?"

"By design!" She holds the tray out for me to see, and the scent of bacon and eggs nearly overwhelms me. "'Tis so late, this was all I could salvage from Cook."

"All? It's a feast." And a rare treat to have in my room. My nose tells me of toasted cheese and tea. I sigh, "'Twill have to do. Will y' join me?"

You do not have to ask Isobel if she wants to eat twice. I was lucky to get what I got, for when the getting of what was to be gotten was done, there was naught to be had.

Isobel scoops up a smear of marmalade with her finger. "Now that we know each other better, I would speak w' y' of something."

"Say on." I lean back in bed feeling full and happy.

She climbs up and, leaning against the piled pillows beside me, she gets right to the point. "Have y' iver loved a mon?"

Surprised to find this new intimacy, I lift my chin and say, "I think we've known each other long enough for intimate subjects. Of course. I'll be fifteen at the end of the month after all."

She lifts her eyebrows and wags her head in mockery. "Och. Such a wealth of experience wi' so many men?"

"One will do, thank you." I plunge. "Well then, your mother is dead as is mine. And does your father not miss her, also? And do you not remind him of her? I am sure he loves you as much as mine does me." I am so very happy to have someone who will understand.

Her lips press together and she blinks. With a tight smile, Isobel reaches for my hand and we sit awhile listening to the rain. Then, soft above the storm I hear her murmur, "Och."

In the months I spent with the Baxters, I came to appreciate another form of knowing, where before my Scottish idyll, reasoning from evidence to conclusion was my paramount form of knowing the truth. From then on, these touchstones I learned from my father coexist with the importance I place on listening to my emotions.

Chapter Seven

Home Again

London in 1812 bustles with the commerce of war. Her quays are packed with people and goods. The river has warships anchored waiting the chance to tie up to port or making way downriver with the tide. Only the English Navy stands in Napoleon's way, so no hint of fallibility must be heard. Sailors shout news to the shore. "Don't believe an American ship overcame Guerriere! It never happened. Britannia rules the waves!"

Daily, the flower of our young men leaves for the wars. Adding to the bustle of war, gold flows into our island from business interests that span the globe. Cargoes from our possessions in Africa, India, and the fabled islands of the South Seas pour into our ports.

As by agreement with Father, Christine accompanied me home for the winter. Our little ship is nearly lost amid all this. Home! London! Dundee has a place in my heart now, but home is still sweet. Though we all revise our memories to enrich our personal stories, I did not think for a heartbeat that others might find London less wondrous than what I remembered or that their impressions might not be the same as mine.

So I learned the way we view the world is separate for each of us.

Thus do the days of the far north summer pass into autumn. Time spent 'neath the trees of the grounds, writing, gives way to weather both chill and damp, and we abandon the Cottage to return to the winter home of the Baxters', Ellengowan.

Christine speaks to me at breakfast. Her smile is comforting and her hand upon my hair is soft as a breeze. "Y've been with us a six-month, Mary dear. Father would have you journey to London."

Six months already? Did I wish to go home? I'm sure my surprise shows, for she chuckles and says, "Only for a time. If y' wish to come back, I'm to say you will be welcome." She smiles, "Best of all, I am to accompany you. A young beauty such as you must have proper chaperonage after all."

"Did I not arrive alone?" I challenge.

Isobel holds her nose. "Barely."

I have to admit the justice of that.

"I fear the voyage." I blurt out my distress as I think of my arrival in Dundee. "I much dislike being helplessly sick."

"Ill?" Christine says. "Nay, sweeting. Put that out of your head. At this time of year, the wind blows propitiously from the north-west; waves canna' form when the wind blows across the land, and we shall sail close in. All which means the sea shall lie before us as a quiet road."

I look into the distance and smile as I consider what going home means. "I would like to see Father," I murmur.

Her words about the state of the sea are true. I do not feel so much as a twinge of the motion sickness that assails me. I'm able to stay long hours on deck thoroughly enjoying watching the land go by. We reach the mouth of the Thames, wait a few hours for the turn of the tide before we proceed up river to our berth near St. Thomas Hospital. Christine stands at the railing, flushed from the spectacle of the river and the city.

We secure a coach, and as I view the cityscape flowing past the windows, I am struck how much my conception of London has changed. Where before I felt such a joy at the might and order of the city, now I contrast the sterile stone angles with the freedom and purity of Scotland.

We alight upon the curb and no more than begin to collect our luggage when the front door opens. There is Father. Still tall, his shirt still stainless, his weskit stiff, and his coat brushed as though to receive visitors. My one constant among the many changes. I fly to him. We embrace and cover each other's faces with kisses there in the street and in view of all. Our ears drink in softly murmured endearments. Father! His arms around me! Lifting me so my feet leave the ground!

"Oh, Mary. My Mary," he whispers to me, and my heart soars. When at last he sets me down he pushes me back so he might view me entire and says, "You've grown! You're a woman!"

"I am!" I say laughing and crush into his embrace again. "And one who joys to be where she belongs!" I raise my face to meet his kisses.

Some time later, we manage introductions.

"Father, this is Christian, a sister of my heart."

"Welcome!" my father says warmly and reaches to take her hand. I tilt my head for I cannot help but sense a certain reticence on her part. But then I am distracted by the sight of Fanny standing at the top of the entry stairs.

Extending my arm to Christy, I say, "Come meet another of my true-mother's daughters." Fanny, wearing an apron and a servant's cap, descends the steps and smiles, opening her arms.

"Mary wrote of new sisters. Most welcome." Her smile is gentle. "Please do come in and be comfortable." She turns to me, "We've company aplenty and there will be a salon this night." I see she has grown to be the gracious mistress of the house. She takes naturally to the role.

Jane appears so I ask her, "Who's to speak?"

"Wordsworth, tonight, but," Jane smiles as though she reads my mind, "young Shelley may attend. Do you remember him?"

Oh yes. Of course I do.

Small William peeks around the skirts of Stepmother whose harpy's voice thunders her version of welcome. "And perhaps, Princess Mary, you'll allow us to see what good your vaunted education has done for your family? Will you so much as sit to write sommat for us to publish and thereby make contribution to our welfare?"

"Christine, this is my charming stepmother," I say and note that though Christine waits for the older woman, the wife of the house, to extend her hand as is her right of place, she might stand thus until New Year's Day.

"Go on then!" Stepmother says with a pointed sniff in our direction. "Clean the stink of travel from you, and stay in your room till you're called." The woman has managed to mortify me within five minutes of my arrival. She spins on her heel and retreats into the house, leaving me to embrace William.

"Is there a servant who might carry our equipage upstairs?" I ask Fanny.

Fanny says in a small voice. "Come let us each bear part of the burden and 'twill soon be done." She lifts one bag, William takes two to show how he has grown, and

Jane and Christine and I bear the rest. We've no more than placed our luggage in my room when Fanny says, "Ask no more for servants Mary. They are gone in the name of economy. We've still a cook, for which may we be truly grateful, and two maids to tend the household, but all else is to be undertaken at our hands."

Times change, and fortunes with them.

"How do I stink?" Christine asks, looking into the large ewer of day-warmed water in our room.

Jane says, "That's mostly Mother," but standing close to us, she wrinkles her nose. "Though I am sure a swipe would not be amiss." But at the door, she turns. "And Christine? Do be welcome here."

Christine and I bathed each other, exchanging light words while I hoped this homecoming was not an augury of events to follow.

Chapter Eight

Observations

I found in Christine the sister of my heart that I named her upon our arrival. No small comfort, as Stepmother made my life as much a toil as Father made my mind brighten in the light of my new-learned discipline.

Father took delight in questioning me of Baxter's teachings. Yet, though I cherished being close once more, I often surprised myself by wishing to hear Mr. Baxter's voice call me "Wee Mary" again.

Another surprise, I began counting the days till I might return to Dundee.

When Christy and I have a moment to ourselves in the days after our arrival, I say, "Father confesses his expenses are at ebb."

She blinks in surprise. "I see scarce evidence of it in the near nightly entertainments y' enjoy. Bright candles of wax and lanterns light well warmed rooms, and there is food aplenty lining table. These speak of sufficiency, not poverty."

"As did the ancient Greeks, so Father looks for support from those who feel enriched by philosophy, but though there are fewer these days than in the past, he feels he must carry on his salons as before." I stand with my hands behind my back, one of Father's favorite positions for speaking, and say, "Polonius thus to Hamlet: 'Appearances oft proclaim the man.' So prosperity must be evident for men to give ear to what I say."

O'er the course of the winter, many guests arrive and depart. The evenings run together in a continuum of readings: philosophy, poetry, politics, and discussions on the art of writing. Mr. Coleridge is one favorite, and not only nostalgia is the main source of his attraction for our guests.

On one such night, Shelley appears. I come upon him by chance as he's speaking with another guest in the hallway, and I take the liberty of watching him. *He's unchanged.* I look again. *No, that's wrong, He's grown in confidence and shows this from his easy laugh though surrounded by the toast of English philosophy.*

As though he knows where I am, he directs his penetrating gaze to me. A slow smile creases his mouth as he steps forward to grasp my hands.

"Here is who I hoped to see tonight. They told me you had lately returned."

Feigning a need to check with the kitchen, I fled the instant he released my hands.

Stepmother is particularly odious the next day with her the constant harping that I "do something remunerative," so I escape to the kirkyard of St. Pancras and the solace of my mother's grave. Here in the center of the graveyard, summer daisies spatter the grass, and tiger lilies make islands in the sward between the pools of shadow cast by ancient trees. Blue sky and green grass are leavened by my presence. My dress, white with a pattern of gold Bourbon fleurs-de-lis, features an unbroken fall of material from an Empire waist cinched with a blue ribbon that allows my blossoming bosom to be revealed by a low décolletage. Resting my head on the sun-warmed gravestone, I close my eyes. My shoes lie next to me, and my stockinged feet are turned upward. My hat of whitened straw, with a blue ribbon, sits cocked atop the stone. I sigh and lift the hem of my dress above my pink garters, the better to enjoy the sensuous breeze.

Wait! I hear stealthy footsteps close by. I flinch and open my eyes prepared to condemn whoever interrupts me in this private moment, but I see Percy as he kneels next to me and hear his whisper.

The Body and the Soul united then.

A gentle start convulsed Ianthe's frame;

Her veiny eyelids quietly unclosed;

Moveless awhile the dark blue orbs remained.

She looked around in wonder, and beheld

Henry, who kneeled in silence by her couch,

Watching her sleep with looks of speechless love.

I tilt my head upward and lower my eyelashes almost to my cheekbones with artistic deliberation.

"Who is Henry?"

"Me. Poetic license. Your sister told me I would discover you here."

"Jane or Fanny?"

"Fanny."

"Ah." *Fanny loves me. Jane might have tried to stay him for herself.* "As you have come to find me you may as well sit." Pushing up and propping my back against the stone, I pat the ground. His smile as his eyes take in my legs is…intriguing. I am careful to pull my skirt down until the fabric brushes my toes.

He looks about. "This is an unusual location for so beautiful a young woman to while away a warm day."

Beautiful? Glancing meaningfully over my shoulder at the headstone I say, "I come to be close to my true-mother, as much as to flee the discord of my house."

He reads the stone and nods. "They say she and your father are poorly matched for intellect."

"Naught but true, but… my father is both patient and kind to me. He loves me as he loved my true-mother."

"And your stepmother does not?"

"No, nor has she ever. I believe she is threatened by the love my father still feels for my mother."

"Does she show her jealousy, for so I conceive it to be, in any ways deleterious to you?"

I try to keep my voice light, for this conversation is more personal than I think proper, but it feels good to express myself to someone other than my sisters, so I mutter, "In what way does she not?"

"One as beauteous as you cannot be many more years without a suitor." He moves close and his lips come near mine but he stops an inch away. My breath flutters. I close my eyes and move toward him.

I giggle as we touch.

He pulls back. "And what do you find amusing?"

"Kissing someone without whiskers feels oddly bare."

"Pray you grow used to it," he says, moving toward me again.

A moment later, he sits back and glances at the headstone upon which I lean. "And what would your, ah, true-mother say of my being here now?"

An imp upon my shoulder makes me intone, "Geeet offff myyy toooooeeees."

Other than kisses he behaves with respect, though his attention fires my imagination. When I make an observation on the meaning of one of his poems, we grow lost in our conversation until the shadows lengthen.

At last he asks, "What would you be, Mary?"

I think, *No one else has questioned me about my intentions for my life.* "A philosopher," I answer him readily. "Though I have far to go. I must school myself to write better."

He purses his lips. "Perhaps I might help you."

Thinking of the time brilliant Percy first paid me heed makes me smile.

I listened, rapturously is the word, when he read at salons. My eyes never left him as I sought to discipline my feelings that others might not see the effect he had on me. Was I ever so young?

Soon enough it was time for my return to Dundee. I freely confess, despite my new formed infatuation with Percy, I looked forward to that homecoming.

Chapter Nine

Ethics and Ethos

Ignorance. A child delights in the rush and pull of the ocean and the glimmer of sun upon the waves, never thinking of peril in the current. How do we know a thing is right before we do it? Or how do we know what is wrong, especially when one we know and love tells us what we do is correct and proper?

"I did not know better." A phrase often used to absolve us.

But I learned.

Again a pleasant journey north with the waves obedient to my wishes. Mr. Baxter is waiting for us at the docks with Isobel. I spy them when the ship is still far downriver. Tears sparkle my sight. I blink in surprise. Though I thrill to be again in Dundee, I had not thought my heart so full.

Once we are in the carriage, he holds Christine's hand a moment, then reaches to mine. "So, you've come back to us."

On the ride home, it comes to me how I thought his interest in me is virtuous, paternal, a man who values me for my mind, but I did not think until this moment that he loves me the way his daughters love me. Sitting across from him in the carriage, I say, "I do return to you, yes, for I believe you are honest enough to know 'there are more things in heaven and earth than are dreamt of in philosophy.'" I would need to add a new definition for love, one that included someone aloof yet, indisputably, valued. I should have noticed afore this. Once I am breathing in the scent of the Cottage, polished wood and pines, I say, "Here is a world I have learned to appreciate."

"And what is there of our little Dundee to which y' would ascribe such virtue?"

I lift an eyebrow. "You promised me mountains if I returned."

He places his hand under his chin as he pretends to think. "I may have."

"You did and I am sure of it!" I cry.

"I did, an' y' shall tread upon their mighty slopes. However, d' ye not romanticize the natural world? Many do and draw meanings that tilt the scales toward the untouched world."

"At times I compare what I find here with the city, to London's detriment, but on the whole, I think I treat both equitably, neither labeling one good nor the other bad."

He puts his hands behind his back. Associating the pose with an impending lesson, I sit upon a chair with my hands clasped upon my lap, frankly wondering at my eager anticipation. It comes to me how much I have missed this.

He says, "There is a conceit abroad in the world called 'The Noble Savage.' Philosophers oft ascribe an effect that a corrupting influence of modern culture upon mankind. Th' proposition states that all human beings, when raised in a state free of th' deleterious influences of cultivated society, may be perfect in themselves.

"When report of early explorers of th' American Continent filtered back to the homeland, the aboriginal peoples were described as tall and of upright mien; an openhanded people who, ownin' nothing, coveted nothing; a people who freely gave help to those arrivin' starving upon their shores.

"In attempt to explain them, the concept of a human untouched by society's ills was invented: a being uneducated, illiterate, but nae-the-less for tha' a human being possessed of nobility. An apparent oxymoron, a 'noble savage.'

"But when reports mentioned th' wars among these people, which were both brutal and vicious, we retracted the name of nobility from them. Still, the concept lives on." He chuckles. "But here y' are not a day in the house and your luggage all ahoo and I keep you with my natterin'. For now, 'tis enough y' know y' aire welcome."

"My thanks, Sir." I curtsey to him. My heart beats a little faster as I slide my hand over the smooth wood of the banister and climb the well-remembered steps to my room.

I'm home.

Mr. Baxter encourages me in developing a sense of the fictive voice as Isobel and Christine said he would.

"Nah, nah," he says, shaking his head as he reviews my pages. "Y' plod along here asking your readers to tread weary miles. 'He does this,' and 'She does that.' Dinna *tell* me wha' they do, use the language to *show* me their actions. And more, think you of how your prime character *views* the scene. What does he *see*? And give y' thought to what senses other than their eyes tell them? What scent is there? How the surface under his or her fingers feels? Neither you nor your audience will live this story but through the senses of your characters. Craft those w' skill."

In my pages, the boughs near the Cottage become dark shadows of impending danger; the slope of the earth from Ellengowan toward the waters of the Tay urges my characters forward.

Baxter suggests I use my personal experiences to inform my descriptions, but my own existence seems a pale and sterile place. Slowly, I learn I can put my flights of fancy, as Mr. Shelley calls them, to paper. On the sides of the woodless mountains that ring Dundee, I learn both the desolation of being alone and elation at having solitude be enough.

Another lesson awaits. I learn no matter how beautifully these words flow across my page like birds in flight, they must say something worth the reading. My message must be as important as the words themselves, and a world of thought opens. *I must learn all I can about...*I shake myself in frustration...*about the world entire,* and that's too much for my head to hold. But I resolve to pay more attention to Baxter's discourses on the nature of things.

"Come y' in, Wee Mary," Baxter says. "There are lessons of the science of living things I'd impart. We shall address animal husbandry."

I can see he's selected some books for me. I pick them up one by one and turn them toward the light from the open window that I might read their titles while he tells me what is in their pages. "This one's by th' Swede, Carl Linnaeus. A practical taxonomy of how things are related. I find the poems in his *Botanic Garden* an entertainin' way to deliver his thoughts on plant reproduction. Y' see, Linnaeus wants his audience to know sexuality in humans is neither sacred nor profane, but a part of the natural world, nothing more."

I'm eager to learn another new subject. "Should not Christine and Isobel be here?"

"This is a lesson I've delivered afore to all my children, one that is of import when a young woman becomes old enough to bear young."

I sit quiescent at that. How surprising it is to think I could be a mother someday soon.

"We'll begin with the study of genetics," he says. "The science began when men sought to improve their stock of both plants and animals through selective breeding. Farmers throughout time thought this was a method to improve their stock through allowing only those living things possessing preferred traits to procreate."

Days pass upon the subject and I, a fascinated student, work as hard as I've ever done to understand. How men might purposely alter the flora to produce more useful foodstuffs had never occurred to me. Wherein did the thoughts arise that led through step after step to produce the wheat that makes my bread? If the tomato is cousin to deadly nightshade, why is it not poisonous?

And when he has done with vegetation, we begin the fauna.

"Consider the dog, canis lupus familiaris. Using Linneus' classification scheme, 'Canis' is the Genus, rather than family. The two names that follow describe the species and *the sub-species,* which indicate a close relationship between the common grey wolf and th' hound who even now snores upon the hearth."

"The name implies a close relationship," I muse. "But dog and wolf are as different as morning and night."

"This is of much import, Wee Mary. For in study of the life upon the Airth y' must be aware the tiniest changes may portend great results."

Now when I think of that time, it seems the biggest lesson was that things closest to us are the most difficult to see.

Chapter Ten

Two Lessons of Biology

Heretofore I did not think truth could be cruel. Blunt, or tactless, I'd seen those, but not cruel.

Baxter was as patient as he was inexorable in his desire that I understand a truth he felt I needed to see.

———————◇———————

One night late in October, I struggle with dissecting a partridge when Baxter says, "Y've the gentle touch of a chirurgeon, Mary."

I use my fingers to pry open the cage of the ribs and view the heart. "The minute qualities of the inner processes make it difficult for me to secure a good view."

"Aye." He nods agreement. "Was this fowl enormous, y'd an easier time with your knives. Larger animals are easier to work with."

There is another lesson Baxter would have me learn. Animal husbandry begins to occupy our lessons. He starts with breeding schemes and their results.

Baxter teaches me two methods of improving stock in addition to selective breeding: line or in-breeding. Both of these offer the benefit of emphasizing certain characteristics deemed desirable. In the case of the dog, domesticity and loyalty or size and speed to assist with the hunt. In other animals, there are many other traits as well, such as milk production in the cow, or fleece quality in sheep.

My suitably primed mind leaps ahead. "Are humans also bred for characteristics?"

He shrugs and sticks his lower lip out. "Have y' heard it said that a person is well bred, or a family shows good breeding?"

"I had thought it only a manner of speaking—the effect of culture rather than blood."

"Often it is both. Legions of the poor cover the world. Of the rich there are few and of royalty there is a very small number. By examination of the lines of marriage, we may find effects similar to line breeding in livestock."

Of all the revelations attendant to enlightened thinking, this one amazes me in its audacity: that aristocratic hierarchy can be studied as we do the bloodlines of horses. And yet, after all was said against the concept, why not? If indeed we were the paragon of mammals, why not examine us as we do the quintessence of dust? In this light may we not discuss royalty the same as we speak of other living things?

He straightens from where he studies my face as I think and says, "Think you of the Pharaohs of Egypt."

I say, "I know the Ptolemy rulers married brothers and sisters so that the dynasty could continue unbroken."

"They did, but I believe there was a cost. Such breeding can engender defective offspring in those societies which practiced their choice of mates to exclude all but a few families. Members of the European royal houses suffer from this. There is the falling sickness and the bleeding sickness. It is whispered among the enlightened our King George is mad. Did he not pursue the American colonies to the detriment of our nation? The Regency was forced upon us to deal with him."

"Have others considered the breeding of humans?" I ask.

"Aye. The Catholic Church constructed a chart listing degrees of unhealthy associations accordin' to relationships. As far back as the 1200s under Roman Catholic Law, marriage was deemed sinful if it fell between cousins. Such association is termed the fourth degree. Relations to the third degree are listed as half brothers and sisters and relationships between grandparents and grandchildren were characterized as that of the second degree. Worst of all is the connection between parent and child, do y' see?"

I go still.

"I believe I do."

"All for the reason of eliminating the defective, or the infirm, or the deformed, and not always as a rule, but often enough, Mary. Often enough."

I am silent awhile digesting the import of this. At last I look up. "But not always."

Though one may hear of an event, direct experience can be a far more unsettling level of discovery.

"Y' must hurry your brekkie, Mary, for we go visit a farm nearby," Isobel chirps. "Father has the carriage ready." She grabs a piece of bread and slides her egg upon it. "'tis oot the door wi' us, we are!"

A day with a high, fine sky greets us as we roll to a nearby farmstead. "Y're in time," the farmer tells Baxter, shaking his hand. "She's goin' to calve any moment."

We go into the barn and step up to peer over the wood of a stall, and see there a cow lies upon a thick bed of straw. Our farmer enters and seats himself behind the animal as her distended belly gives heave after heave. At last the farmer reaches into the animal and pulls with all his might.

"Ay, me," whispers Christy.

"Och, fie," mutters Isobel.

The cow has birthed a monster with two heads.

Baxter puts his hand on my shoulder. "She was bred to a bull that was her offspring. The result lies before y'."

I look to Isobel and see on her face not shock, but sorrow.

My mind leaps.

"Are we not animals?" I ask.

He hesitates. His eyes search mine. "As I have said."

A shift, the smallest change of position, and all one sees changes until what was beauty becomes hideous.

I have known men, perfect in their apprehension, who will call an apple an orange should the subject touch their beliefs.

"I believe!" they say in defiance. "And what I believe is so!" No amount of evidence to the contrary will dissuade them from the course of their beliefs.

You see, there is a cruelty to truth when applied to oneself.

Chapter Eleven

The Sundering

I was, for all my acumen, only fifteen years of age. Baxter misestimated my capacity to process the letter I found that day. What I read profoundly shocked me. I suppose I acted badly. Even from this remove of years, I remember the events of the time as though my senses are submerged in deep water.

October comes to a close. Throughout the day, the temperature rises on a fitful south wind. Clouds begin to build in the north, and thunder marches toward Dundee.

"Mr. Baxter?" I call as I knock at the door to his study. "Sir?" I open the heavy dark wood a crack and lean my head in to look. Late afternoon sunlight slanting through the tall window falls across the bookcases lining a wall, but I still see no one in the room. What I do see is his desk piled with work.

Near the center of the green blotter lies a folded paper, a letter. I suppose I cannot be blamed for seeing that, but once I see it is addressed from my home, my curiosity will not be sated. Despite the intrusion upon this house, I open it.

From the first, it captures and holds me.

> *From: Christian Baxter*
> *C/o William Godwin*
> *Somers Town, London*
> > *To: William Baxter*
> > *Ellengowan*
> > *Dundee Scotland*
>
> *Dearest Father:*
> *I write to you in the hopes all is well at home. I grieve to say,*
> *all is not well with me.*

Because I could not fathom what might have been amiss, I read on.

> *I confess I was troubled by your instructions to me. You*
> *charged me with close observation of Godwin's house. I felt*
> *my task to be a great indiscretion of propriety expected of*
> *being a guest.*

A spy then? A viper in my home? She began her description with our arrival.

> *Upon alighting from the cab that carried us from the quay*
> *to Godwin's door, I witnessed what at first I thought to be a*
> *display of love that occurred upon the walk before Godwin's*
> *door. Affection replete with cries of joy and kisses, but a*
> *display that quickly became so pronounced in its intimacy and*
> *protracted in its duration it passed the bounds of propriety*
> *and drew the stares of passersby.*

Other relations between my stepmother and me, and then she told of a night I well remembered. She told of waking, of finding me gone from our bed, and of searching our house to find me. Until...

> *I heard a deep voice murmuring that was Godwin's, and a*
> *lighter voice I knew to be Mary's. Though I could not hear*
> *what they said through the door, the tone was at once of such*
> *intimacy, I did not need to know the actual words. There*
> *were silences as well. In time, I had no need to see within to*
> *know what occurred.*

Her reaction is clear enough.

> *I whispered "Fie!" as I fled. "Fie! Fie! Fie!"*
> *An half-hour later the bed moved and Mary pressed her*
> *frozen self to my back. "Christine?" she whispered. "I'm cold."*
> *I could nae speak, but I rolled over and held her and stroked*
> *her hair until she ceased to shiver.*
> *She smelled of cigar and gin.*
> *I long to return to Dundee with all my heart.*
> *Your dutiful and loving daughter,*
> > *Christine*

There is a pressure in my ears. Sounds seem muffled as through cotton. My anger kindles. Her letter condemns me. Why would they do this? My Father and

I love each other with a love that surpasses most fathers and daughters, but what of it? And what business is it of anyone else's?

I stop as a thought occurs to me. There in the study, the lessons of genetics come home. Step by step has Mr. Baxter sought to teach me the consequence of such actions, but...Oh, but I love him. What must they think of me? Why do they pretend to love me?

I turn and find Baxter standing in the doorway. "Well," he says, "t'is well past time y' should be thinking on a husband and a home of your own."

"I have no wish to stay here!" I spit.

"Och," he murmurs softly. "That's your way, is it, to throw away all rather than hate wha' has brought y' harm. I know y've taken sore hurt from me. What was done was done for the best."

My anger shows upon my face. "And how often has that excuse been spoken?"

With sadness he says, "More times than there are stars in the heavens, I think."

At that, my rage erupts. I make no effort to contain the coldness I feel.

"What more should I have from those who taint my greatest love?" I throw at him. "No, it is worse than that. You've taught me shame, and that shame has made me to understand I must sever with him. Though you've not a shred of proof, you taught me well what that loving may cause. I'll never, never chance birthing a monster. If, however, you think I shall love you for it, you are mistaken, and if you dare to tell me I ought to be grateful for such a gift, you are wrong."

But he does something he never did before: slowly he takes me his arms. Confused, I fall into his embrace and my tears flow upon his weskit. "Fine luck to y', Wee Mary," he whispers as he kisses my hair. "Send a letter when y' can."

I find Christian and Isobel out of doors seated on a blanket reading. Christian looks up and scans my face. "You know, then."

My voice is flat. "I found your letter."

"I'm thinkin' y' blame us."

I'd hurl that truth at her, but I'm too tired.

"Who else thought she saw shame and never spoke? Who else but the family Baxter to teach me to hate what I am?"

Christian considers this calmly. "And what could I have said?"

"Are y' truly gone from us?" whispers Isobel.

"I am."

She sighed, "Even so, our father did so well in teaching you to eschew your unnatural feelings for that mon. I think we may fear no repetition of this, this..." she looks as though she has something filthy in her mouth, "devotion."

Isobel looks over to me. "I think you not the same person who came to us. You were quick enough then, and grown formidable in using your faculties. N'more will 'y tread that road."

Did I have it wrong, or did they? Should one be condemned for that which is no fault of hers? What might Father do if I avoided him? Or where I might go did he toss me to the street? Who would have my care?

In time, I learned the limits of blame and guilt, but my best lesson ought to have been forgiveness, and the value of providing for myself.

Chapter Twelve

In My Father's House

Learning was where you'd find it, should you keep your ears and eyes and mind open. So said Mr. Baxter, "Will you, nil you, your lessons will find you." I thought knowing when to open my heart and when to close it, or when to let go and hold close, were lessons I knew already, but these were things I would go on learning my entire life.

As I return to London, for a wonder, the winds and waves are both propitious, sending me smoothly southward. Northwesterly breezes blow but steady the whole of my voyage. They allow the captain to keep his ship close to land by day, and not much farther off at night, letting the sea, and me, rest quiescent. A mate explains the sights to me.

"See there, young miss," he tells me the second night of the voyage as I stand by the railing. "There be the light at Tynemouth near Newcastle. Were we to be passin' the point by day, y' might behold the old priory what defied William Rufus, whose ships plundered the place. A monk sent a prayer to St. Oswin, who ran the ships to their deaths on the rocks of Coquet Island in weather no worse than this. Such is the way for the uncontrite."

I may be uncontrite, but I have learned unemotional rationality is not the totality of wisdom.

The mate tells me many things in the days we travel south and I am grateful for his company. And so I come, well entertained and in remarkable health, to the mouth of the Thames early one morning and near enough to the flooding tide that the captain makes for London that very day. I shake my head to cast out the thought of how Christian cared for me when last I voyaged here and resolve not to turn my mind to the Baxters.

Soon enough, we make the quay and tie up. I receive permission to stand out of the way upon the quarter deck while the cargo unloads. Seeing a lad, I lean out to bespeak him.

"D'ye know the house of William Godwin the philosopher, boy?"

His answer is diffident. "I do. What would you?"

"Run you to my father's house and inform him of my arrival. Surely he will pay you for your trouble, lad."

"Walker!" he says with distain, and he turns to go.

"Wait. I've a tuppence if that will do."

The bargain struck, I wait no long while for Father's reply and soon see him on the quay, waving and pushing through the crowds. Upon reaching the side of the ship, he ascends the gangway and crosses the deck to where I stand, and then I am wrapped once again in his arms and he seeks my kisses.

I place my hand against his chest to hold him away.

"What's amiss?" he asks.

"Not in front of the sundry," I whisper.

He looks around, and at last we part. Though he seeks to hold my hand I do not return the pressure of his fingers on mine. His eyes on mine search for what is different between us.

"I trust you've a good voyage. Here, I'll secure some aid for your equipage," he looks at my few boxes, "such as may be. Though it's not far. We've moved, you'll come to a new home."

Father has removed to another set of buildings, he tells me, the better to house the family and the publishing concern he now owns. I spend the next days taking note of other changes. Without any need of asking, my observations allow me to understand how my family's situation has changed as well.

The house is not grand. Not a tenth of what life in the Polygon had been, and the neighborhood, redolent with its odor of cess, is not the only thing that stinks. My Stepmother, ever the shrew, proves my absence has not made her heart grow fonder of me by the width of a single hair.

"Y'r a woman now, and an eddicated one, at least by repute. Y'll contribute to the family by assisting in our publication concern. Would y' assist with labor, or do y' harbor pretenses of authorship? Sommat to fill pages would save us the cost of hiring a hack. We do well with stories for children. I mind you like those."

I told her such a request will be thought about.

"Put on no airs w' me, miss." Her face turns ugly. "Mr. Baxter writes your arm is healed. You'll work and that is that!"

It would seem Baxter's betrayals have not ceased.

Once I am in my room with Fanny, she reluctantly tells me the tale of our fortune. "Father tries to write, but no one is publishing him now. I fear the cares of our situation eat at him."

"I've noted the house, the neighborhood, and the lack of servants."

"All but a few have left, and those who stay are not the best." She shrugs, but then she smiles. Years drop from Fanny's shoulders when she smiles. She is again familiar. "Mother threatened to let Cook go, and Cook went. As far as to her sister's and as long as for a week. Dinners being what they were, when Father sent for her, Mother kept her tongue and so we're able to eat what is served."

"Our money?"

"Little. Remember that handsome Percy Shelley? He tenders Father a goodly sum, but he is near the only one to do so. He still comes to dinner, not often enough for my taste. And salons are few. Perhaps one in a month, if that."

A sharp rat-a-tat on the street door sounds all the way to my room. "Someone using a cane to knock." Fanny's face clouds. "'Twill be a creditor." She turns to me with a resigned sigh. "I must deal with them. Mother says it is beneath her, and Father says it disturbs his work to listen to 'the importuning of peasants.'"

With that, she hugs me and leaves me listening to her voice muted with distance conciliating and cajoling. I hear clearly, "Might I seek more time, good sir. Fear naught, you shall be paid." A man's voice loudly says, "I will not be robbed. Perhaps a tipstaff might make Godwin aware of his duties."

I sigh and think, *Such is life in my father's house.*

The next day such cold grips London, I dare not toss in my bed for fear of losing the warm fug I have built up in my cocoon of covers. Just before dinner, near three o' the clock, I seek yet another slip to wear beneath my dress for what warmth it will keep.

I had just lifted my dress and donned thicker stockings when I hear the door to my room open. Father has found me. He says, "Mary, y' did not come to me last night."

"Dear Father," I begin slowly for I know this will be difficult. "As I am no longer a child but a woman able to bear children, we must show to the world as daughter and much cherished father."

He steps behind me and wraps his arms about me saying, "Is this Baxter's teaching come between us?"

I take a breath and my eyes close at the well-loved scent of him.

"It is, Father. I've become aware of...consequences."

Turning me to face him, he holds me tenderly.

"Yes, you have indeed grown into a woman."

With my nose buried into his shirt, I breath him in and think it has been too, too long since we have known each other. He dips his head to kiss me softly, as he did when I was little. It takes my breath from me. "There will come a time when you must go your way, my Mary dear." And he places another kiss upon my no longer resisting lips. "But not yet, dear one. Surely, not yet."

"As you love me, Father. Not ever. Now let us sorrow for the loss, but champion each other for the gain."

"What gain?"

———————◇———————

What gain indeed? My self respect? No, I'll not play the hypocrite. But there was relief a hair's breadth from pain and I knew, unless my situation changed, I would soon fall.

Chapter Thirteen

Percy and Love

So passed the winter while I contrived to avoid Father's embraces with lessening conviction and to deal with Stepmother's demands. Many times in those weeks, I plead a need to pay a daughter's homage to the St. Pancreas kirkyard. As the year turned to spring, I stayed longer.

This day, the first warm day of spring, when jonquils are sending their thick shoots toward the sky and sunlight upon my mother's tombstone lends a warmth to my back, I think about my situation.

If Father contributed naught to pay for my education in Scotland, I know there will be naught for a tutor now. Stepmother begins a refrain, "Y'r old enough to be a wife and out of my house." What I see and hear at home convinces me my time there is through, but should I seek to leave, my keeping will be at my hands or none. Hopelessness overcomes me and I shed a tear that falls upon the new grasses of the grave.

"Well, now." A voice breaks upon my reverie. Looking into the sun I shade my eyes with my hand and behold someone standing over me.

"Once again, I find you here," says Percy Shelley.

I turn away and wipe at my eyes. Thank whatever fortitude I had that I formed a notion to cry in earnest only a moment before his appearance. At least my visage is neither reddened nor swollen and I am able to face him and answer forthrightly, "You come upon me unlooked for in this private place, sir."

He tilts his head. "Am I forgot? Do you remember neither voice, nor kiss? Can you tell me you do not dream of the wonder of that, even as I have done?"

Oh yes. I remember that day.

I bite my lower lip and scan slowly up the length of him. Percy is not a tall man but one slim in girth. His trousers tightly encase well-formed limbs.

I remember Fanny saying he contributes much to my family's welfare. She says he replied to her query regarding his generosity by saying, "One must pay for what one receives even if no price is requested. I despise the parasites who feed upon your father's thoughts without compensation. Then, there is the chance to speak with you and your sisters."

She says, "The man *will* flirt."

Jane has previously freighted me with the gossip surrounding him. "Percy will soon contend as laureate of English poetry if he does not kill himself with his libertine lifestyle. He's put aside his wife since you left. Harriet is devastated to be abandoned with their child." Licking her lips, I think her relish at another's failing reminds me of her mother. "And so, young Percy becomes fair game." She smiles saucily. "Aye me! Is he not beautiful?"

Perhaps I am more in need of someone to share confidences, but in justice on any other day I might have welcomed him to the cemetery for more kisses.

"Come." I extend a hand to the mound of earth next to me. "Sit and reveal to me what passes with you. I've naught else for intelligent companions." I attempt to play the coquette, tilting my head and wrinkling my nose as I say, "You'll do, at least 'till one appears."

He looks around. "I think I must enliven your company. Your friends are indeed of grave disposition."

At first, we spoke of Harriet.

"She was a vivacious, clever, and pretty girl. One trapped in the dullest of surroundings. Her father ran a tavern. Conversation? Typical tap room sallies as she set the tankards down is all she might hope for." He shrugged. "For my part, I was very much in love with her, but after the birth of my first child, she grew distant and neglectful." He looked into my eyes. "She began tending to the child far more than she did me. Now she holds me to my marriage vow, while ignoring my need for love." He tilts his head back. "There hangs a sign over the gates of Hades that applies to her. Do you know it?"

"Abandon all hope ye who enter here. I've read as well as most." I lift my head and smile as a ribald meaning occurs to me. "Wait, do you imply innuendo?"

He laughs and puts his hands behind his head.

One thought leads to another and before I imagine it possible, I tell him of my dissatisfaction with my house.

"...and as for my stepmother, I, I..." I fold my arms and wrinkle my brow, and a thought occurs to me. "Do you ever find an a-religious life inhibits our ability to curse like a Christian? Think of the number of invectives that are rooted in the deity or the pantheon of myth. I fear our language impedes my ability to adequately damn the woman. She is, is..."

Percy smiles and leans slightly toward me. "Execrable?"

The joy I turn upon him is like the dawn after a storm. "Percy! You've a facility with language!"

He quirks his mouth to the side. "A few have remarked upon it."

Taking my hands, he says, "Mary, mind me. I have seen the chaos of your home, the unreasoning anger of your stepmother." He pauses. "And the way your father looks at you."

My tears threaten of a sudden. *I must guard myself 'gainst this growing honesty between us.* "You are overly bold, sir."

His hand beneath my chin softly turns my head to face him. "I see how you must run from your door thinking a cold kirkyard superior to the walls where your family abides."

My tears overflow.

"And I tell you this, Mary Godwin: I think you a paragon of thought and heart."

I come to him in a rush with my arms full open. My arms circle his neck to hold him to me. I feel him kissing the tears from my eyelashes. I thrill to the contact, and do not pull away when his lips touch mine.

When I return for supper, Jane follows me upstairs to my room.

"How now?" I ask.

"Did you have a good day, sitting alone on her grave?"

"I had my book. The day passed."

"And was it warm?"

"Passing so. Warm enough."

"And were you alone?"

My head comes up. "Did you tell Shelley where to find me?"

"I did not." She turns and takes a step away while her hands untangle a nonexistent knot in her hair. "He may have stopped by to see me, but before I could come to him, I heard Fanny mention where he could find you."

"Then, you know I was not alone."

"So will everyone else if you do not change your stockings."

"And what do they have to do with people knowing my business?"

"You've grass stains upon your heels."

A chaperone is needed, not one to prevent either the kissing or other things I would gladly essay, but someone who will prevent visitors to the cemetery from seeing us and sending word to Father. Jane, I believe, though discomfited that Percy pays court to me rather than her, might be cajoled into our conspiracy.

One day in her room, she holds her hand out to me from where she stands before the mirror. I step to her, and we face the glass together. "Between the two of us, Mary," she says, "I would think me the more fair."

I stop the retort my lips are already forming and, mindful of my need I say, "Dear sister, of course you are."

"Men are idiots," she says, smiling at my recognition of her superiority. Arranging her countenance into that of a happy conspirator she says, "Of course I'll help you."

The next day, and from then on, she accompanies me to the church where Percy and I carry on our assignation.

"Father wishes the two of you be chaperoned," she lies to Percy as she walks between us to St. Pancreas.

"Sweet hypocrite!" Percy cries. "Scant years past, he wrote of marriage as a repressive monopoly! He's said many and many a time that one must, his word, *must,* be free to love as one will."

"Perhaps it is your passion to which he objects," Jane says thoughtfully. "As to my role here," she looks to me and places a finger to her cheek. "I think your reputation is all that is left to preserve and so," she straightens to attention like one of the King's Guards, "I shall stand watch outside the gates that none may see."

Though she proves an adequate guard, I catch Jane peeking between the headstones to watch us, often. Sisterly competition being what it is, when Percy closes his eyes above me and a wondrous thrill invades my being, I tilt my head back and moan loudly so she might hear.

On a day in May, when the sun warms the earth and the scent of grass crushed beneath us is fresh, our clothing artfully disarranged, and I sit astride him, Percy says, "I love you, Miss Godwin." I arch my back and thrust my hips happily atop him that I might enjoy his gasp of pleasure and say, "And I, sir, love you as well."

———————————⦿———————————

Percy and I began to visit friends and be seen in public together. Out of respect for Father's reputation, we continued to have Jane with us. Her presence gave us the semblance of propriety and spared my father more embarrassment.

Step by step, I moved closer to my freedom.

Chapter Fourteen

Percy

Long ago, I thought men's attention was a simple thing. Now I needs must think of a way to keep the focus of Percy's mind upon me. I misdoubt I was ever one to simper or to wheedle a man like Jane. She had a thunderous subtlety.

But could little Mary Godwin be alluring, enthralling, or beguiling? Well, there's a subject for the ages.

Percy Shelley finds me interesting, I think as I look into the mirror to check my dress before walking to the Kirkyard.

Unlike Jane's heavy-handed coquette, I favor a direct approach as the best way to take the measure of a man. Though I knew the elements of love, spring becomes early summer as I learn the art. The flowers of our trysting place at St. Pancras change from daffodils to iris and the walls of our bower under the willow fill with bright green leaves that shield us from casual view.

"What attributes does a person like you find attractive in women?" I'm lying on the sward beneath a willow.

"And what am I?" Percy murmurs. "Though I will say this was a subject often discussed in my younger days."

"What an ancient you are? You have not more than twenty years!" I frown at him, adorably.

"Twenty in August."

"Were we both made in Ceasar's month?"

"At its beginning."

"And I at the end."

"Bookends." His smile undoes me. "But to continue," he purses his lips and says, "my best friend and fellow student, Hogg, and I held forth on these qualities of uppermost importance to be found in a woman," he shrugs, "in times when other investigations were not pressing, and a bottle or two was to be found."

"I believe I know these feminine qualities," I reply with a trace of that sardonic tone easily overlooked by one who does not know me well.

Percy knows me. He smiles and lays a finger aside his nose. "A considerable cadre of women ascribe no greater intellectual acuity to the appreciation of their persons beyond physical lust." He looks into my eyes. "I assure you, this does not apply to you."

"No?" But I think, *Does he say he finds me original?* I bow to acknowledge the touch and then let him know my point is not corked. "Perhaps it is only when you are sated that my appearance is not the," he tilts his head, "sole cause of your attention."

"As you will," he murmurs with that direct gaze that caresses me. "But I say truly, when I am with you finer thoughts inhabit my mind. Mary, listen; in my youth I spoke of the ideal woman as one who combined strength of mind with ardor of heart."

"Perhaps you wish beauty combined with adequate admiration for your person?" There is a tone of challenge overlaying my words.

"Admitted. That too. For what man in the power of life would not wish his lover to love him in all ways?" Percy tries changing the subject. "Harriet, however, possesses little if any of this."

My exasperation flares. "Then, pray, why did you marry with her?" I wait, sitting purposely silent a long while for his answer.

His head is averted and down. His brow furrowed in thought. But then, he lifts his gaze to mine with such open honesty, I know he tells the truth.

"She needed me."

"Was Harriet so beautiful, or was her life as an innkeeper's daughter so terrible?" I ask.

His eyes meet mine again. "Harriet does attract by virtue of her resemblance to the faerie, being both petite and energetic." He continues with more genuine honesty than any man I have known would reveal. "She wanted a rescuing knight, and I suppose I wanted to be that. Now, I inhabit a painful summer, for when love reaches an end, lovers, family, and foes seek reasons for the failure of a promised life together, all different though alike in force according to their opinion of their judgment. For me, the cause for the estrangement of my affection may be that the attachment she displayed became..." he spreads his hands in a gesture of helplessness, "overpowering."

"You take no responsibility for this dependence?"

Thoughts, questions chased across his features. "That had not occurred to me." He goes on, "I rather believe Harriet unwilling to open the lock that frees character to become a unique individual. Having thus entangled myself, I fear she feels me bound by her chains of obligation to love her forever," he lifts his hand in priestly benediction, "and ever, amen." His eyes bore into mine. "What think you of the philosophy of free love?"

"Like my father, I feel no mere piece of paper ought to make one married. Love, freely given and received, ought be the measure of a marriage."

"And if one is married, can one love another?"

This bears on his marriage to Harriet and his burgeoning love for me.

"I see no contradiction in loving several."

He sits back, nodding as if I answered a tutor correctly. "My father estranges himself from my company because of my marriage. He does not love Harriet."

And how should a marriage be the cause of distance between a father and his child? I wonder. But then I think, *Oh, there is sweet hypocrisy in that mirror!*

Percy puffs out his cheeks. "In motherhood, Harriet became her true self, a dedicated and complaisant matron, and, unfortunately, a chaste one, too."

I will not keep my irony from showing as I raise my eyes to his. "I do pity you. So many women, so little Percy." The man, for all his complaint of others' lack of decisiveness, seems not to know what needs must be done.

"Harriet knows my intent toward you, and gives out to people her complaint saying, 'There was nothing amiss between us. Nothing but that her name is Mary, and not only Mary, but Mary Wollstonecraft, and Mary Wollstonecraft Godwin at that. The man leaves a devoted mother and a natural child to chase a chimera.'"

"But what can you know of me rather than Mary Wollstonecraft Godwin? We've not loved more than a dozen times. I would you not think of me as an angel upon a column and, far worse, a prize because of my name."

Father's reaction to my news of Percy's suit is to shout, "Mrs. Godwin! I require your immediate council!" The two of them vanish into Father's study, but I overhear their voices discussing my future from where I stand to the side of the door.

"We must take measures to ensure our livelihood, wife."

"How are we set upon?"

"My daughter dallies with my principle backer."

Stepmother ever saw the simplest solution to Gordian knots. "Then we must prostitute her. He may have her for his continuing support."

I draw back as though cold water splashes in my face.

"Still," she sighs, "we must preserve the family's appearances."

"There is another way to preserve our finances and keep Shelley, though hazardous. Here, I shall talk to him and inform him to leave the girl alone, as he has not yet made name enough for my daughter."

"Will that not cause his funds to leave with him?"

"I think not. I shall couch my remarks in such a way that extends the promise of her hand when he has made his mark upon the world."

"Meanwhile there is another way to profit." Stepmother's voice is sly.

"What?"

"I can lead my friends by my words. I'll assist the boy in shedding this unwanted wife by letting it about that Harriet is to blame for the dissolution of the bonds of marriage. Word will reach him that he will know who helps his cause. And you shall inform the boy that although you will not allow Percy to call on her, he ought not consider himself a rebuffed suitor, simply delayed. At least until he finds himself no longer married."

I have no doubt my stepmother will aid Percy to be shed of Harriet. In the destruction of another's reputation, her natural gifts for cruel gossip are unparalleled.

Percy and I stand outside Father's study for a few minutes until the time appointed arrives. I squeeze his hand and Percy knocks.

"You may enter." Father sits with his back to us at his desk in what he calls his working dress. A pair of oversleeves, two thick tubes of canvass fabric with ties at the wrists and above the elbows keep ink smudge from his shirt.

Father turns his chair around to face us, but he does not ask us to sit. He neither stands for us nor does he remove his protecting sleeves. A statement indicating we are not worth the effort of further interruption of his work.

He goes directly to his purpose.

"The two of you have been reported consorting in the kirkyard. Word comes you pay un-respectful court to my daughter, Shelley."

Percy lowers his eyelids and his response is freighted with the languid intonation of Oxford. "I assure you, sir, I am most respectful."

Father's mouth clamps down. "Do you respectfully lay her upon her Mother's grave, and, do you most respectfully, mount her?" His riposte, aimed under Percy's guard, would have gutted another young man, but Percy parries.

"I am, sir, respectful in all particulars."

"Save my good name, I'm sure." But then Father loses his temper and his rationality. "By what right, oh very young man, do you estrange my daughter's rightful affection from her father?"

Father is hotter than the situation warrants and I know the cause, but so does Percy.

He says, "Rightful? Excessive and public!"

"My family is my business." If father was angry before, he is now snarling.

Seeing himself the injured party, Percy is eager for the fight.

"You spoke no word of your objections to paying Mary court when I was most free with sustaining contributions. Had you practiced frugality as I suggested, I would be pleased to offset any debts you might build. Economy rather than outrage would become you, sir."

Father's face goes a dark red and he sputters, "Get you into the street you ass, and do not return."

Even Father knew he had gone too far, but he felt the loss of my attention to be Percy's fault. Stepmother assured him all was not lost. Using me as bait, she would continue with her plan and win back Shelley.

As though through a glass do we know such situations as the basis of tragedy. What happened next was predictable.

Chapter Fifteen

Escape

Push any reasonably intelligent person hard enough, pile on injustice followed by injustice with neither recourse nor hope, and what happened ought not be a surprise. Ah well, seek a perfect garden and you'll find a serpent got there first.

With the signing of the Treaty of Fontainebleau, Napoleon was exiled to Elba, and the Continent lay open to us. I did but seek to augment my education. I had nothing but the best of intentions.

I was that young.

Jane however...Jane had no excuse.

27–28 July, 1814

Near the end of supper, I tell my family the heat of the day has put me out of sorts, and I retire. The truth is I can barely keep my stomach still for my nervous anticipation.

Long do I lie awake listening to the sounds of the household subside. When the clock downstairs strikes two, our agreed upon time, I rouse. As silently as I can, I begin to dress when Jane opens the door.

"Mary?" Her voice holds a tiny tremor. "Are you awake?"

I whisper in exasperation. "What will you?"

She pulls the door wide enough to slip into my room. "I'm going with you."

"You shall not!" I hiss.

She sets her legs apart and her arms akimbo and plays her trump. "I am! Do you not take me with you, I shall cry and awaken Father!" Jane's tears bedew her lashes and threaten to fall.

My lips compress until they hurt in utter, helpless frustration. It appears from the way her eyes are glazing over and her lower lip trembles she is preparing her best wails. We must be away before Father can object.

"Cry, and be damned! It's certain you'll not go then."

Her eyes dry like water spilled upon the sidewalk in summer. She begins to bargain, "I should be most useful…"

I fold my arms and shake my head in disbelief at this self-justification. "In what way, Jane, can you be of use other than the expectation of continued blackmail?"

"Well, there is that," she murmurs slyly. "But hear me out. Keep in mind my facility of language that neither you nor Percy possess."

"Percy speaks French."

"Poorly, and you do not. Also, I might be useful later with Father."

"How so?"

"I can tell father I chaperoned the two of you on the road the same as I did at the cemetery."

"He knows how well you kept us apart."

She shrugs. "Men often believe what they wish."

More points in her favor, and ones I am loath to argue right now. Father will be upset enough at my departure, and Jane has earned trust standing watch for visitors while Percy and I pursued our aims.

"Mary, please," dropping all pretense she entreats me with the truth, "I want to leave this house almost as much as do you. Now that Boney has been sent to Elba, I would see the Continent."

Her pleading sways me. As much as she has the ability to exasperate me, I do love my sister, and so I relent. "Go. Get you ready then. Wear your black silk that we may blend with the night."

Throwing her arms around me, she kisses me, is gone, and returns in less time than it takes to tell as I finish dressing. She must have had her box packed and waiting outside my door. She helps me pull my portmanteau from beneath my bed. Piling hers upon it we haul up on the end handles.

"Uff! Oh!"

"Hush now, Jane, and lift."

"Ought we repack?"

"No time. Percy will be waiting. Now, will you hush?"

Then we are out the door to where Percy sits in the darkness with a coach. He and the driver help with our boxes.

"At last," he whispers, holding me close and kissing me. He grunts as he picks up one end of our boxes as he shifts the load to the coach. "Did you bring everything you own?"

"They're not all Mary's," Jane says in a conspiratorial undertone. He glances at her and quirks an eyebrow to me.

"We'll speak later when there is time," I murmur, my mouth askew. "For now, I bid you welcome our fair traveling companion."

His mouth opens and his eyebrows climb to his hair. "Ah, well..."

I run back inside to leave my letter on the mantle explaining how we shall visit great sights and so enhance my education, and we are off.

Difficulties mount from the outset of our journey. Upon reaching the river, we learn our ship will not sail today. Our captain tells us he will not be leaving with the tide as promised due to, "Expected weather in the Channel."

I look up to see the sky as the dawn shows red in the east. "Father will soon rise and read my message. There can't be many ships departing for France. It will be only a matter of moments for him to find us."

"Oh, Percy," Jane's voice trembles and she lays her head on his chest as though she is a maid in most dire need of a hero. She licks her lips so they will glisten moistly in the dawn before lifting her eyes to him. "We must away, ere our parents discover our absence and thwart our designs."

She does have uses.

Checking with the office, Percy finds the Dover packet scheduled to sail on the next tide. By repute that boat's crew seldom remains in port for storms. He leaves our boxes at the custom house. They'll be delivered by a later ship to our hotel in Calais, and we secure a carriage to Dover to wait until the tide changes.

Oppressive heat building throughout the morning goes ill with us. Jane and I in our thick black silk are condemned to suffer worst. Sweat beads upon my face and neck and stings my eyes. My back is soaked and my legs are slick upon the fabric of my dress. I suggest we spend our time cooling our bodies by swimming while waiting.

"I don't know how," says Jane.

"You do not have to swim," I tell her. "Let your feet remain upon the bottom and immerse your body as you will. Come, it will be well."

We pick our way down a trail cut into the chalk cliffs to an isolated strand a mile or so above the harbor where cooler air infuses the atmosphere.

"Oh glorious!" I say, turning my back and lifting my hair. "Percy, do you loosen my buttons!" That done, I sweep my dress over my head let it fall on the shingle. Pulling off my shift leaves me clad in my stockings and shoes and in a moment more they join my clothing safe above the tide line. Skipping into the waves, I rise as Venus minus her shell above the waist-deep water and turn to where Percy and Jane stand. "Come! The waters are a delight!"

Jane's glance at Percy is shyly sidelong.

"Come," Percy says laughing. "Fear not, for I already think you beautiful."

She turns while he undoes her buttons, and raising her voice that I will be certain to hear, she says, "I fear I shall disappoint, for I have not the familiarity with men that my sister possesses."

Witch.

"Careful sister," I say quietly when she joins me. I turn her about to face a horizon empty but for a far-off wall of clouds. "Only the religious eschew sexuality. When it comes to those possessing a sophistication regarding the arts of love, much knowledge of nothing be worth little."

But the cool water feels too blissful for jealousy. Yawning broadly, I mind I've not slept in many an hour. We find a grassy knoll and drowse.

In time, I feel much restored. It being past three of the afternoon, we eat dinner at a small way house which I find we appreciate all the more for having missed our breakfast. Finishing our repast by five we seek the docks, only to find the packet departed and the next packet not scheduled until the following day.

"Here now, gentle people," the rasping voice of a man on the docks says. "By the way your faces look I'd say sommat's awry. Can I be of service?"

"We've missed the packet to Calais," Percy says. "And need is hard upon us to reach the far shore."

The man places a dirty finger against his nose. "Fate often hides her favor that a greater boon befall y'," he says with a wink. "You might take passage with a true flyer." He points to a small boat on the other side the pier.

Black and low with one tall mast and a boom that extends well past the stern, her rig tells of the spread of sail she can carry.

"Captain?" Percy addresses the man.

"Aye, what would ye?"

"Can you outrun the storm?"

He looks to the sky, "I doubt it," he drawls, "But I moight try were there pay enough."

Percy smiles and says to us, "When a man begins to talk price, the thing may be had."

A bargain struck and sealed, the pirate then raises his voice to summon his men, and three stalwarts who are nearby come quickly aboard to cast off. They raise the sails, the little craft heels with the wind, and the water sings along the hull. The cloud bank I noted earlier has grown with the passage of the hours until it towers over the northern channel with its dark underbelly the color of onrushing night.

Our sails shape to the southern wind as we make our way past the breakwater. Percy looks to the horizon and murmurs a thought from Shakespeare's Ceasar.

> There is a tide in the affairs of men,
> Which taken at the flood, leads to fortune.
> Omitted, all the voyage of their lives
> Is bound in shallows and miseries.

With his one arm about my shoulders and my cheek to his, I speak the next lines.

> On such a full sea are we now afloat.
> And we must take the current when it serves,
> Or lose our ventures.

And so I leave England, not knowing when I shall return.

But as the hours pass, the wind fades and our sails flap uselessly in the dying air. We see the water darken with ripples as they sweep toward us.

"A tempest sure," mutters the captain. "Three reefs in the sail, boys."

At first, winds flow toward a cloudbank that nearly covers us, allowing only a scrap of sky for the sunset to gild our faces. Then, with a sudden gust from the opposite direction, our little boat heels over. Jane gives a small scream, and my eyes fly wide at the speed of the storm descending upon us. In minutes, the wind strengthens to a gale, shrieking in the rigging. My inclination toward seasickness overwhelms me, forcing me to retire to a tiny cabin in the bow to become violently ill.

29 July, night

Some time later, I become aware Percy is at my side, pulling my hair away from my mouth.

"How close to shore?" I manage to wheeze out the question.

"Each time we ask the sailors they tell us we are not quite halfway, yet all will be well. They tell us we make for Boulogne, which lies at no great distance."

But hour upon hour, the flashing lightning gives them the lie. The east wind greater than any before strikes us. I open my eyes as I feel a hand touch my brow. Percy is by my side.

"Mary, I needed to tell you I love you, for the sailors say our condition is perilous, and our boat cannot last."

I find an advantage to seasickness. I do not care to live any longer.

"And I love you as well, sister," Jane quavers. "Please say you love me."

"Fine," I spit. "I love you." But I relent when the lightning lets me see their terror. "It has been grand." Hand and foot, I cling to the wood of my cabin like a spider spread in her web, but I am determined to go down without a coward's protest.

But fortune favors the bold. With the sudden shifts known in the Channel, the wind changes direction, drops, and bears us straightaway into Calais. Sensing in my comfortless slumber an easing of the motion of the boat, I arise to find us entering the sheltered waters of the harbor as a golden sun lifts over France.

We thank the men for our passage and, though I am exhausted, my excitement at being in another country overbears my fatigue. I am improved by finding a pump to swill me off. Percy knows where our hotel is, and we determine walking to it will aid my restoration.

Even though we stroll the dockside shops, we see so much! And hear more!

"Oh, what joy to attend to the language all about us!" Jane rhapsodizes, but she furrows her forehead and says, "Though these do not speak with the clarity of my teachers."

I find myself in thrall as much to the incomprehensible voices of those native to this shore as I am by their costumes. I chirp in surprise the first time I spy a man wearing a gold earring! Gentle ladies wear short jackets and high bonnets perched jauntily above their coiffures.

"Look you how brazenly these women show their ears!" Jane says.

I halt in mid-step. "Of course these natives are superior," I say. "Do you not remember Edward III took Calais during the Hundred Years' War? Calais is peopled with good English stock."

Seeking the Harbor Master's office, we inquire about our boxes. A clerk barely glances at us and mutters some mellifluous statement that Jane, imitating his accent, translates once we exit. "He most rudely says, 'Unfortunately ze storm 'as delay ze London ship weeth your equipage, ze Eenglish being timid sailors. Rest you in your rooms and be assured it must arrive in a day,'" she spreads her hands in an uncanny mime, "'or so.'"

We arrive at the hotel, enjoy a bath, and, although there is but one bed barely big enough for three, exhaustion allows us to sleep without waking.

30 July

By next noon, the clerk proves good to his word and our boxes arrive only slightly behind the time we expect, but with them is another passenger.

The concierge standing in our doorway jerks his thumb over his shoulder. "Zere is a fat woman downstairs demanding entrance to your rooms."

Stepmother explodes into our room. Planting her feet apart like a pugilist, she makes a quick scan of the three of us before focusing on Jane.

"Your father discovered your plans because this tramp (a curt nod in my direction) had the brazen effrontery to leave a letter. I'll leave her here thinking good riddance to bad trash. You, however, shall return with me to London."

When she inhales, Percy says, "Mrs. Godwin, lower your voice, if you please."

Oh Percy, you'd best stay out of it.

She rounds upon him and through some agency unknown manages to raise her volume. "You shut your mouth, you seducer of little girls!"

Unused to her ways, Percy draws himself back as though struck.

"Where would you all be were it not for my economy that allows us passage home?"

"Better off!" I snarl. She may balk Percy, but I am familiar with what passes for family conversation, and I am angry. "And your miserly penurious conduct is scarcely economy. For economy, you rely on my sister Fanny, and scant thanks she receives!"

Percy, although somewhat stunned by his first full exposure to her, comes back as game as any.

"I beg you remember where much of the funding you and your husband receive originates. Desist this unseemly display in rooms that are under my good name."

He might as well have addressed a rock.

"D'you believe your money gives you any right, look you, ANY RIGHTS to my daughter?"

"Daughters," he corrects.

"The hell!" Her voice rises yet again and grows shrill. She stabs her finger toward my heart. "That one never was mine! More like she is a bastard by-blow of her wanton, bitch mother!"

We are in full heat now.

I raise my finger to her. "I have never, never considered myself any kin to you. I tolerated you for my father's sake."

Her eyes go sly. "Oh, aye!" Her voice quiets to an ugly lilt. "You and your precious father. Don't believe for a moment I do not know all about you and your darling father!"

Jane earns my love by changing the subject. In a voice many years older, she says with conviction, "Mother, I am going with them. They need me."

The hateful woman reaches out as though to grab at her arm, but Percy leans forward with his face inches from hers and in a sure, calm voice says, "I've but to summon the Gendarmes. On this soil, she is a woman, not a girl, and the laws of France protect her. As she has spoken her wishes before witnesses, there is nothing for you to do but leave."

Stepmother shouts with a volume that shows how much she had previously restrained herself, "Jane, if you go with these, come you n'more home!"

Jane summons her patience and, in the voice of saddened reason, makes her cast. "Mother, I shall chaperone. All will be well. You'll see."

"Oh yes, the services you've rendered these two are well known throughout London." Mrs. Godwin's hand lifts as though to clout Jane. "What they did in St. Pancras Cemetery is the best kept secret since the one about the Thames flowing to the sea."

The harpy's hand trembles with the force of her emotion, then cuts toward me. Her nails close on my throat. I heave back and my flesh rips. My hand on my wounds comes away crimson, and I begin to fall. Percy drops to his knees and holds my head from the floor.

Jane does not waver but steps protectively over the two of us. In the face of Jane's determination, Stepmother lowers her fist. She turns to Percy and snaps, "Y' prevail but for a moment."

With her back to the door, her last sally is aimed at me. "Be you with child?"

"I am not!"

"Then soon enough you'll seek your father again."

Her meaning is as clear to me as it is filthy.

Slowly she crosses the threshold and slams the door, leaving the bloody field in our possession.

Percy looks down to me. "I'll see about a cloth for your neck." And with a quick kiss for Jane he says, "That for bravery. I must find the landlady and apologize."

"Jane," I begin, seeking to both praise her and offer comfort.

Trembling, she jerks at my voice and raises her head. "No, not Jane. Never again the name that woman gave me. Clara. That is my name from now on. I shall be Clara Clairmont." She turns to me, showing her teeth. "A melodious name, is it not?"

Not the most auspicious of beginnings, perhaps. I remember well reaching my arms to Jane, now Clara, and the two of us holding tight against our shaking. We passed a look between us, and with a resolve I had not thought part of me, I knew, to live or to starve, this night, my most loved sister and I were women.

As with all young people who go on a fledgling flight, we were young enough to call it adventure.

Chapter Sixteen

Innocents Abroad

We did not starve, immediately. That was a treat for later.

The days rolled by too full of sights and sounds to hold more. The highways opened on vistas green and golden. Carts and wagons rumbled toward the capital. Buildings and houses, barns even, echoed centuries. And discoveries lay around every curve in the road and each turn of our lives.

It was wondrous, it was grand, we were beautiful and in love.

Late that afternoon, Percy and I walk the fortifications surrounding Calais.

He's tentative. "What did your stepmother mean when she said she knew about you and your father?"

With a soft cry I bury my face in his shoulder. *Not yet. Oh, not yet. This love is too young for such a truth.* The gentle man does not pry, but he pats my back, holding me in silence awhile. We look out at the haying going on in the fields of Calais.

Returning to Jane, *who wants to be called Clara,* I remind myself, our evening becomes a celebration. We share a bottle of wine and the laughter of the victorious with my bandage a badge of courage.

31 July

Next morning, Percy goes to secure a coach, telling us to rest while we keep watch upon our baggage. Upon his return, which takes some time, the reason for his delay becomes delightfully apparent. After much searching, Percy found us a shining black cabriolet for our journey to Paris, and soon the miles flow by to the melody of horse's hooves and delicate red wheels against the road. We ride seated three across and facing forward with me safe in one corner of the seat, Clara in the other, and Percy between us.

But what rides with us will out like a febrile tooth.

"Percy, about my father and me...you must see...oh, my father suffered so much when my true-mother died. And an hundred, and an hundred times more, he tells me I am all he has of the greatest love he ever experienced...he thinks me the embodiment of her wit and says he knows me the image of her...and, in me he finds that lost love again, and more..." Percy rounds my shoulders with his arm and Clara reaches over his lap to hold my hand, her earnest face giving me evidence she knows my story though we've never spoken of it.

"I have said that I love Father. I thought there was no impediment to our love, that we might love for all time in the way of men and women. But I know now, the consequences of consummating such love are more than the censure of society, no matter what the poets say. I...am I not Mary still? Are we not free to love as we wish?"

Percy looks off over the fields as he digests this. At last he nods. "Indeed we are." And he kisses my hair.

Jane, Clara, who, though she has had a similar education to mine, can hardly conceive of corollaries to Free Love. Instead she focuses on what she deems the salient facts to my ideals. "But if you are so dedicated to the principles of free love, what of marriage?"

"Women must have livings the same as men, in their own right, for them to be as happy; however, I misdoubt any change will occur if women simply ask for their due. No, let me not ask, but use my abilities to take."

"Sister, I've never heard you speak so forcefully."

"May you never hear me speak softer. I will speak my mind instead of another's."

Percy says, "I have a philosophy, which should be shared, that touches yours.

"Endeavor to approach each day with excitement, approach each individual, man or woman, with respect and in anticipation of learning. I will condemn nothing, and I seek to recognize that, while an event or experience may not be to my taste, I shall respect that others may find it enjoyable." Again, he kisses me, this time on my mouth. I breathe him in.

Our exertions and the lack of sleep the night before cause us to seek an inn early in the afternoon.

We have a most pleasant corner room with enough of a breeze blowing through the windows to cool us. The plaster walls are unadorned, save but for their beige color and an amateurish painting of a man in a red cap standing on a barricade of furniture.

We request three horses from the landlady that we might explore the town, but so fatigued are we, we fall asleep as one. Waking later still, we find we are barely capable of ordering a cold supper of bread, cheese, and some vegetables with *vin ordinare*, which we eat with pleasure and return to bed to sleep away the dark hours.

You may imagine our surprise the next morning at finding our landlady has altered our *addition* to reflect not only the room and a full supper rather than the little we consumed but the cost of the horses as well.

"But non, zee 'orses deed not know you would not come. Zey waited all night for you."

A hesitant Percy breaches the subject of our expenses. "We should give some thought to economizing," he begins. "I was so grateful at finding passage to Calais I agreed to the Captain's accounting, which was usurious—although in justice, I ought not begrudge him his fee. He did safely deliver us through one of the worst storms I have seen. However, there have been other charges I had not foreseen. The French seem inclined to revenge Napoleon's defeat by bankrupting any English they find. In short, although I brought the full amount of my allowance from my father, my purse, like you," he says, patting me, "does have a bottom."

1 August

We reach Paris late the third day of our adventures in France to discover prices for hotels are dear. We are obliged to rent a small suite of rooms for a full week. But they are clean and airy with lace curtains covering the windows. White chair rails, wainscoting, and baseboards contrast with the lavender walls hung with pastoral paintings. Immediately behind the entry is an antechamber we can use as a sitting room. "Here we shall conduct our little salon," I say.

"I'm sure we shall pass happy hours reading and reciting poetry," says Percy. "I have several small volumes of George Byron's."

"That famous rake?" Clara is all attention to gossip.

Percy pulls his mouth to the side. "He courts scandal as a road to fame."

I say, "And I brought the works of my true-mother, who knew this city after the revolution but before the depredation of Napoleon."

"Here, see!" cries Clara. We follow her into a retiring chamber with a closet containing a bed for Clara that is separated from the rest of the room by a curtain hanging from rings.

But before we do anything else, we must bathe, for we stink like natives. "I wonder whether the French can find a bathtub," Clara says. While the manners of the French are amiable, their hygiene is execrable. We request the landlord for a tub and hot water that we might wash the dust from our bodies and hair.

When I hesitate, looking from Percy to my sister, Clara prompts me. "Sister, it is foolish to pretend modesty after our time together in the sea," and suiting word to action, begins to disrobe.

I glance at Percy who sits happily in the large comfortably stuffed chair with the fingers of his hands tented beneath his chin.

"Be you of more use than lechery," I tease, handing him all the clothing we have worn in the past days, which in truth is nearly every stitch we have. "Give these to the porter that they may be cleaned." I stop a moment, my nose wrinkling. "You'll want to add your own."

Clara and I stand behind the door to the bed chamber as Percy exchanges our clothing for two large ewers of steaming water, towels, a tub, and a small bottle.

"What is that?" Clara asks, looking at the pale yellow colored liquid.

"Ah," he says lifting the stopper and sniffing. "Our landlord included a treat. Mademoiselles, here is perfume."

Clara lifts the stopper and wafts the bottle beneath her nose. For a moment, her mouth opens in surprise, then her eyes light. "Ohh! What invention the French have to bottle ecstasy."

I inhale. "Flowers, honey, and, something, some spice?" I hand the bottle to Percy. "Myrrh, I think."

Clara smiles. "This may have aphrodisiacal powers, Mary," She says with a naughty grin. "We may want another bottle."

For the next half hour, we glory in the sensation of warm water, soap, and wonderful smells. Percy, as though in front row at a play, most thoroughly considers us. By and by, a thoughtful expression crosses his face.

"Having discovered many of those who consider nudity objectionable, I learned they demand both nudity and obscenity to be equivalent in meaning. It appears to me that philosophy is a blasphemy. Are we not, as Hamlet said, 'the paragon of animals?' Did God not endow us as the pinnacle of his creation? How then obscene?"

Clara stops running the cloth over my back, leans close and whispers in my ear, "Wouldn't you think he would find the sight of us enjoyable enough? Does he often philosophize at such inopportune times?"

"I have known him to discourse upon a thought during the act." We, conspirators in intimacy, giggle.

She smiles toward him. "Maddeningly adorable."

"Just so."

But Percy's mind is not finished. Percy's mind is ne're finished. "It also occurs to me..."

"Oh, enough, you smelly man! Hush!" I run, dripping, to where he sits and, laughing, pull him to the tub where Clara and I force him to submit as we perform ablutions upon him, she attending to his hair and I to, well, to the rest.

That night Percy and I take each other. Loving indoors, in a bed, is a novelty. So released are the tensions of the past week, we fall asleep in each other's arms.

2 August

Next morning the weather continues hot, making late afternoon the preferred time for exploration, so we determine to salon until the day cools.

"What is the best way for one to begin a poem or a story?"

Percy sighs and glances out the window. "I must tell you, of all those questions asked of a published author, this one rankles most, as the questioner invariably demands a considered yet easy-to-follow set of instructions."

He sighs. "However, I took upon me the responsibility as teacher when I accepted the two of you as companions, so I'll give you an answer. All good poems, all good stories are as notes in a bottle cast upon the waves. I begin by thinking of one thing I wish people to know."

"But," Clara quivers, "What if you do not know what message you would tell?"

"Ah," murmurs Percy, considering. "So much road before us." He thinks a moment. "Have you ever made a list?"

"I have," I say. "That was one of father's most often-given assignments. I made lists of many things. Blue things or red things. With time, these became more involved. Things I like and things I abhor, ephemeral things, permanent things, things for which I would give my life, and he would question me to determine the depths behind these feelings and why they held import."

"But I could not use those," says Clara, "for those are Mary's lists. If I attempted them, mine would be but copies."

"Not so," objects Percy. "Here, the two of you, think of a tree. Now, of what tree have you thought?"

"A pine," I say. "Reaching toward the clouds."

Clara puzzles a moment. "An oak. An honorable English Oak."

"One question, but two answers. Clara, your message might touch duty or reputation. And Mary, does not your message go to the heart of achievement or fame? Here, take an hour or so to write in your journals on these themes. You may find the beginnings of a story."

By the time the sun reaches a hand's breadth above the horizon, we don dresses of lighter, flowing fabrics more appropriate to our comfort.

"Hmpf, Sister," Clara says, cupping breasts that strain her best dress. "I have not worn this in months. Either it has shrunk, or...I think I have blossomed."

"Surely it must have shrunk," I wryly address her as I twist in the mirror. "See? My dress fits me still."

Her eyebrow lifts and, hooking a finger into my décolletage, she examines how much room is left vacant in my bodice. "I warrant 'twill not much longer."

I toss my hair and resolve to mind my posture, quite pleased by what the mirror displays.

Percy is resplendent in a bright green coat and his omnipresent poet's blouse. In this wise do we stroll the streets of Paris seeking our suppers.

For the next week, we visit as much of Paris as our feet can carry us to. On one day, we see the Tuileries Gardens, or as Clara calls them, "*Le Jardin des Tuileries*," which enjoy a far-flung fame for their beauty. I find them pleasant enough, I suppose, though I see no evidence of the tile making I had hoped might provide me a keepsake.

Better by far are the Boulevards. Though there are several of these wide ways, a promenade running in an eight mile circuit around the inner city and lined with

3 1308 00354 6645

shady trees on both sides most captures my imagination. Brilliant and beautiful, the grand boulevards of Paris thrill me. *Not the least reason being that I am in love.*

"There, that one," Percy inclines his head at a comely young woman. "Is she one?"

"How would I know?" I reply, with my arm in his. "I am not familiar with those who procure the favors of men for coin."

"Oh, fie 'pon you both," snorts Clara. "She is simply a beauty much like us. Do we look like prostitutes?"

"One could wish," sighs Percy, wagging his head like the rake he would be. "Then would I wish for a purse as deep and full as the sea." Then, recalling himself, he looks from one of us to the other. "I pay her no mind, greater beauty is with me."

"Oh, he's good," says Clara, insinuating her arm in his on his free side. "There!" she declares. "Now you'll be the envy of every man."

The week speeds by, and one morning we find a remittance arrives from Percy's father, as welcome as it is small. "I posted him a letter the day after we arrived in Calais telling him of our journey thus far and my intent to show the two of you some of Europe," Percy says with a frown. "His answer is this allowance, along with a note saying we should return, as we can expect no more will be forthcoming." Standing tall and foot forward, chest out and head high, posturing heroically for us, he says, "Paris is too expensive, ladies. We must be on our way."

"Do you say you propose to walk to Switzerland?" Our landlady places her hand over her heart aghast at the prospect. "Non! These two flowers will have their stems spread by every lately disbanded soldier roaming the countryside!"

"Thank you for your concern, Madame, but I am with them."

The woman's face reflects her disbelief. "*Oui, mon brave,*" she looks him up and down. "The soldiers might enjoy you as well." She shrugs. "You might distract them enough to allow the women to escape."

"Tell her my mother walked the length of France after the revolution," I beg Clara. "If she could do it in safety with my sister tied to her hip, I can do as much."

When Clara translates for me, the woman mutters, "Oo says she was safe?"

To assuage the woman, we leave in a cab which we dismiss at the city barricades, procuring a small ass from the stall of a carter. We think we might take turns riding upon the luggage, which we strap to his back, and so preserve ourselves, but we feel so sorry for the little beast once we see him struggle beneath the load of our cases on his back, we resolve that all of us should walk.

8 August

League upon league, the road winds ever before us through as bucolic a summer's rural setting as ever I have beheld. There are songs to be sung as we bathe our feet in streams and verses to be spoken in cool woods that call us to rest awhile. Topping a hill as the sun sets, we are gratified to view the destination we determined upon before leaving the city. Charenton lies displayed for our pleasure in the gathering dusk, though in truth it had taken us several hours longer than we intended.

"Oh!" exclaims Clara. "This is beautiful enough." She turns to us and, placing her fists upon her hips, says, "Let us live here!"

I smile at her, but the beauty is undeniable. My chest swells as I breath in the rolling hills, the white cottages, and the little stream running over a gravel bed. As we arrive, late, to the inn, we find it has but a single room for the three of us available. But the keeper is willing to provide a familiar cold supper and a bottle of the local wine with our room. On that we feast until we fall asleep on the one bed.

12 August

We wake to a bright day that promises more heat in the afternoon. Our innkeeper feeds us a breakfast and packs a luncheon for us to carry. But before we leave, he repeats information that lately furloughed soldiers roam the countryside as well as his poor opinion regarding our safety. He is so sincere in his solicitous attitude for our safety we take pause.

"Perhaps," I venture, "we might mitigate our appearance through a ruse."

"Should we dirty our faces and so appear French?" inquires Clara.

"I doubt it is your nationality that draws these men," Percy says.

"Look, you," I continue my thought. "We have the black dresses in which we left London. Were we clad thusly, we might appear grieving widows. Were we to tell the soldiers our late husbands were veterans, their respect ought to provide us safety."

Clara looks out the window at the bright street. "But the day promises to be terribly warm."

Warm it is, but our enthusiasm over my plan overcomes much of the heat of the day. Much, I say, but not all.

Selling the donkey and buying a mule more suited to carrying our burdens, we leave Charenton intending to pass the evening in Guignes.

14 August

Hour upon hour we trudge the roads, and though the luster of our holiday still shines undimmed, the effort especially in these dresses oppresses us. Perspiration causes the fabric to cling to our legs and arms when we walk.

"And still," I say, "our progress today is better than yesterday. This noble mule stands good for many miles."

"Well he might for his cost," mutters Percy.

At noon, we repair to a large wood for our luncheon. The sound of water draws us deeper into the shadows, and the shade is such relief we revel in the cool darkness.

"A stream. Look you, a pool. Oh this is like a painting," Clara calls. She turns to me. "My laces, sister? This is the very spot for a dip to cool ourselves."

"Sister, do not be more foolish than you can help." I rake my eyes between the tree trunks. "We do not know but that there are soldiers close by."

"I'll keep watch." Percy looks around through the trees. "And should any of the army appear, I'll signal to give you time to hide."

I shake my head. "By the time you sight the enemy they'd be upon us."

"Listen." Percy tilts his head. "Not a sound. Surely we would hear them if they were near. Turn about and let me ease your laces. I'll watch you most carefully..."

"That I do not doubt. And I am sure you will keep such a watch on us, an herd of elephants might pass us unseen."

Finding a shady spot, I lie down until it is time to resume our travel. When I revive, I look for them and find them near the stream. "Fellow travelers. Are we ready to resume our journey?"

Clara touches my arm. "Do you take our friend mule and essay the road again. I wish Percy to keep watch for me," she holds her hands to her stomach, "for I experience some distress."

"Stay then, sister. I'll wish for your relief." And sweeping up the halter rope, I stride to the road.

My imagination fires at finding myself alone on a French road. In my mind's eye, I envision my mother as she treks with that tender burden who is my sister Fanny. *What courage she must have had! Then as now, bands of soldiers prowl the byways looking for, well, for beautiful, young women like me.* I begin to search for howling *soldats* emerging from the shadows under trees. *What might they do at finding me?* My heart pounds. *And how often?*

I stop in the road with the mule's lead clutched in my hand, but then I laugh at myself. Turning around I see my companions cresting a small hill hand in hand. "There you two are!" I call.

They stop when they are no more than at arms length from me. Clara breathes as hard as she had run a race. "Sister?" I seek to present our canteen to her lips. "What's amiss?" She looks to Percy and raises an eyebrow. He looks anywhere but at me, he puts his hands behind his back and scuffs at the rocks in the track.

Ah. I cannot say I did not see this coming.

Clara screws up her face and begins to wail. "What shall poor Cordelia do? Love and be silent. Oh this is true—Real Love will never shew itself to the eye of broad day— it courts the secret glades."

Percy holds her. "There, dear one. Look you, all's well."

She turns her head to me and gazes into my eyes. "Is all well, sister?"

I step close to them and circle them with my arms. "If we reject the values society imposes upon us, then we must put into practice those values that seem sensible to us. I support the ideal of loving whom you will without censure. Should I balk at the first test to put my philosophy to practice?" I take her hand and say, "There, Clara, enough. All is well." And I resolve to think no more on't.

We arrive in Guignes trooping down the last yards to the town in the early evening and learn we are early enough to eat in the common room with the other guests. On the whole, it is a pleasant place with a low ceiling of wood darkened by decades of candles and lamps and the smoke from a broad stone fireplace.

Perhaps there are fewer sojourners to this place, because the woman who runs the inn stands at the end of our table and regales us with stories. Clara translates nearly as fast as the woman can recite the history of the inn.

"'Napoleon himself slept in the very rooms you occupy this night.'" ("Which explains the expense," mutters Percy.) She points to the wholly unremarkable, unpainted piece of furniture where Percy sits. "'And you, young sir, you rest your laurels in the very place of the Little General.'"

"Can that be true?" I whisper to Percy so as not to interrupt Clara's concentration.

"It could be, although every innkeeper throughout France will likely tell us the same story." He quirks his mouth to the side and looks down into his lap. "But I have never heard them called laurels."

"Ahem," Clara hushes us and continues her translation of the woman. "'Josephine, Empress, and she who is the Duchess of Parma, Mary Louise, who was wife to the Emperor and so an Empress too, passed along the road that runs past our door.'" The woman gestures grandly to the dusty way, then points to the window seat and says, "'I sat right there and saw them.'" She nods and, clasping her hands in front of her, hangs her head reverently that we might appreciate the moment's significance.

Percy lifts his head and produces a small coin for the woman as he says, "Perhaps you will someday tell of Percy Shelley who sat here with two empresses even as Napoleon?"

The next day gifts us with a treasure for our eyes. We crest a hill to see Provins lying in a valley below us with its cathedral rising above all other buildings. On a cliff above the road before us climb the ruins of a citadel with a great tower.

"Oh!" exclaims Clara. "This is beautiful enough; let us live here!"

"Did you not say so about the last town?" Percy gently laughs. Nor is this the last of that paean we will hear, for she repeats it as often as each new vista presents itself.

But in this case, I agree with her. "After the last two days of country, while pretty though without interest, this is matter for a painter!"

Whitewashed buildings line narrow streets that climb a small hill capped with a church. The whole appears cool and inviting to weary travelers. Each home is draped with an hundred hues of green ivy.

We eat a coarse dinner much as peasants, and though our rooms that night lack the amenity of comfortable beds, I fall asleep remembering the scene as we approached the town.

So used to finding beauty are we that we are shocked next day when we arrive in Nogent. The town lies in blackened burned ruins. Clara inquires for us the cause of the devastation and learns when the Russians arrived, they destroyed as they went.

I declaim, "I hate, above all, both the love of war and the waste it begets."

Here we leave the road, intending to strike cross country upon a track that winds through the hills to Troyes. However, we misjudge the distance and darkness finds us a league from our destination.

"Ahhh!" Percy cries, falling and rolling back and forth in pain clutching his ankle. We are upon his sides in a moment. "I fear the worst," he hisses through his pain. "I may have broken the bone."

Helping him as best we can to sit upon the mule, we decide we must continue to Troyes. When we arrive an hour later, we are so late it takes some time for the keeper to answer the hammering upon his door. His manner is surly, but we are admitted to a poor room, with but a sheet upon straw for a bed, and given milk and sour bread for our supper.

As we lie down, Percy says, "Place your shoes where you can find them in the dark."

"Do you think we shall have to flee?" Clara asks.

"I do not, but we will in all likelihood have to throw them. This place is sure to have rats. A good aim will save your toes a nasty nip."

For all that, I fall asleep directly, though I have dreams of Clara's giggles.

We wake late to find Percy's ankle badly swollen and elect to stay another day.

"Mary," he beckons me, "Clara did not sleep last night. Do you go find us some food in the town by yourself? Here is money."

"I'll not be long," I whisper not to wake Clara.

"No," he says with his lips to mine. "Please. There is no reason for you to deny yourself the pleasure of the sights. You stroll the town that you may relate all you see to us."

I smile at the dear man who thinks of my pleasure. "I shall remember what I see well enough to share."

I walk from street to street wondering at the construction of the shops and houses, at last finding a market and returning hours after I left.

"Look you!" I say, opening the door to our room. "I managed to find enough sustenance of such variety our feast ought to be jolly." As we eat, I beg Clara accompany me that afternoon. Our effort is successful, we are able to find a four-wheel wagon with a driver who agrees to carry us to Neufchatel. He is... unimpressive, stooped with age and the loads he has transported.

Conveyance is not a luxury as Percy cannot walk. At the next town, Percy pays over enough coin to the innkeeper to cover the man's shelter and board, but he shakes his head saying, "My purse will never stand the pace should this continue. But, have faith in me. I am sure I can procure more funding."

In Bar-sur-Aube we have a straw pallet for sleeping and a fireplace for both cooking and light in a small room for the three of us. The ass sleeps with his horse in the stable.

16 August

We note a change in the manners of the French the farther from Paris we travel. Guests surrounding the fires seem unwilling to make way for us when we arrive at inns and, as the rain does not abate, we stand far from warmth.

Our driver appears affected by rudeness as well. The acrimony between us and our man grows in the miserable village of Mort. His obstinacy forces us to submit to his demand: he not sleep with the other animals in the stable, but he would share our room. Sitting near the fire, his eyes glitter as he watches first Clara, then me, then Clara. To our remonstrance regarding his stares, he answers, "*Je ne plais pas.*"

Throughout the night, his farts jerk us back from the edge of sleep.

"Perhaps he will expel gas close enough to the fire that he will explode," whispers Percy.

"Could such a thing happen in truth?" Clara inquires with her eyes wide at the prospect.

Percy puts his hand over his heart. "And naught be left in the morn but ashes."

At three in the night, Shelley rises and hobbles close enough to the man to kick him awake.

"We may as well take to the road as listen to your French horn blat all the night," he bellows. We ride sitting up in the cart, pillowed on each other, and watch the cloud-covered sky lighten.

As we top a hill, our man stands and points to the south. There, shining in the rays of the sun, are what I take for bright clouds.

He turns and speaks a short statement to Clara, whose mouth forms an O of surprise. She lifts her hand in the direction we are traveling. "He says, 'Behold the peaks of the Alps.'"

"How far?" I ask, my heart in my throat and all inclination to sleep banished.

"He says, '*Un cent milles,*'" Clara tells me. "An hundred miles."

May I forget a thousand other sunrises before I lose the memory of my first sight of the Alps. Their very whiteness upon the vault of a blue-painted background by a master artist could not more capture their majesty or their light. I thought them clouds ere I knew them to be the stern peaks dividing Italy from the rest of Europe, but the uncommonly clear air made them seem only minutes away rather than the days it took to reach their feet.

Would that my sight had been as keen to those around me.

Chapter Seventeen

Switzerland

Wonder followed wonder. I suppose they do when a person of sixteen years travels to places far from home. Everything I saw was either beautiful or ugly, but new, and in novelty there lies marvel. Like the mountains. Great thrustings of the earth that called to me, peaks whose cloaks of snow could not hide the jagged dark grey rock. Their crests disdain the might of men and the power of them resonated inside me.

Shining, serene, the mountains lie before me. The rain quits, the wind blows from behind us, taking the carter's farts with it. We fly the hundred miles in four days.

As we draw up to the French barrier at the Swiss border, profound differences 'tween the nations and their peoples begin to manifest. Certain contrasts are notable: cleanliness, and manners.

Swiss cottages, neat and orderly, dot the landscape, and Swiss women as tidy as their homes go about their family tasks. My impression of cleanliness forms quickly at the sight of the volume of white linen they affect for dress. We debate whether these differences between the French and the Swiss in hygiene are generated by their religion.

"I suppose the evident changes in cleanliness may be attributed to Catholic France versus Protestant Switzerland," I say. "These people are clearly superior."

The land, as if to distinguish itself from that country to the north, changes as well. Now, mountains reach for the stars. Piney forests, which cover the lower slopes, terminate in barren high rocks, and these in turn wear mantles of snow. Between the peaks, verdant narrowing valleys allow passage deeper into a country delightful in all aspects.

Percy's ankle is so improved we decide a horse will do to carry our boxes, and determine to sever our ties with the driver at St. Sulpice. Upon rising the next day, we find the ingrate importuned the host for the cost of his shelter, and is gone having given no notice.

"And good riddance to him," Percy says. "We'll find a better guide, I wager, among these people."

"One better smelling at the least." Clara sniffs.

We consult the innkeeper and before we can finish our breakfast we engage the services of a Swiss cottager. A difference in class is evident. Not only clean, but for the price of the horse we once thought all our purse could afford, he volunteers a somewhat humble but well-kept carriage. Added to this, he is able to converse in English. Looking at our table, he confirms the bounty of the glades around us and assures us the butter, milk, and cheeses of Switzerland have no parallel in the world. We smile with pleasure at the evident pride he derives from his country.

"I scarce thought it possible, but, look you," I breathe from my seat in the carriage as we progress toward Neufchatel through a valley which our driver says divides two mountain ranges. "These mountains rise higher than the last!"

Even the most magnificent of sights will not keep ideas at bay. "Percy," I say. "I took well your meaning that an author ought to have a message in mind when she conceives a tale, but, well, what then?"

"Ah, you wish to know how to cloak the bare meaning with trappings that will make the reader enjoy a story rather than a bald moral? There, you must think of a plot. Think of some incongruity, a disharmony, which can be of interest in itself. Just now, I think of a time I saw a woman dressed as a lady, but begging alms from passersby. What could have happened to give her such a blow?

"Or the opposite. Two people who are so fundamentally different we cannot see how they could be connected: a wealthy man and a poor one.

"Another is a memory that lives within you. Think for a moment of episodes scratched upon the metal of your mind without diminishment. Use that for inspiration.

"And then, there is revenge. Revenge is always good."

I'm stunned as I have never heard of these methods, or have heard them but they made no impression at the time. Percy is a better writer than I thought to parse this complex problem. As my mind sorts examples of each, I begin to see what he means by stories that move from the first page to the last.

While I ponder, we descend to Neufchatel for the night, where we part from the superior Swiss driver with expressions of thanks.

We stay another day but Percy can obtain a loan of only twenty-eight pounds from a banker of the town. "And there will be no more," Percy tells us. "My name is not well enough known to fatten our purse more. When the man asked the state of my finances, I was able to answer I was free and clear of any debt, but I'll not be able to say that and be truthful again. This banker assures me without solvency no one will lend us more."

He must sense our distress from the looks of our faces, because he smiles and says, "Be of cheer! We are not destitute. If we practice the strictest of economy, we may spend a few days here and still cross the 800 miles that lie between home and ourselves on this amount, though I fear it will be on short commons."

Clara reached for his hand. "We shall be happy with little," she says, looking up at him, "for our company is worthy."

21 August

Arriving on the shores of Lake Lucerne, our first sight of the lake confirms our hope for rest and beauty. We hire a boat as a mode of transport more comfortable for Percy. At night, we seek shelter on shore in houses called "Chateau" and pass the time in conversation and philosophy.

"Something occurs to me, Mary." Percy lays the book he reads on his chest and turns his face, which wears a questioning expression, to me. "Do you see anything in your mother's philosophy applying to our present circumstances?"

I need think only a moment. "Circumstances, mmm. I would note my mother recited on many occasions how enamored she was of nature. Like her I thrive in the open air and relish picturesque aspects of nature and find these at present most beautiful." I sweep my hand to indicate the breadth of beauty that forms our surround. "But there are two parts of her character and her written philosophy that have recurred to me during our travels, which are related. For one, I have thought upon the value of capital, for money is what allows us the time and conditions for thought, and for the second, I have given thought to equality.

"As to the first, I find poverty not conducive to reflection. Imagine if we had to find the wherewithal to live each day? When could we find the time for conception of ideas higher than necessity? Would we travel, or be content with finding a house to shelter us? I think it is our possessions that imprison us by restricting us to their maintenance. Now we are free of want and the care of possessions, and see what thoughts arise! The glory of the mountains will live in my heart, and my philosophy is the better for it."

Percy attends to me intently, which is a thing that endears him to me. Now, he inquires. "You mentioned equality?"

"The second of my thoughts does relate to the equality of women and men; I am aware I live upon your grace. You have placed yourself in debt for me. Mary Wollstonecraft put herself in such a position with men many a time for her sustenance, and was excoriated as an adventuress flitting from man to man, yet what other choice had she?

"And yet..." I pause at this remembrance. "There was another way as model for her. My mother met a woman only a year older than herself, Francis Blood, Fanny."

"Our sister's namesake?" Clara asks.

"The same. Mother dwelt with this Fanny for years without the patronage of men, and the two of them made a living for themselves together. They formed a school, sought pupils, and were rewarded without the need for a man's benefaction.

"Still it was a hard life. In the course of events, my mother did seek patronage with a number of men as expedient to her wish to write and reflect. My father was her last, and I think her best. His respect and their like-minded approach to the needs of those who seek a life of thought offered a place for her."

I smile at my speech and run out of words so I ask, "But Percy, what thoughts has our journey engendered in you?"

Percy lies upon his back and, pillowing his head upon his hands, he speaks to the sky.

"As to philosophy, religion has been on my mind."

"How so?" This surprises me. Few are those I have met whose minds leap about the way his does.

"You two have made me mindful of the power of religion to shape a culture, and how difficult it is to shape one's personal view of our world through application of reason."

"And how," Clara's smile shows her incredulity, "do we cause you to reflect upon religion?"

"It is not so surprising as you might think, as I am in the company of two angels well in advance of my time in heaven." He smiles in return. "Thoughts like these began from the time we flew from England's shore. Remember when we plunged into the waters of Dover? I never beheld such beauty and innocence as I did that day. I thought how the religious would have deemed the sight prurient, for does not the Bible teach us to view such sights as from the devil? I blame religion for that. The disparagement of nature is often found in those discussions that emphasize sexuality as a sickness rather than beautiful and natural.

"The Protestants say Catholicism, by justifying its authority as the only Christian religion, became too corrupt to support itself. A logical extension of reasoning leads Martin Luther to split from the church over corruption and gives the movement its name as a protest of Roman Catholicism. Then Henry splits from the Church over papal defiance of his divine right. It follows, there are no limits to dividing the Church according to philosophical differences."

He raises his finger. "But what is left to protest? Philosophy becomes secondary to human practices. Sex becomes a target for Puritans and Calvinists who dwell long on sins of the flesh, leading to a skewed vision of biblical interpretation. If humans are His ultimate creation, then to object to natural sexuality as sin is a special case of twisted logic."

He lifts his eyes to ours. "The prevailing opinion is that sexuality MUST be perverse or obscene, per se, with no thought as to reasons for labeling it as sin. For the majority of humanity, the mores are simple concepts, the better to be understood as a set of rules with no thought of exceptions and less for the reasons for those rules."

I ask, "What of the idea of providing sin as an injunction against disease?"

"Or incest?" Clara says, causing me to turn my head to her, but she will not meet my eye.

"To promote celibacy as an exercise in health strikes me as an unreasonably harsh and simplistic way of dealing with normal passions. I think celibacy is no friend to health." Percy will not be distracted. "Clara, you mention incest. There is little wrong with incest save a risk the act produce progeny that is deformed, but do not all relationships run a risk of producing unhealthy or defective children? There is also that as the child matures, other relationships will fail because he, or she, cannot sever the family tie. This is, again, simplistic. Do not all relationships risk separation?"

"Little wrong with incest?" In light of my time in Scotland with a natural philosopher of excellent repute and with women of intelligence I cannot abide by this. "How many of those with power over others speak of their transgression as only a little thing? Those despots never feel the pain they cause.

"I think you say 'there is little wrong' only because you'll never carry a child beneath your heart for nine months, only to deliver a malformed being. Do not forget that a baby may be crippled or condemned to the bleeding disease when it should be an object of love.

"Nor ought you to dismiss emotion. Confused and warped into an excessive affection for a family member obvious to all," I sneered my sarcasm lest my meaning go awry, "and intrusive of other relationships. The objects of such attentions must find a way to live a whole life having been deprived of an example to mold their actions.

"Fie on you, Percy," I spit, "you do no credit to your gender!"

Percy shakes his head. "I still say the practice is condemned beyond its detriments. Condemnation being at the heart of religion—disparagement rather than reasoned argument. And so we go into our first act of normal exploration, expecting sex to be perverse. There is no *sin* but a denial of experience for the reason of naming that experience evil." He looks to me. "Tell me Mary, what did your mother say concerning relationships between rational beings?"

"She held with the responsibility of the individual without the consent of society. We ought to be free to love who we will, when we will."

Percy and Clara glance toward each other.

"Would you say Clara and I love each other?"

My heart hammers within me. "Though you change the subject, we've come to the crux of the matter, haven't we?" I lean forward. "My conviction that all men and women ought to be free to love without certification or censure will not be overridden by the two of you."

They kissed me, and Percy praised me for my integrity. And I felt noble.

Late in the night, however, when I lay upon a pallet by the fire and heard them sporting in the bed I admitted, to myself alone, there were limits of philosophy's ability to console.

Chapter Eighteen

Downriver

Could we travel the 800 miles to England on so small a sum as what was left in our purse? As well ask, what cannot be accomplished when one is too young to know better.

---

28 August

Having determined the cost of taking downriver passage on a barge was the most economical, we resolve to drift upon the Reuss and the Rhine through Germany and the Netherlands, thus saving enough money for the voyage to England.

A passenger boat trip takes us to Lucerne. Violent rains drench us during this first part of our journey home, but a storyteller among our company heartens us by telling a tale of a priest and his mistress who died at the foot a glacier. He assures us that, would we but travel to the glacier, we might "still, today, hear their voices calling upon travelers for aid."

We sit in silence watching the beauty of the shore and thinking on the lovers, the priest and the beautiful wife of his rich parishioner, their inevitable discovery, the flight, the pursuit. I shiver.

Percy takes over the storyteller's role. "Our present location minds me I had occasion to ponder Paracelsus and other alchemists of note while I resided at Oxford.

"Shall I tell you the story of the Devil's Bridge or Teufelsbrücke?" Percy asks, taking a turn at storytelling. "And how it relates to the great alchemist Paracelsus? Yes? Well then...

"I had occasion to ponder him with some avidity when I dedicated some time to the arts of Alchemy—and of Agrippa, Magnus and other alchemists of note. This was but a few years ago while I resided in Oxford.

"The story of Paracelsus begins darkly," he lifts a hand with two fingers pointed upwards, "and, like the man, fabulously.

"Attend me, now. Once there was a shepherd who sought to cross a river, not all that distant from here," he says, pointing through the rains. "Said Shepherd discovered the waters of the river were much swollen with the rains of spring. Upon beholding the cataract, he feared, and in his fear he did a foolish thing. Eschewing the Lord God, he bespoke unto the Devil, entreating Lucifer to create a way for the Shepherd and his flock to cross the raging stream."

"And why," Clara looks askance, "would he seek the aid of the Prince of Light rather than the Lord God?"

"Perhaps he did not wish to trouble God with so trivial a task." He sticks out his lower lip and shrugs. "Perhaps he knew this action would make a better story. Regardless of motive, let me stipulate he entreated the Devil to aid him in crossing the rushing torrent.

"Beelzebub considered and, nothing loth, accomplished the task in typical demonic time, an instant.

"'Oh, what a great labor that was!' the Devil said, slumping in weariness. 'Such was my effort, for I must have compensation.' He looked to the Shepard. 'Do you pay,' he cried. 'I require the soul eternal of the first to cross my bridge.'

"Our Shepherd, albeit grateful for the conveyance, bethought the toll too steep and sought a way to cheat the Father of Lies. To wit, he allowed one of his sheep, we may be sure the sheep was the poorest of his flock, to cross the bridge before him.

"We may postulate thus: the self-worth of the Devil did not allow for him to be the subject of a defeat by the wits of a human. We may, therefore, assume the wrath of the fiend knew no bounds."

"We shall so assume," said Clara folding her hands upon her knee.

"And so I content me." Percy patted her hands and continued. "In his anger, the Devil sought to hurl a boulder and destroy his creation the bridge, the sheep, and the Shepherd at a single effort."

Here Percy looks from one of us to the other and, placing the back of his open hand next to his mouth, speaks in a conspiratorial air. "A Shepherdess enters the story at this time. She somehow," he lifts his hand to forestall our objections, "by device unbeknown to this respondent, bore witness to the covenant between the human and the daemon, and as she was wiser than the Shepard..."

"As is the case 'tween many a man and woman," I mutter.

Percy sighs and continues with hardly a pause.

"As I was saying, the Shepherdess, who was wise, entreated the Lord God for aid. God, perhaps having no other task at hand, encumbered the boulder the Devil still held in his hands with such mass that he could not shift it. Beezelbub, having been bested by Shepard, Shepherdess, and God Almighty, slunk back to his domain but left the bridge intact. To this very day it bears the name, Devil's Bridge."

"What's to do with Paracelsus, alchemist supreme?" I asked.

"This." Percy raises his hand in benediction with the pride of a storyteller who springs an unlooked for conclusion on his audience. "Three hundred years ago, a young woman, married and a mother yet weary of life, did hurl herself from this bridge and so end her existence. Her husband, seeking to spare her young son the stigma accruing by gossip that associated the family with the Devil, removed him from the vicinity. And yet, and yet..."

"And yet? And yet?" Clara entreats.

"The child was Paracelsus. Upon growing in years, he was schooled in the alchemistic arts by his father. The gossips had it he was to have made compact with the Devil for ultimate knowledge. He wished to know the formulary for life eternal."

"Ahhh," I exhale. "A worthy bargain."

"Most worthy, but, in full disclosure, he increased his bargain to incidentally include the secret of turning baser metals to gold."

"Less worthy, but still, the one pact remains as it stands aloof without augmentation. He did bargain with the devil for endless life."

Percy looks off through the rains thoughtfully. "There is within these apocrypha a thread of truth, or half-truths, indeed of quarter-truths, but a thread of truth nay-the-less. Harken to me now, a mentor I knew, Lind was his name, James, whose fame were made as physician to King George..."

"The Third?" Jane asks, turning her head and lifting her lip in disdain. "He was a less able physician than a conjurer I have heard, unable to treat the King's madness."

"The same. However, our King did recover, it is said, and Lind received the credit and thus earned a living for his remaining years, becoming a teacher. I sought him out, and he spoke at length to me of subjects to which I was inclined by my nature to attend. It was he who enlarged my knowledge of Galvanism to the extent of personal experimentation, where I produced on several occasions a blue nimbus about my body.

"I could say it was this experimentation and the protest of the neighbors, who included advanced students, rather than the subjects of my poetry, that caused the dons of Oxford to seek my removal, but I know it was not."

"Tell me more of these." This is of interest. The rage of the Devil, the combat with God, the sparking nimbus of electrical discharge in the night, here is the very stuff of a good story.

Percy smiles and murmurs some lines from Othello,

> When I did speak of some distressful stroke
> That my youth suffered. My story being done
> She gave me for my pains a world of sighs.

In this manner do we occupy our soggy time upon the lake. By the time we reach the town of Lucerne, the sun comes out, and we dry ourselves in the heat of the day. Before boarding the river vessel that will bear us upon the Reuss, I look my last upon Lake Lucerne, at the rock-bound shores with their o're-towering cliffs and the bright snow-caped mountains shining against the clear blue skies.

At Loffenburg, we engage a boat for our transportation down the Reuss. More a barge-like conveyance, it had seating for many passengers upon the low roof of the cabin which spans its length. From the line of those waiting to board, we see these seats are quickly filling.

Our appearance bespeaks hard traveling. My feet are bare as I lost my shoes, I know not where I left them, but I think I owned them still when we had a picnic a day or two ago. Clara's shoes are drenched ruins. We have but two small, tattered boxes tied with water-soaked silk ribbon, each containing a spare dress and two shifts, the rest having been jettisoned along the way. The boatsman requires but one look at us to know us for that peculiar breed of English youth who ramble the continent with more enthusiasm than money. His face gives evidence he does not approve of young British. "*Quarante* (forty) *sou pour un passage*," he spits.

In contradiction to our bedraggled appearances, we mark a difference between our classes: our upright posture and direct gaze to his shifting eyes and slouching stance. The look all three of us turn upon him cows him. He knows we stand upon the brink of seeking better treatment from his competition.

Percy informs him the three of us will occupy a single cabin while he provides food and wine, "*Forty sou*," but, he adds, "*pas un tout*." A bargain struck, Percy extends his hand, and the man eventually takes it.

"*Monter. Allay, allay. Tout suite*," the man enjoins us. He helps Clara over the gap between the quay and the hull. Percy steps aboard like a sailor. But when the boatman holds out a hand to me, I glance, pointedly, at the dirt on his fingernails and smile as I step over without aid.

"*Merde*," I hear him mutter behind my back.

Here I should speak about the insufferable Germans who, though they sit upon the same boat, are not our fellows in the journey. They stink. Did I heretofore think the French odiferous? They are as lilies to horse manure compared to the Germans.

We think ourselves fortunate in securing seats on the forward part of the vessel so that the slight breeze of our passage brings fresh air to our faces, but when we stop for lunch at one of the picaresque villages lining the shore, we find our seats occupied when we return.

We look at each other in surprise, but the rule appears to be first come first served, so we shrug and seek three other seats together. However, we are no more than settled when the previous tenants, Swiss as evident from their attire, return from the town and begin to assault us loudly with their abusive words. Though we cannot understand them, it is evident from their shooing gestures they demand we vacate. We demure and the assault escalates to the point where one man grabs at Percy's coat. Percy may not appear dangerous, but he has been tutored in the English art of boxing. One second to set his feet, another to raise his hands and another for three quick punches in succession, quickly settling the matter by knocking the man down. The master of the craft, now sensing the angry mood of the passengers and having seen Percy's ability to defend himself, quickly entreats us to different seats.

"These Germans are an affront," I mutter. "And the Swiss are fit for nothing but slavery, but as they possess an abundance of stubbornness, I doubt anyone will ever overcome them."

We happily part company with them at the next stop. Finding a small boat or canoe for hire, we load our poor boxes and propel ourselves down river with paddles.

Great cliffs of rock often crowned by ruins rise many feet into the air and flank the water as it flows. At one point the water surges strongly through two rocky outcroppings, foaming and churning for some distance.

Percy cries, "Strike out with your oars and aid our passage."

"Are we not going along fast enough?" Clara shouts over the roar of the rapids.

But I see the problem. "'Tis not speed, sister, but accuracy. Look you! By using this oar to push against the water we might miss that rock before us!" And suiting action to word I paddle furiously, thrusting our craft's bow aside from certain destruction. "Huzzah!" I cheer as we surge past the jagged obstruction and rushing waters.

So we shoot along the passage atop waves that mount between serrated rocks and whoop with delight in overcoming obstacles.

When we reach the next village, we make for the shore to drain the water that slopped into the bottom of our little boat. Clara and I clamber out and wait for Percy to make his way to us, but he stops halfway along the boat to look at us with his face a mask of amazement.

"Goddesses! Muses to tempt Homer. Do I not see before me Diana and Artemis, in their awful beauty, exquisite beyond the most choice courtesans of Paris?"

"Muses?" My mouth twists in chagrin. "Medusae, more like, with our hair hanging in sodden snakes about our shoulders."

"Is the plural not Medusas?" Clara lifts her hair. "Look not upon us lest ye turn to stone."

"I speak of your accomplishment and beauty. In those the two of you are lovely past the eyes of man to behold!"

I think a moment. "Percy, how is your stamina?"

He holds his hands to the side. "As good as any man, I suppose."

"No better?"

"I am as you see me."

I turn to Clara long enough for her to see my grin, but compose my face before returning to him. "If you are no better than the next man, the best we can hope is for you to pass with a smile."

"But," Clara puts an arm around my waist and lays her head upon my shoulder. "In years to come, we shall think of you."

"At least until we find someone of suitable stamina."

Percy, seldom at a loss for words, stutters. "W-we must find a room."

On unsteady legs, we totter up the bank. A man inquires whether we have lately come down the river as he gazes incredulously at us. When we gesture to where our canoe is visible, he says. "Your luck must be great. Storm rains have swollen the river unduly high. A boat with twenty-six passengers overturned yesterday where you passed. All were drowned."

We may have been more lucky than skillful.

The next day, Percy has that far-off look of one who has seen great sights and done fantastic deeds.

4 September

We are fortunate to find seats in the diligence in company with some merchants who appear, from the cut of their clothes, to be of a better class or are at least polite. In Cologne, we secure another crewed boat for the last part of our voyage upon the Rhine.

The current, while quick, is still more placid than before. It is evident the men who guide the boat are well versed in their jobs. The leagues pass as rapidly as the current flowing between the high cliffs, and our journey is pleasant. For entertainment, we read a draft of Lord Byron's *Childe Harold's Pilgrimage*, which the publisher gave Percy to review. We happily read the passages of the third canto and compare the poet's description with the view of the river which presents itself to our eyes.

"I believe our time on the river to be paradise," I remark. "These boatsmen exert themselves so their craft turns, and turns with the current, and so we are presented with fresh vistas of wooded isles and ruin-capped crags. They compare well with Byron's verses of the land."

Clara exclaims, "Did we not view his, 'The Castled crag of Drachenfels' frowning down upon us as we traversed 'the wide and winding Rhine'?" I pause and my mind wanders. "What a name for a place, I wondered whether he invented it or not."

"All true, m'love," Percy interjects. "Others near here are just as real. Only a little distant is the castle Frankenstein, for example. But note Byron well, Mary, and read the man entire if you would be a writer; he is a wonder the way he paints with his pen. Though the light of the day reflecting from the waters defies any attempts to capture with paint, he does well enough with words alone. I hope to meet him in some future day, as much as I hope he approves of my notes."

In Bonn, the water flows so slowly we reckon the money expended in food and drink during the days needed to traverse will surpass that paid for a coach to Rotterdam. We leave the river for the last part of our journey by land. Nothing, no other experience, could ever surpass the disgust of travel in a German diligence. A stench of bodies that have known no more washing than rain is a reek augmented by the scent of rotting sausage and cheese from their clothing. Such a miasma infests the interior, it causes us to seek the upper seats to sit gasping in the air.

8 September

Rotterdam, our final guinea buys our passage, with meals, to London on a ship due to sail that night. We are fortunate indeed to have paid before the master declares contrary winds will force us to stay two days in Marsluys, as once we are passengers, he must continue to feed us.

Dutch captains refuse to chance crossing the bar when the wind is not distinctly in their favor because vessels go oft aground there. A firm and following wind is required, and at that they might scrape over the sands even at high tide. At least Dutch ships are clean, and the air is wholesome below deck.

At last a propitious wind sets from the east and we cast off. We repair to our tiny cabin and Percy sits between us on the narrow lower bunk, holding us for what we expect will be our last night together. Without lifting my head from his shoulder, I say, "I feel the crossing of the bar like the end of our freedom, Percy."

"I hate going home," says Clara.

"What will they make of your new name?" Percy asks.

"I care not, but I have been thinking."

"Yes?" he prompts.

"Claire, I think. Claire Clairmont. That is more melodious yet."

"Better," he says into her hair as he puts an arm around her shoulders and pulls her to him.

"Your new name has a nice sound." I take her hand in the brief time I have before my seasickness overwhelms me. Percy wraps his other arm round my waist, the better to steady me against the roll of the ship. But the wind shifting to the Northwest gives me an abysmal crossing. Three days upon the billows of the Channel pass before we reach our journey's end.

13 September

A cold rain falls upon the grey face of the Thames, blurring the buildings that line both sides of the river. As the Dutch ship must wait for space near the Temple Gardens, we are ferried to shore in a small boat. I step upon the stone quay and know my six-week journey at an end. I search around us for one of the idlers who are omnipresent. "When we reach home," I promise a man, "You'll have half-a-guinea for carrying our boxes." And we place what is left of our battered, sorry possessions in his pushcart.

And at last we turn our tired footsteps toward the house of William Godwin, philosopher. The rain stops and the clouds part, letting the sun begin to shine to warm us.

"Your feet are filthy," says Claire, looking to where I stand before the door steps.

"You are ragged," I say.

"Your hair looks like shite."

"You stink like shite."

But then we straighten.

She says, "But I have walked the boulevards of Paris."

"And I have seen the Alps." Despite our exhaustion the smiles on our faces glow as we climb the steps.

Claire bangs the knocker. "Hello?" she calls. "We're home."

So much occurred in that scant month and a half abroad.

Memories of the brilliant architecture of Paris are mine, as are the devastations caused by war. I was present, and party to, discussions that would be the envy of any salon in London but were held in forests, and lakesides, and on rivers passing ancient ruins. Most of all, the sight of the greatest peaks in all of Europe, of radiantly burning sunsets and dawns, lives inside my mind and would forevermore.

Percy Shelley was now my lover and if my sister joined us, it was a matter of loving more and gaining more by it. Together, we found strength and through this we formed a family.

Was I prescient in my love of Switzerland? It is said that a place which pulls at our conscious being will be, or has been in another lifetime, of vast import to us.

Chapter Nineteen

Leaving Home

I do not know what I expected. Perhaps I wanted to be petted for my daring, my fortitude, my courage. Perhaps I thought my life would continue at home with lessons, invitations to salons, the theater, and interesting entertainments. I was that naïve.

We trudge exhausted and famished up the steps to the house on Skinner Street, to be let in by Fanny, who ushers us into the kitchen.

"You appear as gaunt wolves. Go ahead and eat your fill despite Mother," she says, serving us herself, but there is an anger in her, too.

"Call a maid to tend to us," Percy says, reaching out and touching her wrist. "You sit and join us."

"I've let almost all of them go." Fanny puts more vegetables on my plate. "Mother expects me to perform duties such as serving guests myself." But we persist until she sits, placing her elbows on the table and putting her chin in her hands. "Now, tell me what you did without me."

First one then the other, we trip over each other to tell the tale of our travels. With her head at an angle, her eyes wide, and her mouth open, she listens in amaze.

Fanny's gaze goes again to the door and she listens intently at every sound. "Jane..."

"You must call me Claire from now on, sister, for I am as pure as the waters of Lucerne."

"I suppose I shall grow used to the change. Claire and Mary, we must speak. Here is how our house lies. Mother and Father are furious at your desertion. Mother embarks on a letter-writing campaign against you, Mary, and though she seeks to portray Claire as innocent, both of you are tarred by her brush. She's given out that Mary is a trollop who seduced a married man..."

I open my mouth to protest but Fanny holds up a hand. "I know 'twas mutual, but there is worse. Harriet has written letters of her own. I fear the three of you will not find many friends in London."

Since we've been here, no one else approaches the kitchen. No servant comes near, though we must disturb the time for meal preparations, not one of the other children intrudes upon us. *Nor Father.*

Food gone at last, Fanny stands and says, "We've looked for you for weeks." She's obviously troubled by some matter. "Father says do you return I am to show you to your rooms." She glances at Percy. "Alone."

"Ah, my cue," he sighs. "'Exit stage left, pursued by a bear.'"

Fanny turns to us. "Go along with you. I'll send up water as soon as it heats." She glances at our hair. "And lice combs."

We see Percy to the door. "We'll be reunited soon, my loves." And with a kiss for each of us, he's gone. I blink, noticing how much space his departure leaves in my heart.

Claire and I wearily tread the steps to our rooms only to find Stepmother at the top of the stairs.

"So," she says, letting the word hang. "You have the brazen effrontery to return as a starveling dog to my door, have you?" I note how she faces only me.

"We have, Mother," interjects Claire, "and much have we profited from our travel. We are worldly women now."

Stepmother rakes her eyes over my stomach. "How worldly, I wonder? Well, get you unpacked and bathed. You stink like a Portsmouth alley when the fleet is in."

And how does she know the scent of a seaport alley?

"Remain in your rooms until dinner. You will attend and you will be prompt."

I stumble past her, but a new worry intrudes and comes to a head as we sup.

Though difficult at the best of times, on this day dining with family would strain a bishop's patience. My stepmother is seated at one end of the table and Father at the other. We children range down the sides of the board. We gladly share our stories with our brothers. Billy loves to hear of the ruined French villages, and Charlie that we ate dinner in the same room where Boney Napoleon once did.

Father is a stranger to me. Always cold in public, what I feel from him now is like the wind off a glacier. He enters and sits with never so much as a glance at me.

Our parents say little to each other and less to those offspring who are, perhaps, subject to imminent imprisonment in the White Tower. When needful to address me, Stepmother directs her remarks toward Claire in the third person, thus, "Ask your sister, when she is quite through playing with the beans, if she would deign pass them." Father does not speak even this little to us.

Stepmother addresses my sister, "I forget what name you are giving yourself these days. Are you to be clept Claire now? You know you were named in my honor."

My sister lifts her head regally but with a gentle smile. "Claire is where my heart has landed like a robin upon snow, Mother, a herald of better times."

"Claire Clairmont," the round old woman tries the sound of it in her mouth around her food before she shrugs. "May it do you well."

From what I know of the woman, she practiced the art of self-naming years earlier so that her children would appear to have a legitimate father. Mr. Clairmont must have been a man of perception, as he never married her.

"Fanny," Stepmother says. My sister flinches. "What plans have you to adjust our budget in accommodation for the expense your sister forces upon the productive members of the family?" She spits a piece of gristle into her spoon. "That one shows little attention to attracting a mate and so relieving us of her support."

"Perhaps if she had a new outfit?" Fanny assays. "I did see a fine cloth at a shop this morning; cheap, but worthy of being sewn into a dress. The fabric is so white, so light, so perfect for the late summer."

"Mother!" Claire claps her hands, trying to swing the woman's attention from me. "I do think I would so love a new dress of it as well." It occurs to me, Claire schemes to have Percy for herself.

If it were done...'twere best done quickly. "Father, I am with child," I say. *There, it is out.*

"Are you sure?" Claire's face shows her disappointment. She knows Percy's wont regarding damsels in distress. Although I would not have chosen this method, I have taken the lead in our game.

"My menses failed to appear at the appointed time." I look to where my father sits chewing steadily, his nostrils flair and his face turns white. With deliberation, he lifts his napkin to his lips, pats them twice, and places it next to his service. He rises and steps toward the door, but before he leaves the room he stops. "Fanny, as four of the clock has yet to strike, do you send to Shelley. Please inform him Mary is no more my dependent but his. He must make accommodation for her as I'll no longer suffer her within my house."

I run from the room. My tears nearly blind me as I ascend the stairs, open the door to my chamber and, throwing myself upon my bed, I give vent to the pain inside me. My pillow is wet when I hear a soft tap upon my door. "Father?"

"Claire. Do let me in."

"It isn't locked." She enters, her face a study in grief. "Oh, Mary. He doesn't mean it. He can't. You are his natural-born daughter. He loves you."

We cling to each other and in time sobs and embraces serve to quiet us. I post a note to Percy. *All is as scattered dust. Father will naught of me. Do you come to the cemetery as soon as you can.*

What if he will not take me?

Green, sun-filled, and as still as a place within London can ever be, the rank grasses of my mother's untended grave make my bed, and I lie down, listening to my heart.

My pain will out. "Father threw me over," I cry and hear my plaint echo from the walls and houses. *Over. Over.* Never did I believe such a thing could happen between two hearts so close. It is said sharp knives hurt less. Exile, the blade my father used, was dull and dirty, the better to inflict pain both immediate and lasting.

"Mary?" I hear Percy's voice call from the gate.

"Anon," I call. Standing up and dashing the tears from my eyes I see him run toward me. A moment, no more, and we are together. He gives me his lap for a throne, folds me in his arms, and strokes my hair while I recite my story between my sobs 'till all is told. "I am lost, Percy. If you won't take me, I've nowhere to turn."

"Then be glad, for I'll not let you sink. I've nothing better to do but love you, and so we shall love forever."

"You'll have mine as well," Claire's voice draws my eyes to where she stands at the foot of the gravesite. "I'll not abandon either of you," she says, extending her hand to Percy and patting my back. "In our home, we shall make as fine a family as we did on our travels."

I had not foreseen that.

"Shall we feast upon moonbeams and words?" Percy's voice holds a note of joy. "For though my finances will scarce keep us alive, all I have shall be yours," he says, kissing us. "We will be bourn upon a sea of love."

The three of us go hand in hand in hand to the house on Skinner Street that was no more to be mine. Fanny meets us at the door. Before she can speak, I tell her. "We have reached accommodation. Percy and I," I hesitate only a moment, "and Claire. We are to set up house, dear Fanny."

"Cheers sister," Fanny says, "The four of us shall be well together."

That is unexpected, too.

Though upon immediate reflection, I find I understand. Mayhap too well. Did not Claire escort us when I sought to flee to the Continent with my lover? Fanny must have decided a precedent has been established. But another sister to further divide what love Percy possessed?

I'd rather not.

"There is no money, dear Fanny." I say quickly. "Less even than here. Percy is as destitute as only a poet can be. As it is, we have scarce enough for us. Be glad, for you'd not wish a life of poverty upon yourself."

"My life would still be better," she says, glancing over her shoulder. "And as for love," she looks to Percy, "who can see the future?"

Oh this is not needed.

I screw my courage to the sticking point and find my stepmother at her desk, to let her know the gleanings of our intent.

"Gone is good," she says. "Your presence makes it hard for your father to work. It is well that your lover makes a place for you even though he be not yet divorced." The smile she turns on me could curdle milk. "You'll be more than a nine-day wonder for scolds, I warrant."

"I'm going, too, Mother," Claire says.

Cat-quick and cat-furious, Stepmother turns. "Is this baggage not plenty to tramp about without you adding to the meat for the gossiping dogs to worry?"

"Nay-the-less," Claire folds her arms and says, "I'm going."

The woman writhes up to her full height. "I forbid it!"

Her censure works no better than it had in Calais. Stepmother is beset on all sides. Another voice speaks.

"And I," says Fanny. "I'll go with them. They need me."

"Your father needs you, as do I! Great thought must not be hindered by the dross of work-a-day. Who will keep the house while we think? Nay, Fan, y'are most required, and to leave would be traitorous."

Fanny returns again to her plea while I pack, "I can be of such use. Have I not kept this house for years, and do you say there is another with stricter economy? There I am nonpareil."

And so I tell a lie.

"When Percy publishes enough that we may see our way to plenty, then do you come live with us."

"Ah, sister!" she cries. "And when will that be?"

When indeed? Never, if I got my way. One sister in my lover's bed is enough.

Chapter Twenty

Stories

We learned Harriet struck first by having Percy's bank account emptied while we were still abroad, nor was that all that was amiss. Stepmother's letter campaign against us did what she intended. We were social pariahs. However, even though she did not intend to help me, Stepmother came to our aid through not knowing which way to turn her anger. She could not abide ill being said of her daughter, so she put it abroad that Harriet was a less than congenial wife to Percy as the reason for his attachment to Claire.

Percy had friends who were happy to defy convention and allowed us to stay with them. Within the week, Percy found a place for us in Somers Town, not far from St. Pancras and close to my old house in The Polygon. There, Claire and I were introduced to those whose names I knew but had not the pleasure of meeting.

Claire particularly, but I as well, loved it that we had such lively company, and dear Fan joined us when she could. When I cast my mind into the past, I find I remember our first dinner party as though waking up the day after.

"I simply must have a new dress for the party," Claire pouts to Percy. "And the fabric and the sewing, which is nearly finished, will cost so very little. I'll be home early to help Mary."

He gave in, and now the work falls to me. I try not to be disgruntled by Claire, but I cannot foresee a time when she will change.

"There!" Percy says, looking out the front window where he sits reading. "They've started to arrive."

"I'll let them in directly," I say, walking into the front room from my post by the kitchen door, where I have been driving our cook to such distraction she orders me to, "Leave me alone lest I confuse the fish with the squab!"

I recognize the young man who appears in our room as the same as I met in my father's house upon a time. Although he is well made, with a delicate chin and a broad, honest forehead beneath a full head of hair, I fear my initial impression ought to be thought of as the opposite of liking. He has a tendency to flirt with any woman associated with Percy.

"Hogg!" Percy shouts. "How excellent you should be first! Here then, my love, meet my most special friend, Thomas Jefferson Hogg, Mary Wollstonecraft Godwin."

The man makes a short bow and brings his hands around from his back. "Lobsters!"

"Gads, no!" I cry. "You'd have us batten on these when the servants had me write a decree that they should not be served lobster more than twice a week?"

"Ah," he says, "but in addition to being economical, they cost only ha-pence, there is virtue in the taste when they are prepared with generous saucer of melted butter."

"Consult Cook," Percy tells him. "Though she will not sup upon them, if there is a way to make them palatable, she will know it."

I have oft heard of Percy's fellow student from Oxford. As he sidles toward the kitchen to deposit the armored insects, I call to mind he made Percy's acquaintance while at Oxford.

A sharp rapping on our door announces two more of Percy's friends and three women who accompany them, and we are soon adrift in a whirl of introductions and small chat. We find our seats round our table set with a cloth lit with *two* candles, "Hang the expense!" Percy shouts in honor of the event.

I find myself next to Edward John Trelawney. Tall, with long black hair and saber-like mustachios, I judge by the color and cut of his vest and coat and the tightness of his trousers (not that I notice) and his free and easy manner, I think he would be at home upon the heaving decks of a ship terrorizing the Spanish Main.

But it is another guest, Thomas Love Peacock, who catches at my heart. Though he is more than a decade older, he is my poet's future image. Like Percy, he has the slender mien of a writer and a poet. His shirt is of the whitest cloth with a ruffle at his neck, and he wears his hair in a mop atop his head. *What is it about poets and their hair?* I learn he has spent time on the ocean, though not as a pirate, but his years of naval service came to an end, he says, with the realization of what hell a life aboard a warship can be.

"Though I would try to earn my bread with words, the inferno of battle poorly prepared me as a poet, and so I sought long walks on the paths and roads of solid land for inspiration. My friends both ashore and at sea lamented me."

I tilt my head. "And why would they do so?"

He sighs. "They felt it a shame that a man of such intellect be so poor."

Claire sweeps into the room clad in ivory silk. *Oh my,* I think, *a blonde ought not to wear even off-white.* But the color hardly matters as the fabric is of such translucence she draws every eye to her. Percy introduces her to the assembled company as she sits next to him at the table's head. Our guests take seats lining the sides of the board, and I occupy the foot. The first of the bottles are opened, the first of the courses is served, and conversation bubbles as other introductions are made.

Hogg's dinner partner is dressed in so rich a deep green, she gleams like an emerald. Trelawney's companion is in the red of a ruby, and Peacock's particular friend wears an organza that flashes in the glow of the candlelight. I see several of these are beauties who do justice to the rich trend of colored silks in contrast to my long gown of white linen with cap sleeves and Grecian folds now out of date. *Aye me,* I glance at Claire, *what cannot be mended...*but that platitude does little to sooth me.

Eventually, we reach the point of sufficiency in our meal and push back from the table, but not from the bottle.

"A contest!" Percy calls standing at his place. "Friends and lovers, now that we are all assembled, I call for your wit as payment for this feast."

"We brought the feast!" Hogg shouts.

"Beside the point." Percy gives a dismissive wave and returns to his challenge.

"Lead off, then," says Trelawney, slapping the table. "Display the wit of which you speak, and damned be him who first cries hold, enough.'"

Percy places his hand over his heart. "Would you have a mark at which to shoot? Well then, hear the tale of the drowned goddesses."

Percy tells the story of how we rode through the rapids with a storyteller's flair. "We reached the town below the rapid and, beaching the battered little canoe, my companions exited safe upon the shore. Their demeanor clearly indicated they had no notion of the peril we had escaped. To these beautiful innocents, the dangers of the falls were nothing more than a joyous ride. So overcome with glad feelings was I that gazing upon them I called them 'Goddesses' with some reverence, and they, glancing at each other and clasping hands, proceeded to threaten me."

"We never!" begins Claire.

"They told me that if I could call them deities in their present state of sodden dresses and tangled locks, I ought to cast up all account as they intended to exceed the limits of my physical stamina. In short, they meant to violate me to death!" And placing his hands on either side of his plate, he sighs.

"Well don't stop there, Percy," demands Hogg. "Tell us of the method of your torture."

Percy purses his lips. He reached for his glass and lifting it, says, "They did indeed use their best skills." He smiles at us. "I died with flights of angels attending me and the most blissful of smiles upon my face."

"Oh ye of mighty imagination," I say, lifting my glass to him. "Who says those were our best efforts?"

"See with what I must put up?"

"Poor, poor Percy." Trelawney yawns and turns to me, "If he be truly deceased, might I offer my services?"

I pause as though considering before I say, "Nay, for he be a lively shade with one firm part."

Percy retires the field to the thunder of the company's applause, and Thomas Love Peacock clears his throat to indicate he will take up the gauntlet.

"I find a toast is always in order, and so, I give you two reasons for drinking." Peacock sips from the brandy that is his contribution to our evening and says, "One is to cure thirst." He grins impishly. "The other is to prevent it."

"I've walked around the whole of Scotland, traced the length of the Thames and loved a Caernarvonshire nymph." He grins and nods to the company. "And though I be destitute in worldly goods, all in all, I'm having a wonderful life."

"Proof that a life, though one in poverty, can be well lived," I say, lifting a glass to him.

He lifts his in return. "Thanks. I look forward to knowing you better, Mary Godwin. A teller of tales ought welcome the poverty that characterizes those years.

It brings out a valued creativity." He furrows his brow and smiles. "My story is of a time when a beast and I sought each other's lives.

"I was a traveler through the east of Scotland, when one day I came to the shores of a great lake, or loch, as they say. I met a man who loaned me his boat that I might spend a time on the waters in contemplation of many matters, but eventually what my mind turned to was where my next meal might appear. Seeing some fishing gear in the boat, I seized upon it as the probable source of procuring sustenance. I lost no time in baiting the hook and casting it over, then sat back to await results, fishing being not only a way of feeding one's self, but a wonderful excuse for a nap.

"Presently, I felt a tug upon the line. I pulled, only to have the rod bend down sharply. From the way the rod arched, I thought I had caught something that would feed me for several days. So, bracing my feet upon the seat before me, I set myself for battle with what had taken my hook."

He relates his fight with an improbable fish of great size and endurance, ending with the creature's head, with its rows of huge teeth, rising far above the waters until he falls back into the boat, which extracts the hook from the creature's mouth along with one of the finger-long teeth and causes the monster to sink beneath the waves.

"As I rowed toward the shore, I bethought myself to seek sustenance elsewhere than in the cold and dark waters of Loch Ness."

"You have captivated me," breathed his partner, the woman clad in emerald.

She ought to be careful leaning forward and heaving such a sigh, lest she display her charms to us all.

Thomas glances at her and pats her hand. "Fear not, my cabbage."

"I cry the lie!" says the organza dress from across the table. "And call for the evidence!"

"You doubt my veracity, miss? Then look at this." He pulls his watch from his pocket and puts it on the table for all of us to see. The fob, a tooth, long as a hand is wide, thick as a thumb and deadly sharp, lay neatly impaled upon a fishing hook.

"This counts," says Percy. "And by the sacred canon of the game, should you 'cry the lie' and proof be offered, you must pay the forfeit."

"Very well." She lifts her head in challenge. "Name my loss."

Trelawney scarce hesitates. "Show us your legs."

Screeches of feigned outrage! Avid lust on the faces of the men. We laugh at her show of patently false modesty. Then she rises, steps upon the chair, turns her back to us, and slowly, teasingly, raises her skirt until, "There. Will that do?"

"NO!" shout Peacock and Hogg. Percy too, I note. She lifts her skirts another inch, and another...

"Ha! A well-made maid!"

"More!"

"No, you demanded to see my legs and you have seen a goodly bit more than that."

"Technically the arse is part of the limbs."

Her dance of the seven veils over, she dimples and resumes her seat.

"Well, Thomas, your monster will take some topping," says Hogg. "But if truth is necessary for a story, I'll tell you one of our host and he can verify it.

"While we were at Oxford, Percy spent perhaps a week of the entire time in lecture..." Hogg says.

"Less," Percy interjects.

"...but he read incessantly. Oft did I see a light in his room late at night and oft did I see him eat his breakfast with book in hand.

"It was while we were at Oxford." (From that time hence, my private name for Hogg becomes, Old While-We-Were-at-Oxford.) "Percy and I penned a reasoned argument for atheism that has been given out as the cause of our expulsion. That is not the truth." He covers a small belch with his fist and goes on. "The dons said we could stay if we recanted what we wrote. But Percy's character and his conviction would not allow him to recant, and so we left the halls of higher learning, if not enlightenment." Hogg thinks a moment and launches another anecdote.

"While we were at Oxford," *Of course*, "Percy pursued a practice designed to allow the memory of dreams." He turns to face me. "Does he still rise at night to wander your home?" I nod. "He calls the experience while in the state of vision-laden sleep a 'waking dream'."

"I have heard the very phrase," I murmur.

"He describes his practice thusly: 'There is little difficulty in obtaining a state where it is possible to remember your dreams. Upon waking, do you write down what chanced during your reverie. With use you shall grow accustomed to this blurring of lines of wakefulness and somnambulism.' I tried his formula, to rise immediately following nightly visions and commend them to paper. It does provide a record, but I find it most deleterious for sleep. Yet, he attributes this remembrance of dreams for a salubrious effect upon his imagination. Do I lie?"

"Well," Percy mutters. "It is but the unadorned truth."

I glance to my left and see Trelawney considering Hogg's story. "I have found that, in Percy, the bounds between truth and fiction are as blurred as a drunk's speech."

He rises, "Perhaps I might assay a tale..."

As he speaks, I think, *if Edward's saber is as sharp as his wit, ships must have fallen to him the world over*. His story leaves all of us helpless with laughter.

"And so good hearts," he says. "That is the true tale of my time outward bound from Batavia aboard a Dutch East Indiaman with a Sultan's Daughter and the Orangutan who fell in love with her."

"Pax!" I gasp, gripping my waist with both hands. "Oh please, my sides hurt so!"

Claire is laughing so hard she snorts, which sets us off again. When Trelawney raises his finger to make another point, we shout him down. "Have pity!"

"Then cry me the lie and prepare to pay the forfeit!"

His dark eyes find mine, and I change the subject. "Forgive me again, I had thought you a..." I choose a polite term. "A privateer."

I touch his vanity for either pirate he is, or pirate he longs to be. His eyebrows rise toward his long, black hair. He lifts his glass with a flourish and sips the full red wine. "You've a keen eye, missy, there were a time indeed when I plundered the India Ocean."

With that he begins another long story, which thrills us. He tells of his capture of a French merchant with a dark damsel dressed only in gauze aboard, with a peculiar problem. But at length his ship turned for the green isle of England. "And that is the tale of the princess who lost her skirts and gained a husband, though not her own." The company shouts approval.

When he runs down I have a chance to say, "I confess I am jealous that so many of Percy's friends are published."

"We do have something of a circle." Trelawney tilts his head back in pleasure.

"Tell me then, what makes a story wonderful to hear? For I would join that club as a full member with all my heart."

"Would you be a woman author?" simpers the emerald silk.

"Cannot a woman write for men as well?"

"I think not, for it is men who read, and men love feats of daring, danger, and action. What woman would know of these?"

"What of love?" from the Ruby's lisps. "Austin writes the most wonderful stories of love, does she not?"

"I'll tell you what makes a good story." The glass pauses as it rises to the pirate's lips, and he smiles at my gaze.

"Though life be pleasant, with angels adorning every corner of a house, or sunsets gilding the heavens, or sunrises pink as the nipples of Venus," his gaze rises to my eyes, "these niceties of life do not make a good story. Nay, missy, 'tis the crash of cannon people would hear. Or the groan of a hull as it grinds against that of a foe's. A storm's banshee shriek through the rigging is what causes the mob to toss a coin in your hat. It is battle that orders a story as well. Begin with what leads to the fight, a hero and an adversary and what comes between them, work 'round to the bloody confrontation, and last, tell 'em what all that meant." He pauses, looking deep into his glass before he raises his eyes to mine. "That's a story worth the tellin'. I say battle, lass, battle is essential to any story. Listen to what has been told this night. 'Twas the striving against a foe, or the elements, or a beast runnin' through them. Though, 'tis true, these are in a woman's story as well. If you seek battle twined with romance, look you no farther than Romeo and Juliet."

"Surely there was no impediment between the marriage of true minds?" the organza lisps and tilts her head.

"Was there not? Have you forgot the battle that raged round them and caused their demise? Did all end well?" We grow thoughtful when he moves to sip his wine again. "Battle be all to a story, even one of love."

"'Tis late." Percy looks around at the dark windows. "One last story. Hogg? D'you have it?"

Thomas ducks his head and I see the corners of his mouth curl. "Well, perhaps one I ought not tell to guests facing a long ride home." He inhales. "An article in the *Times* drew me. It seems we have a new murderer in London."

Heads turn and lift.

"A devil who stalks his prey, they say. Late into the night, when all is dark, he strikes in the spaces between the lights. Unlike most, who attack the poor for reason of released emotions, he has a penchant for the carriages of the affluent though he takes not their goods." He nods to us all. "From a dark passage, he jumps atop the driver's box and slashes the man's throat. As the horses will continue on, those inside have no inclination anything is amiss until..."

"What?" squeaks the ruby dress.

"Until the fiend rips open the hearts of those who, all unaware, embrace within. From the evidence left upon the bodies..."

"Bodies?" the organza, another squeak.

He shrugs. "When they can be found. Oft-times all that is left is a blood-stained, abandoned carriage. The evidence suggests he wields some diabolical weapon. Not a knife, for the wounds are neither clean nor straight but slashed though—how is as unknown as his identity."

"Slashed?" the edge of hysteria creeps into the emerald one's voice.

"Viciously. Perhaps he uses a long hook," he moves his hands apart, "sharpened at the tip."

He reaches for his wine. "The latest was just last night, but in this instance, the monster was defeated. It seems he timed the leap well, and had quite dispatched the driver..."

"Poor soul."

"...when the horses spooked and ran away with the carriage, which alerted the passengers. They shouted for the driver and received no answer, but the swain was of stern mettle. He exited the door opposite the one where the sound was heard, and reaching up to the luggage rail atop the cab, climbed into the driver's seat, grasped the reins, and stopped the carriage."

"Saved," breathes the organza, laying her hand to her breast.

"The swain was saved." Hogg pinned her with his eye. "But what do you suppose he found when he rounded the carriage?"

"What?" They sound the request.

"Nothing. The carriage was empty."

Small, nervous laughter from four out of five women. I restrain myself.

"All that could be found of the mademoiselle was a single stain upon the cushions. One, both red and wet. Blood."

Which draws a soft, choked scream.

"Well," says Percy. "With that, dear ones, I bid you adieu."

"They'll stay warm on their way home this night." Percy says. The two of us wave from our door watching them depart, while Claire descends to the walk to wish them a pleasant evening.

"Percy," I say, "explain something to me."

"What, love?"

"I don't understand the effect Hogg's story had. It was neither compelling, nor original; I believe it may have been told in Greece, so why the obvious signs of fear from our gentle guests? Surely, they are smarter than to be fearful."

"Of course it is, and they are. There are two, no three, effects operating here. One: as the stories at dinner progressed, did you notice how the way they were greeted grew in intensity?"

"I did, but I thought the stories improved as well."

"Having gone first, I hope not," he mutters. "But, what happened was that the interest that each created provided a platform on which the next teller built. We all know the trick. It is why each author at a salon will try to go last."

I am sure the question in me must show on my face. "This is much livelier an evening that that which passes in a salon."

"A salon is for serious work. What passed at our table were stories to entertain friends, mere wit, but I admit, our friends are some of the finest and most polished story tellers in England.

"Another effect was Coleridge's suspension of disbelief. They are willing to be afraid for the sake of feeling the emotion of fear itself."

"With all my heart, I would be an equal rather than an audience. Far too often women are simply recipients."

Percy smirks. "I think you are as often on top as otherwise."

"You said there was another thing playing upon the emotions of our guests?"

"I did. These women tonight sought the attention of their escorts. They wanted to be thought afraid so that in the dark of the carriage their companions might comfort them."

A light dawns upon me. "And provide a license for what occurs."

"Even so," Percy's grin lit his face. "Only a ninny would be frightened by such a story."

Claire returns to where we stand on the top step. "Oh Percy, I'm so glad we are safe in our house and need not go home through the dark." She insinuates herself between us. "I am most happy to have you to keep me safe in our bed this night. Come, my protector."

As the two of them leave, I catch the look of triumph she casts over his shoulder, intended for me alone.

Though my anger flairs I think, *my sister has always been a purposeful ninny.*

<hr/>

Those parties live in my memory as some of the most joyful moments in my life. In the months to come, I found the depth to which these three, Peacock, Trelawney, and Hogg, supported my poet and I am fortunate their devotion extended to those Percy loves. An example of this can be found in an action I already related but have not shared its significance. The action? When they visit, they bring most appreciated gifts of food and drink that we might not be put to the expense of playing host. What I have not said is that these gifts are far in excess of what we can eat in a night, and so their charity sustained us for a time.

That last story, the one by Hogg, kept coming to my thoughts. If a storyteller wishes to build an emotional response, can there be any more powerful companions than Fear and her sister Horror?

Chapter Twenty-One

Resurrection

There was little to warm me that long winter, and less for comfort.

Caught between moneylenders and creditors, Percy could no longer work. He and Claire left for the country to escape; as my pregnancy had advanced, it was thought best I stay behind. I remember that winter as exceedingly cold.

In the dying of the year, Percy wrote but one piece he thought good enough to publish. He titled the work, "A Refutation of Deism." Though he feared the work might provoke, his enthusiasm for the piece bore him onward.

Our friends were my salvation throughout that lonely time. Hogg visited on the days when I sat alone. Although at first I was loathe to admit Old While-We-Were-at-Oxford, little by little I began to enjoy his company until I surprised myself one day when he made me laugh aloud. As our confidences grew, information about the strange man I love filtered into our talks.

"Has Percy told you of his discovery of Harriet?"

"A bit." I set down my darning to listen better.

"His actions toward her are contradictory to many. The situation he rescued her from was odious." Hogg gazes into the fire. "Yes, he did eventually abandon her, but when he removed his affections he settled money upon her for her care and that of his children." He raises his eyes to me. "Some say he abandoned her for you." He wags his head, "There are also those who say she had a poor concept of a harmonious home."

"I've heard those stories. My sister, Fanny, repeats the gossip my stepmother sows among her friends. I believe that woman created her stories and dispersed them to justify Claire leaving her to live with us." Regardless of her intentions, I grapple the information to my heart as word of Harriet's pregnancy reaches me.

"In my opinion, he did not *desert* Harriet as much as he *fled* from her." Hogg straightens and sips his wine. "Here is meat. Harriet...Umm, you know what phrase he says of her?"

"'Abandon all hope ye who enter here.'"

"A ribald pun." He smiles. "One typical of the man as a justification for putting her off. The truth is, Percy enjoys the company of women in need of a savior and, once they are saved, he moves from one to the next."

My breath catches. "So I have noted."

"That he was married when he met you scarce dampened his ardor. There were several between you and Harriet, even as there is one now."

"To be free to love is freedom indeed," I think he means Claire.

"Are you that committed to the philosophy?"

"If it is a man's right so it is also a woman's right to choose who she will love. Here, now, in this place, at this time, I will to love Percy."

"Ah." He sips his brandy and stares into the fire.

Percy looks up from his desk by the window of our sitting room. I sit as near to the fire as I can get, absorbing the heat like some lizard. His pen as it scratches a tattoo upon the sheet of foolscap is a comfort to me while I read. His chair creaks and looking up I behold his face flushed with triumph.

"I've found the device for my poem!"

"The one that challenges religion?"

"More than that, it is a refutation! I'll set the matter as a discussion between Greek academics rather than a modern discourse and thus allow the passage of time to overcome affront caused by present day's beliefs." He taps his lip as he thinks. "D'y' see?"

"Who are the characters, dear?"

"Theosphus and Eusebes."

"Oh well." I set my book on my lap. "And who does not know those names?"

"Ah, woman, go along with you. Look, I'll set one in favor of Christian mythos while the other maintains a rationally composed argument, a uniquely rational position, in support of atheism."

It is quickly published, and the piece garners praise in enlightened circles and approval by the masses. Even better, the epic poem brings many invites to salons, which spreads Percy's fame. And best of all, it puts paid to many of our bills, though he begins another round of spending, and we are soon in debt again.

November is cold, so cold it seeps into my bones, even when I sleep under as many covers as we own. I'd scarce believe it possible, but the month is made colder by the post. Harriet sends a note to Percy saying she is delivered of a son. Percy goes to her that he might see the baby.

"A beauty, he is!" Percy enthuses when he returns. "And strong, too. He held my finger and would not let go. Harriet says she had scarce any difficulty birthing him. A squeeze, a pause, another, and done! Ah," he sighs. "He is the son of the world!"

For his sake, I do not cry. Despite my commitment to the ideal of free love, as I shiver in the winter drafts I know my heart is made bereft by Percy's reaction to this ultimate paragon of childhood.

On another day toward Yule, when snow covers London and the air bites, Hogg arrives with a cartload of fuel for our fires. I whoop, for it is especially cold when I am alone in bed, although the baby inside me disputes my need for sleep by kicking me without mercy.

Hogg and I settle in front of the fire in our sitting room and share a brandy warmed before the blue flames of the crackling coal. As glass succeeds glass we damn Boney and Parliament, toasting our good sense and the incompetence of both Commons and Lords.

Sliding my stocking-encased feet from my shoes, I hold them close to the warm hearth. "Oh, I've another hole and these are my last pair."

"Fear not. You've adorable feet."

"Base flatterer. Ah, Hogg," I sigh as the flames warm my soles. A moment in silence, then, quietly, "You've saved me, again."

We sit in a companionable silence gazing into the flames, thinking, until Hogg shifts in his seat. "Do you know the cause of Percy and his father's estrangement?" he asks.

"I do not. It is a non-topic for Percy, one I have not pursued." I hold my feet up and wiggle my toes, the better to feel life coming back to them. "Though the pragmatic effects of Lord Bysshe's anger are manifest around us."

"It was 'gainst his father's wishes for Percy to continue his affair with Harriet."

My head snaps in his direction. "Why?" I hate to blurt but the man astonishes me. *Harriet the cause of Percy's father's condemnation?* Though I would know more, rare gossip must not be hurried, lest it be lost. I sip my brandy and keep my peace.

At last the maddening man goes on. "Percy's father thought the woman was low."

I shrug, "Well, so she is."

"There is low class," he says and shrugs as he touches his brandy to his lips, "but then there is also high money. Harriet's father has the chinks in plenty. He owns one of the better public houses in the borough. More than one MP stays with him, and many of those in business meet in his rooms.

"But, as for Lord Bysshe," he says holding up the finger. "Sir Timothy could not stand to see his son with a tavern keeper's daughter."

I say, "I've heard Percy tell of how Harriet was mistreated by her father and how she sent Percy letters describing her desperation to be away. She threatened to end her days should he not save her."

Hogg is quiet for a time gazing into the fire. But then he lifts his eyes to mine. He shakes his head. "Did you not say something like this to him?"

My hypocrisy reveals me for what I am, I attempt to salvage my respect with an old excuse. "It was different."

"And Claire? And Fanny?"

"They importune him with such tales at various times."

Percy's friends often play at logic games, finding the fallacies in reasoning. If thus, and thus, then, what? I confess my misconduct in sorites.

Percy endeavors to save women in distress.

Harriet presented herself pitiable and despairing of her circumstances.

Eventually, Harriet became odious to Percy.

Percy found another pitiable women and abandoned Harriet.

I have presented myself to him as piteous.

"But," says Hogg. "I see at least one fact lacking in your enthymeme." He turns to face me. "You are not as other women. I am sure you know there is more to you than to be the object of a knight's mercy."

"Well, there is venery." I put my hand upon my stomach. "Present evidence implies at least once."

He smiles in sympathy. "Nor are you an object of sexual attraction."

My eyes go wide with outrage.

"At least, not only that," he hurriedly amends. "Besides, a strong sexuality may bait the trap, but sex alone cannot command any man's continued attention."

"Beauty, then? Claire is more beautiful than I." I am disgraceful in fishing for compliments.

"I could argue your beauty against hers." He puts a finger upon my lips when I would protest. "No, Mary. This is hardly the time for false modesty. I have never thought you to be anything but candid. Yes, Claire is the more beautiful of the two of you."

Damn the man.

"But were I to argue from analogy, and were that analogy a horse race, I would set the odds in your favor." My eyes flash again; he will not compare me to a horse! But he holds his hand up again and says, "What I am saying is, though you are beautiful, your appeal for Percy lies not in beauty...oh, you have made me awkward of tongue. Here is what I mean to say. Do you not see you pose an intellectual challenge to him? Alone of all of his friends and lovers, you have the ability to keep pace with his mind."

His words find my heart. *How odd,* I think, *that I should fall in love between sips of brandy with Old While-We-Were-at-Oxford.*

When Percy returns home, I tell him that night in bed of what transpired between his friend and me.

"Oh, Mary," he says. "Are these thoughts so strange?"

"They are, but loving two people at once is wonderful also."

"I find it so. Of course, you must take him. Did you stay for my approval? You have it, but as a rational woman, you ought to feel free to act upon your impulses without seeking approval from anyone."

I rise upon my elbow and gaze upon the face of this odd man who so infatuates me, but understands me not.

"I know that. And I knew what you would say, but I fear you misunderstand my motives for not bedding Hogg. They have to do with reason rather than emotion."

"Educate me."

"Thus. Even as the tide of love rose inside my mind I experienced a recollection of the theater. I stood like Hamlet's mother seeing the likenesses of you and Thomas thrust before my eyes. I asked myself, could I leave the fair mountain of Percy Shelley to batten upon the moor of Thomas Hogg?"

I slide my leg over his and lever up atop him.

"Look you, Percy Shelley, I am in love with the paragon of man and the delight of angels. You blind the sun with your brilliance. Why then should I settle for Hogg? Why make love to dust when a comet is within my grasp? Love Hogg I do, and that undeniable, for when I was deep in the darkness of loneliness, he brought me light. But to make love with such as him? My mind does not pander to my heart. Would I live as Hamlet's mother in the 'rank sweat of an enseamene'd bed o're a nasty sty?' No, I've a sufficiency of him as friend, and I desire no other lover but you. But as a friend, I do love him."

"Enough," says Percy, accepting my cheek upon his chest. "I hear you."

Though I doubted he understood. I sank down beside him with a sigh.

Another evil occurs just when we are least able to absorb the blows of outrageous fortune. Percy is taken with a cough. Day after day, and through the nights as well, it doubles him over and so tears at the tissues of his throat and nose he bleeds into the cloths I give him. I seek out a doctor to tend him in spite of the expense.

"Consumption," the doctor says. The word hangs in the air. "Put your affairs in order, young man, for I fear you've not long to trouble this world."

I strive to present a smile to him as a last gift. I shall not wail to nonexistent beings. But though I cannot seek solace in a deity, I learn a lesson in compassion, and I think I shall not disparage the religious, for when people are beset by intolerable burdens, it is a human thing to find what comfort we may.

Deep in winter I give birth to a girl to set 'gainst Harriet's son, though I would describe her birth as far more than "a push, a squeeze, and done."

"If motherhood is so completing of human kind," I snarl during my labor, "then it would be only just that men experience the phenomenon!" Still, to give birth is part of being a female, and that settles any other argument.

I take much delight in her tiny pink perfection when the baby is placed in my arms by the midwife. I think her a cunning marvel as I show her to her Fanny and Claire.

"Have you a name for her?" Claire asks.

"She is so weak, we think it better to delay her naming for a time," Percy tells her. "Though should she do well, she will be called Clara."

Three weeks after her birth, having not heard her cry in the night, I go to her crib and find the little body twisted and still. My heart stops. I cannot move or speak. Next morning, Percy, gentle soul, says he cannot bear the loss as he fears for his fragile health. Touching my hand, he says he will return when he can and he and Claire depart. Though Percy must have love and admiration it would seem he is incapable of giving those things to me. I take up my pen.

> *My dearest Hogg:*
>
> *My baby is dead.*
>
> *Please come to see me as soon as you can. It was perfectly well when I went to bed. I wish to see you.*
>
> *I awoke in the night to give it suck. It appeared to be sleeping so quietly that I could not awake it. I took it into my arms but it was cold. From its appearance, I supposed it died of convulsions, and nightly do visions of the baby follow me.*
>
> *Will you come? You are so calm a creature it will comfort me to see you.*
>
> *I am alone. Shelley is afraid of a fever from my milk for I am no longer a mother now.*
>
> *Please come?*
>
> *Mary*

Hogg stayed with me and much comfort did I take from his presence. Hours upon hours, he simply read the latest poetry or political commentary to me. I lost myself for a time as much in his calm voice as in the thoughts he brought.

I suppose, following the death of my baby, there were several paths I could take. I'd neither accept the false comfort of a god who could kill an innocent creature, nor the lying succor of drugs, nor the Lethe of sex, nor suicide.

Mr. Baxter said to me once when I inquired of the loss of his wife, "She lives as long as my memory of her. Love endures. Sorrow does nae last."

More and more often as we grew destitute that winter, I found myself alone to entertain our friends. They brought food, drink, and coal to warm the house so often that those who supported Harriet began to say I entertained many men for gifts.

Chapter Twenty-Two

Escaping the Chrysalis

I remember a sailor sitting on a pier in the Tay, one of those amateur wise men who dispense wisdom to any audience willing to listen. Looking up from the macramé he was knotting, he said, "Winds and fortune ne'er blow from but one quarter. Hold your course and you'll get home."

"Or to the bottom of the sea," I whispered as I walked away.

It is better that I should bring to mind a lesson of the seasons as they turn through the long year; spring follows even the longest winter.

As the first warmth of false spring emerges, there's promise in the air. Percy's cough becomes less frequent and easier for him to bear and comes the day when he holds me and says, "I believe I am the healthiest consumptive in the world." He snaps his fingers. "Mary, we ought demand our payment from that doctor."

And Claire shouts, "About time we had something to spend!"

As rubbing a cat the wrong way can cause the animal to hiss and spit, so Claire's presence grates on me these days. We begin to snipe at each other. I refuse to speak her name. "That woman is in her room," I say to Percy when he inquires of her, or, "She is out, again."

A letter of significance arrives before spring can clear the ice from the roads.

"Mary, Claire!" Percy shouts with the post still in his fingers. "Come and hear!"

"What news, love?" I ask, trotting down the hall.

Percy raises his head from reading the letter and murmurs wonderingly, "My grandfather has died."

"Ah, Percy," Claire says holding his arm, "I'm so sorry."

But I know better. He is not overly fond of his family due to the ill treatment over Harriet. Percy might feel a loss, but he would also sing, "Adieu and Farewell, old *Père*."

"I'm, well, I'm unsure what I feel." Percy disentangles himself from my sister, and steps to a window to stare into the sky. "Sir Bysshe was ever stern, but the man was also just. I suppose his seat with the lords in Parliament will devolve upon my father, as well as the bulk of his fortune." He shakes himself. "I haven't the foggiest what will happen to the family seat at Field Place. Perhaps Father may have to abide there, for the sake of the borough, either there or at the house at Goring. We ought to go to Sussex to learn more."

"Percy," Claire cries. "It is winter and Mary neither abides travel nor cold." She smiles at me sweetly. "I shall go with you."

I could have spat in her hair.

Percy says, "You are right. Mary, you are hardly recovered. Claire, do you give thought for the two of us."

Her plans to focus Percy upon her during the trip are foiled, though. Roads are so bad this year the journey must be postponed until spring should dry the ruts, and while we delay other shoes begin to drop.

A solicitor forwards a second letter, one Percy's grandfather wrote before he died. In it, the old man encouraged Percy to reconcile with his father. The missive is filled with advice toward that goal. The gossips have had more than enough time that long winter to discuss the various household arrangements of young Percy Shelley, et al. Word of our ménage had reached Sir Bysshe. "Marry that girl, and be done with the other." *Perhaps the identity of "the other" is Harriet, or perhaps Claire.* It could be that I am not considered completely objectionable.

However obscure the letter is, a second letter from Sir Bysshe's solicitor admits no ambiguity. Percy tilts the paper toward the wan light from the window. He lifts his head in surprise.

"A moment more, dear ones, I..." He sets himself to read it again. At last when he lifts his face from the paper to us, astonishment is writ plain upon him. "Mary! Claire! We are made! Grandfather settles a thousand pounds per annum upon me. Father shall be named 2nd Baronet Shelley of Castle Goring. As he is the eldest son, Grandfather had the right to knight Father upon his 21st birthday. He knows Father and I have become estranged and he supposes Father will never create me Sir Shelley. Perhaps that is why he settles such grand monies on me after he put paid to the rest of the estate. Father is to have six thousand per annum from which he'll maintain Goring and the staff! I do not doubt he'll go straight away to Sussex."

To make known our new status we sent a round of invites for a salon to be held next week. Percy orders a carriage for me to hire staff that we might appear appropriate to our new station. We already have a sometime cook. It is a pleasure to see her reaction when we ask her to be our chief cook and move in with us. She is pleased enough to change her role, "An' if you might, miss, a girl to wash up?" I think a maid, or two, will be welcome.

That week is lost in frenzy. Percy's other woman and I are measured for new dresses, there will be a coat for Percy, and food and cakes, such cakes, and the makings for a pudding, and a thousand other things for which we previously had no money and now lack time to do, but done it is and on Friday our guests arrive to cheer us our fortune.

Peacock, of course, and dear Hogg, and Trelawney with his huge burgundy hat, and twenty more besides! Cook, released from making do with little performs a wonder. Our sideboard groans with delicacies to be freely sampled.

Walking through the crowd as I extend greetings, I smile to see there are those who arrive with pages strategically tucked into jacket pockets that the host or hostess or guests might inquire of them.

"Oh, this?" said with a slight nod to where papers protrude from a pocket as their owner seeks, artistically, to push the pages from view. "A nothing. Well, perhaps, if there's time..."

And the women! Such dresses! With the end of the wars, the seamstresses of the Continent have been hard at work for the victors. Long gowns of such delicate stuff flow below rounded bosoms scarcely concealed by sheer fichus. I note many demoiselles cinched by corsets that they might better retain a perfectly erect posture. I whisper my congratulations to the mirror that my posture is both erect and supple without lacing.

There is light to lift the mood that weights my heart since the baby died. Candles, wax not tallow, reflect their clear white glow from polished sconces that line our walls. And warmth such as this house has not felt the whole winter! For the sake of light, our fireplaces are filled with wood instead of coal and the chimneys are roaring with unaccustomed blazes.

Candlelight and firelight are women's friends; they make skin glow. To speak of skin, I am listening to Hogg when I notice that other woman playing the coquette with Thomas Peacock. A pause, a sip of her cup, a laugh as though she hears a jest, and she steps as though all unaware 'tween the flame and the room, casting an erotic silhouette.

"Claire," I call to her. She turns to me, smiles and performs a slow sway, exiting the stage in a manner designed to leave the audience sighing.

"Sister?" she says, standing by my side.

"Dear, have you forgotten something?" I murmur.

Wide eyed innocence is the look she turns to me. "What ever can you mean?"

"I mean, your shift? The firelight shining near unimpeded through your dress casts a most provocative shadow."

"Oh, good! Such was my intent." The minx wrinkles her nose and giggles into her cup. "Provocative. I like that. It has been forever since I had such fun." But then she turns sharp. "Or do you mean I steal the light from you?"

Like that, our truce is ended.

"Percy!" Peacock, his face reddened either, or equally, from the punch or from the fair miss who attends him. "Do you read this night?"

Standing aloof and inclining his head he says, "Alas no, Thomas. My situation demands of my time such that my flights of fancy must be postponed. I am working, though, on a long poem."

"Tell!" he shouts.

Percy bows. "I've in mind a metaphor for my late absence from all my friends. Narcissus and Echo warning us to take care of one's social obligations for, as Donne says, none of us are solitary islands. Remembering to be in touch with those of our society is the meat of the matter. I'll title it for the spirit of solitude. 'Tis near finished."

"Most cordial congratulations!" Peacock lifts his glass with one hand, "For your inspiration and fortune. And now that you have the chinks, do you chance to travel?"

"We've scarce had the time to ponder a destination, but soon, soon." He glances at me and pats the hand I place upon his arm. "We ought to shake off the dust of poverty with at least a small trip."

"I have such a place," he says, with a conspirator's smile.

"Whither, Thomas?" I laugh because people do love to be the first to discover a holiday destination.

"Torquay!" he crows. "It lies in Devon, a long road through Cornwall in late spring when the rains are not yet gone but then," he pauses dramatically, "O, the town! The Romans knew it and called it Torre for the hill that rises next to the water. Over the years, a fine harbor grew there behind the long stone quay. D'y' hear it?" He laughs at the jest. "Tor - Quay! Torquay! A word play upon geography. Did y' smoke it?"

"And what so commends this place, other than the name?" Percy asks.

"The navy used the harbor there to victual their ships during the wars. Good water is there in abundance."

"Good water then recommends it?" I ask.

"Ah, Mary. Good water drew the sailors of the fleet. They so loved the spot, they sought to live there when the war was done. Inns sprang up and inns brought gentlefolk who partake of the fare from captains' cooks lately set upon the beach now that the fleet is no longer needed. Their dinners are seasoned by spices fetched by friends who crew the East Indiamen."

Trelawney, his face alight, enters the conversation at this. "D'ye say the true riches of the Indies, pepper and paprika, and cinnamon and cloves, may be found in this town?"

"All that and more. These cooks know where saffron grows. "Oh, yellow saffron rice!" He rolls his eyes lost in epicurean memory. "And remember," he winks at me, "The wares of the Continent reside in the shops! All this to be had from those who are conscious of being set ashore with only their sea chest. A room in an inn may be had for a farthing."

That night as I lie with my head on Percy's chest and as our breathing slows, I ask, "Percy, might we go to Cornwall, just the two of us?"

"Torquay?" his voice holds a gentle humor. But then in a rich tone that speaks of his love for me he says, "Aye. You've been benighted so long a holiday would do you good. But..."

"But what?" He breathes deep and as he holds it, I sense there is something amiss. "What's to do?" My voice is gentle.

"Do not tell Claire."

"You fear she will hinder our departure?"

"Not so. It is that she must spend some time in the country. I've arranged for her to stay down south in a cottage in Lynmouth."

I know what it means when a young woman is to be sent away for a time. But I'll make him say the words. "Why would you have her leave?"

He falls upon his pillow. "You know there is enough talk about us. Were she known to be with child, all speculation about us will cease."

I am not done. "And what would be the import of people's opinions?"

"I am not as talented as Lord Byron. His fame keeps approbation at bay. So much scandal will damage me." He looks up as that Claire enters without knocking. "Ah, I've just told Mary you'll be leaving us for a little while."

"Gone and good riddance, is it?" There is a resemblance to her mother as she stands, spread legged and arms akimbo, before us. "I hope the two of you will enjoy yourselves without me."

Percy rises and steps to her with his arms open. "Claire, love, we've talked this out. You know we'll be awaiting your return." She turns away from any comfort with her shoulders shaking.

"Give you joy," she says through her sobs. "I'll soon be banished to the country."

Ah me.

By and by, spring flames forth and we depart for Devon, and so my love and I are alone upon the road. A most welcome change.

Our coach rocks up one hill and down the other, affording glimpses of Cornwall rolling into the horizon like a sea of green. 'Tween one rise and the next I lean out the windows "to port," as Trelawney bade me refer to the left side of any vehicle, and behold the ocean sparkling silver.

Percy, surveying the view muses, "'Now is the winter of our discontent turned glorious summer...'"

I turn to him. Placing my head upon his shoulder and taking his hand, I murmur, "It pleases me to hear you say so."

"It pleases me to be able to say so." He lifts my face and kisses me softly. "But perhaps the time was not so much a waste. Though you may doubt it, I've given thought to you, my Mary, many times o'er the year past."

I say nothing to this, as remaining quiet often leads to more admissions when such moods are on him.

"Have you suffered much?" he asks.

"I dwell on our lost child, but less and less do the visions of it come to me."

"Do you begrudge my time with your sister?"

Ah. "But little. You are free always to love where you will, and how, and well do I know how beautiful she is."

"I do not feel as Marc Anthony did for Cleopatra. Beauty *can* grow stale." He rolls his shoulders under my head. "I note you're reading Shakespeare. What occupies your thoughts?"

"Writing and skill. I think of the way his plays hold up more than 200 years. I'm attempting to discern how the Bard holds an audience."

He shakes his head. "There you go awry."

"In what way?"

"His audience was Queen Elizabeth. As for the rest of the nobles and groundlings, they were lagniappe. If the people took to the work, so much the better for his purse, but make no bones about it, the Queen was the only audience that mattered. Her approval made some men, her disdain broke many. Attend me in this; 'The winter of our discontent...' D'y' recall the rest?"

"I do. '...by this son of York.'"

"Good. And was the hunchback king a hero or a villain?"

"Evil, yet thrilling in his daring."

"Remember that, for a worthy antagonist is always brilliantly daring. Consider Iago or Macbeth, but I stray from my thesis. Elizabeth. The Bard knew how to lionize a ruler. He wrote an elegy pouring scorn upon Queen Bess's enemy, and praise upon her house. In return, she saw to it his plays were performed many times. And that is how he was allowed to win the people's favor." He shrugs. "Of course, talent helps. I've said your writing grows in skill. My point about the Bard is that it is as important to know your audience as it is to parse a sentence. The one is a tool, the other a connection between minds. A story, a novel perchance, must touch the hearts of your audience. Seek to know for whom you write and tailor your ideas to suit them. So the nascent author rises from the morass of scribblers. Though some may accomplish this by happy accident, knowing how is always better than chance."

I thrill at this. Months have passed without his tutelage while I ask my pillows whether I am forgot. In speaking to me as he is, I know my Percy has returned. Devon may not be the best of England, but I have cause to love it well.

Though happiness be fleeting, this journey will shine an eon in my heart.

Percy sits for some time looking from me to the window and back again. At last he says, "Have I told you how precious your mind is to me?"

"Seldom of late."

"Of late there has been little time for us."

"There has been time for you and my sister."

His eyes sharpen. "I thought we were above jealousy?"

"I may advocate free love, but who says I will not wish the exclusive attention of my love?" I shake my head. "I but state a fact."

We've become playful again in another way.

Torquay is situated on the western shore of a large bay. Being thus sheltered from the worst of storms that sweep across the Atlantic, the port was favored by the navy during the war. A stone quay curling around toward the east knocks down what waves ride in from the south and west, making it easy for shipping to tie up in front of the buildings that line its inner reach.

Everything we've heard of the town is not wonderful enough. Even the buildings of the city find complement in their natural setting. Both are worthy of attention. A cave, Kents Cavern, we are assured, was quarried by the Romans. Clambering into it, we fancy we hear the ghosts of Caesar and Trajan echoing among the stalactites and stalagmites and undulating stone veils caused by rain and time.

"A face is there!" Percy exclaims pointing to a rocky wall. "D'y' see it?"

I strive to piece together features within the outcropping stone and finally a rugged visage emerges to my senses.

I smile and, gripping his arm, I ask, in a voice all breathy and girlish, "Perhaps that is the spirit of the place?"

His lips split in a naughty smile. "One that doth live upon moonlit midnights to pursue the footsteps of beautiful girls who trespass here!"

"Oh!" I cry, putting the back of my hand to my head in imitation of the actress upon the stage who plays the virgin in distress. "What ever shall I do?"

Percy nods and points to me. "Quickly! Cast off thy clothing! We must sacrifice to him!"

"What?" I clasp my bosom. "Wouldst plunge a dagger into mine heart?"

He crosses his arms and looks at my hips. "Nay, love. Not thy heart." His grin tips me there is wit to come. "My sword lacks sufficient length to reach thy heart from the angle I have in mind."

I sigh, putting one foot forward and bending to grasp the hem of both my dress and shift. In one motion, I lift them over my head and let them flutter as they fall. My shoes clatter on the stone floor of the cave, leaving me in naught but stockings with their pink ribbon garters. I thrill to hear his breath catch at the sight of me, and straightening, I pose with my arm beckoning even as Eve must have welcomed Adam, but with a wicked grin I say, "Poor, poor Percy the Short. You'll have to do the best you can with what little you have."

There is wonder in plenty to occupy me. Percy returns to discussing the craft of writing with me as we stroll sandy strands bare of foot and open to a universe of thought.

"Mary, d'y' remember our discussion of Shakespeare?"

"Which one, dear?"

"Any of them. All of them, but I'm thinking of the one we had on the road here."

"Be specific."

"You said his work held a glass to truth unchanged 200 years after he writ. How do you think he accomplished such a thing?"

I tuck my hand into the crook of his arm. "Remember you told me I must have an idea I wish to express before I could form a story? His ideas must be relevant to people now as then. But in answer to you: Does truth change?"

"It's more than bald truth. People do not change. At least their hearts, their emotions, do not."

He holds out a cupped hand in front of him. "Idea, then, what is the lasting merit in idea? Canst hold it? Canst spend it? Canst pet it? Like love, it cannot be seen but the effect an idea can be of such value the stars are unable to outshine it." He laughs at his mummery and his voice returns to normal. "Idea begets culture.

Look you, this sceptered isle, this England, many a philosopher will submit it is nothing more than an idea in an ocean of darkness." His eyes narrow and he goes still with the nearness of his point. "Where do ideas originate?"

"Where indeed," I say, turning and stepping away with my hand to my chin in thought. Then I quickly turn to him and say, "Where but in the actions of those whose ancient brows were rounded by gold, those who strove upon antique battlefields and so created England distinct from any other country. Where but in the royals themselves?"

He nods. "Many will answer thus. But the politics of the sword last only the life of the knight. What happens to the actions of the great and puissant, were they not writ down for the ages? Their ashes are blown by wind and so lost. It is writing that preserves idea, and idea that creates culture when it finds a heart and moves a reader to do great things. Remember your responsibility to the craft to present and preserve an idea, even as you strive to make your words flow like a stream or thunder like the storms.

"Shakespeare, now, there was a writer who could capture the idea that reaches us men the way a falconer calls his bird." He cups his hand to his mouth and imitates the call. "Hi, hi, haloo! That is what separates him from the mediocre." He turns to me and I behold the sun illuminating his face. "That is what we who write strive to be."

We are no more than settled back in London when Percy comes home to tea and delivers another prize from the cornucopia of our new wealth.

"I've rented a house off Bishopsgate Road, my girl!" he crows.

"Where?" I lean forward where I am sitting in surprise.

"If you look along the edge of Great Windsor Park, you'll find a cottage of two floors." He smiles and gives the words she said many times when the three of us walked through Europe. "When I saw it, I said as Claire did, 'That is beautiful enough. Let us live there!'"

"Oh, glorious!" I bounce up in my excitement. "Such an address will make our friends know our worth."

As 1815 dies in a glorious burning sunset of wonder for us, we take residence in Eden. Percy completes *Alastor*, his epic poem upon the influences of politics.

And I? I add to our happiness. Our time in Torquay flowers with the fruit of the tree of Shelley. I glow with the knowledge of a child inside me.

As though all Percy touched turned golden and he could not sup enough of the bounty, he wrote, and edited, and rewrote and thirsted for more! More ideas, more rhyme, and above all, more time.

But I dissemble like a young girl. Yes, he gave me to know he wanted more of me as well. Aphrodite, Grecian goddess of passion he called me. Did I worry my rounding belly might cause him to seek another's slender arms? He named me, Belet-Ili, Sumerian goddess of the womb, and Hathor, the Egyptian goddess of pregnancy, and worshiped me in my bed.

Would you know devotion? Find a man like my Percy.

Chapter Twenty-Three

Claire and Her Lord

Though I reveled in Percy's attention and my newly found motherhood, when my sister returned to us, free of encumbrance, she chafed at his changed attitude toward her. Oh, to be sure, he went with her from time to time—great beauty does have some appeal—but on more than one occasion he said to me her love clung while mine set him free. When I asked him about the differences between us, he said she lacked imagination.

There's a lesson.

Percy's friend informed us she would live in London. "I'll have more to do there than here." Though in Percy she had the best of tutors, it was another who taught her one must never beg.

Late in January, I am delivered of a son. Percy insists we christen him William Godwin Shelley though we are not married.

One morning as I am sitting in the front room reading, my sister strides into the room like a fencer stepping onto the piste. She's wearing a morning dress of dove gray that brings out the blue of her eyes, which are fixed on mine. Neither greeting nor preamble is offered, yet I think this is not unexpected. She has been secretive in her letters to Percy these last months.

I sigh, again.

En garde. "Has Percy told you ought of me?"

He has often compared Claire's chattering to the birds in the ivy covering the walls of our cottage. Frankly, I think him grown tired of being importuned each time he goes to town to see his solicitors or creditors. I set my book on the small table next to where I sit with my back to a window and say without asperity, "If you wish to know a man's mind, perhaps you should speak with him. Now, do ring for tea."

Her mouth lifts in the slow smile of one with a secret that may draw blood. "May I sit with you and relate what has come to pass?"

"Again, call the girl, have her bring tea, and I shall listen to all you say." Parry.

She harrumphs and leaves to find a servant. I have waited weeks to hear what chances with her.

She returns soon enough, and sitting on a low couch opposite my chair, leans toward me in a semblance of familial intimacy. She creates her voice throaty and low as she says, "Sisters we are," she inclines her head, "and rivals too, as all sisters are. But now I have taken a lover."

"Indeed? I wish you joy," I say with a smile that is neither unfeigned nor unforced. My heart lifts at her announcement like a lark ascending into the morning.

A soft tap announces the girl who brings a tray to us. Claire waits until the things are set out on a table between us. When we are alone, I nod for her to continue her story.

"It began in the spring," she says, staring out the window, "when a letter arrived saying my book would not be published." She looks up to the ceiling and clenches her fist in frustration. "I thought, what good is Shelley that he can't help this little tale along?"

"But he worked with you on it for weeks."

"He couldn't get anyone to print it, could he?"

"I suppose not." But I remember Percy telling me that all the editing in the world cannot help a flawed writer. Claire is too lazy to spend the time needed to polish a story.

"Fie on't! I *am* as good a writer as you, Mary."

I think, *There's venom to sting a mouse* and raise my cup rather than say what I think of her assessment. Watching her with narrowed eyes over the rim of my cup, I say, "I did not know you harbored literary ambitions."

"Always, and I told you many times. But as yet, no volume bears my name." Her voice vibrates with emotion. "It is a lack that causes the past salons I have attended to be less than satisfactory."

She pouts prettily, a well-learned art, and shifts into one of those non-sequiturs she affects.

"Do you know we are a wonder of the moment for gossips? The three of us are become their target? 'Ah, Shelley's conquests!' they purr with a smirk and speak of bedroom matters. 'How does he satiate such nymphs?' I overheard one such remark aimed at us. As though the great rolling barrel of lard would be offered the chance.

"'Oh, to have the stamina of youth,' another man returned. At least he had the grace to be envious."

Remembering how much she likes to wound, I disdain to show my dismay at having our names sullied. I slow my breathing and sip my tea.

She sets her cup down and smiles naughtily. "Though I ought not have done, an imp on my shoulder whispered in the porch of my ear so I crept close behind them and said, 'Both at once is fun.'" A giggle escapes her. "It is so satisfying to make someone obnoxious jump. 'And how does one go into two?' another wit bold enough to ask to my face inquired. 'Same as one goes into one, only twice, if you be man enough.' I was in rare form."

She lowers her head and her eyes slide sideways to mine as she smiles malice at me. "I was not alone in being the object of such gossip. In one of those lulls in conversation when words carry farther than intended, I heard this:

> Shelley entertains Godwin's girl,
>
> Often and well,
>
> And so, for thanks,
>
> Her stomach swells.

I withhold the outrage she clearly expects and shrug. "Thanks does not fit the rhyme. Girl, well, swell."

Claire misses the thespian effort it takes to deny her a point. "Said salon was held at Hogg's home." She shakes her head dismissing it. "Only the lesser lights attended. I held my tongue. However and, to the point, it was at that salon I heard Lord Byron has returned to London."

George Gordon Byron, 6th Baron Byron. The name is well known to me. Years ago, when Percy and Claire and I rode the Rhine home from Switzerland, we read the man's *Childe Harold's Pilgrimage*. I can still hear Percy reciting even as we floated on the storied river.

> The castled crag of Drachenfels

Frowns o'er the wide and winding Rhine,

I remember crying, "There be the very cliff and see how the ruins crown it in majesty!" The memory of so happy a time brings a smile.

Claire's remark at the time? "As he is even more difficult to follow than you, Percy, he must be the more acclaimed."

Neither noticing nor caring for my reverie she continues her story of what chanced at the salon.

"Thus I determined to meet the Lord Byron. 'And where might this pinnacle of creation be?' I asked."

The man ran his eyes over my figure. "'You *might* find him at the rebuilt Drury Lane Theater. He is on the board of directors this season.'" She turns her head to me. "I harbor aspirations toward the stage."

"Really? When did this occur?"

"Oh." She fanned the air with her hand in a gesture as dramatic as it was false. "I have ever thought I could tread the boards. I'm surprised you do not remember my telling you. At any gait, the next day I asked Percy how came Lord Byron to his title."

"'Baron,' Percy said. 'His father died and George inherited before he reached his tenth year. While in his teens he took his seat in the House of Lords, where I hear he spoke well for one so young.'"

"'How should I know him? *Quel visage?*' I asked Percy." She turned to me, "*Est-ce-que vous comprenez francais?*"

"*Certainement.*"

"Ah, then your French *has* improved, though your accent is atrocious. To return to the thread, Percy, frowning in thought, answered my question. 'I'd say he possesses a face to make the angels jealous. Not overly tall, near my own height. Slight, but vain of his figure, the man must have been teased in his youth. You must have caution, my Claire.'"

She scanned my face to judge how I might react to her sally but all she saw was my small smile. When she judged it was another miss, she continued. "Percy said, 'He is reputed to engage in unsavory habits which he affects to solicit outrage. The man courts personal condemnation in the hope of gendering infamy, as fame and infamy are but two sides of the same coin. He thinks an evil reputation a must for those seeking to remain in public view.' Percy thought a moment before he said this, 'George says, "Scandal is not the most terrible fate that can happen to a writer. Worse by far is to be obscure."'"

My eyebrows go up at the truth of this. "Say what you will, Byron is not obscure." But even as I mutter the remark, I think Percy, too, understands the game of courting scandal. *Does Percy think our* ménage à trois *a way to attract attention?*

Claire continues, "I asked Percy what gave the Lord such bad character. 'The gossip says he will bed any woman he can outrun.' But then he said, 'This is a patent libel. There are far too many stunning females who run toward him for the man to bestir himself after those who flee.'"

Claire smiles a conspirator's grin and says, "Beginning with a letter, I asked the Lord for advice to advance my career in the theater. Only a few days passed before I had a reply."

She mimes holding a letter and says,

> *Claire Clairmont:*
> *'Please attend me in two days' time at the theater on Drury Lane.*
> *I remain yours faithfully, G*

"His real name is Gordon, or George, I get those mixed up, but d'you hear, Mary? 'Faithfully'" She tosses her head. "Using the interval to good purpose I selected a song from a poem written by him and set to music. It was sure to flatter him." She tosses her curls. "More importantly, it suited my voice."

Cupping one hand in the other and thrusting her elbows out, she sings,

> *She walks in beauty like the night,*
> *Of cloudless skies and staaaarry sights...*

"It is said he penned this for his cousin." She wrinkles her nose and strikes, "You know familial love, do you not?"

That bait is so old it has lost its scent and I refuse to rise to it, so I ask, "What was your first thought upon meeting him?"

She looked as though remembering a marvel. "Here is a god come down from the heights of Olympus. Handsome is a word beggaring any description of the man. As Percy said: thin, regal, older, wise, and..." she sighs and places a hand to her heart, "most suitable. He stood in the proscenium before the stage, watching the players rehearse. I saw he noticed my entrance with the corner of his eye. I should say he was in his late twenties, perhaps some few years senior to Percy, but so beautiful. When the cast paused, he turned to me and said, 'You are Claire, is it Clairmont, or Godwin?'

"'I am m'lord,' I said. 'And it is Clairmont.'

"'Your name connects with a young poet of some talent, Percy Bysshe Shelley.'

"'I'll allow I have that honor, m'lord.'

"'I had hoped so. Let us begin…' He gestured me to the stage. I sang, I read, and I, a poor player, strutted my moment upon the stage." She closed her eyes and took a deep breath. "A poor player, wealthy only in talent…yet I felt myself transform beneath his gaze. At the end of my time, he murmured, 'Perhaps you'll do.'

"Tripping down the stair to the groundlings' level, I leaned close to him and raised my lashes. I am, you know, sufficiently worldly to be well aware of the effect my appearance has on men. Mirrors do not lie, after all. I used my best devices to lure him," she smirks to me.

"''Tis nearing time to sup.' He looked down his perfect nose at me. 'Would you care to join me?'

"And so, we began the oldest dance. He, most gallantly, proffered his arm. We walked to an inn that catered to actors no great distance away. Although I kept my eyes straight ahead, I took note of the stares directed my way from those habitués of the theater who noted our pairing, sure they would repeat the sight to eager ears. I saw he ate only a bit of biscuit with water but he watched me as I nipped the tips from my asparagus. 'So,' he said. 'You are a member of Percy Shelley's house?'

"I said again that I owned that honor.

"He said, 'Shelley is one of the few rising stars I follow. His talent is a talk of London, but I allow it is his politics and philosophy that intrigue me.'

"'He admires you, m'lord, and admits your poetic skill superior to his own when speaking to others of you.'

"'Does he?' His head came round of a sudden and his gaze narrowed. 'Did he send you to tell me so?'

"I sat back, meeting his gaze and placing my hand upon my bosom I told him, 'He did not, m'lord. Nor did he suggest what I might say.'

"'Your, ahem, arrangement with him and Mary Godwin, do you find it acceptable?'"

She leaned toward me. "I said, 'We three are friends of the heart. I value their company and they mine.'"

I smiled as though her devotion touched me. *Oh sister, speak but little of matters* en famille *to others. You know not what damage you might inflict to Percy's reputation.*

"Byron said, 'Much of what is said about me is untrue.'

"Shelley says you ought not heed gossip for you are supreme among poets."

"'Indeed?' he tried a sally, 'And what does he say of the way I conduct my affairs?'"

"I laughed like one younger than my years. 'Oh, m'lord, he calls you a most delicious rogue. But you do know you are ever the talk in the salons. Why do you so seldom attend? I think I have never seen you, for surely I would have noted the occasion.'

"'Salons bore me. Most who speak are sheep bleating for approval or pretentious critics, and I admit no criticism of my work from amateurs.'

"I said, 'The stars in the heavens do not depend upon those who slouch as they go upon the ground.'

"He smiled into the distance. 'I like that. Say instead, "those mired in the mud," and you have it. Hmmm, I may use it.'

"Letters flew from me to him, and on occasion he wrote to me as well. I learned he was affected with depression, as much due to his marriage ending as it was to the memory of his lost love for his sister, Augusta. Seizing the moment, I acted and arranged a rendezvous at a country inn. There did I, at last, console him."

As my cup had gone cold, I leaned forward as much to refill it as to avert my face lest she notice my lip curl. Prurient gossip is so distasteful.

All unknowing, she continues. "Several times before this, I noted he walked upon his toes, but it was not until I bedded him that I discovered his clubfoot. He wears a special boot and goes about on tip-a-toe with his other foot in compensation. 'A birth gift from my mother,' he said. I lowered my lips and kissed his deformity. 'Poor foot.' When I looked up, I read wonder on his face."

I began to feel I was at the mercy of a woman who will dispense her story no matter the muck.

"Caroline Lamb wrote a quip which caught the minds of the jealous. It was bruited about she called him, 'Mad, bad and dangerous to know.' I thought him pursued by many, owned by none. But as I knew him, he was not invincible. He says he lives as a little boat in a tempest. Lady Oxford affected disinterest, though she also disdained to set him free. He says, 'I wrote of her husband and me, "Thou false to him, thou fiend to me!"'"

She straightened in her seat and lifted her cup. "A lesson, Mary. Have a care for a writer's wrath, for they shall have the last word."

She snapped at a biscuit with her white teeth.

"The love that dwelt in his heart for his half-sister, Augusta, is one that never faded as far as I know. A pure and selfless love that Lady Caroline dragged through the sty by rumoring he fathered a child with his sister. It hurt them both. Augusta said, 'To have such a thing said of us is utter destruction and ruin to a man, from which he can never recover.'

"Lady C. also originated the gossip of his predilection for sodomy. His response? 'I ask you, what kind of lady would want the world to know how she came to such knowledge? Such are tales from a scorned woman. These are the mounting attacks of packs of dogs as they seek to bring down a lion.'

"He sought my confidence, sure I would not betray him. 'Little fiend who inhabits my drowsing hours,' he murmured into my hair one night, 'I must away.'

"'From me?'

"'From London. I go to the Continent. Switzerland haunts my mind. The tranquility of Lake Geneva...'

"'Lake Lucerne is beautiful enough for me to live there,' I said, holding him. 'I would accompany you. That is, if you think I might soothe your heart.'

"'I think not. I go to escape all of London. And to heal, for I am taking a doctor. This doctor will also chronicle me and my triumph over the burdens heaped upon me by outrageous fortune.' Then, he gazed down into my eyes and said, 'Look for me to rise like the Phoenix.'

"He was gone before I could induce him to attend so much as one of Percy's salons. I wished so much for you to see me with him."

Thus spake Claire Clairmont of her time with Lord Byron.

Claire was to play a most important role in the story of bringing my book to print. It was she, you see, who linked us to Lord Byron for that cold summer on the shores of Lake Geneva. Without that, then I most freely admit, I would ne'er thought upon my story.

Chapter Twenty-Four

Words Upon a Journey

Percy's sense of economy always outstripped our finances. Although his inheritance and the income from his writing could have kept other families in comfort, his idea of entertaining ruined us.

We determined to offer an amount to sustain my father, and did so, but little good did it do us. We received a terse note stating although the fact of our offering was in keeping with what we owed the philosophers who coined the ideas Percy uses in his writing, the amount we gave did little to match the benefit Percy received. He closed by reminding us of our duty to continue his support.

Just when it appeared Claire's time with Lord Byron was at an end, to our surprise, we would be the cause of their reunion.

Glancing to me to be sure of my attention, she asks "Have you determined a date of departure for the Continent?"

"Perhaps soon, I think."

We sit in our front room where the maid serves us. Thomas Peacock joins us for breakfast this sun-filled day as winter breaks.

"Ah." she straightens and looks into her cup. "Do you know, Byron has a villa on the banks of Lake Geneva?"

"You've said so," I answer.

"Think of this," she says, "were we to journey to Switzerland it would be travel most beneficial to we three scholars." (I note the promotion she gives herself.) "And you say you want the chance to meet the lord poet." She's all innocence as she sets the hook. "Were I to write to George, he might be persuaded to be our host for a time."

"Oh, to be a guest of Lord Byron," Thomas breathes the name. Like every other literary man in London, he is drawn to the man like a boat upon the tide.

Percy pulls his lip. "We have exchanged our work."

Thomas' his head swivels to Percy. "And how do you find him?"

"Brilliant." Percy sips his coffee. "I made a few suggestions." Speaking of a studied performance, Percy shrugs as though correspondence with England's premier poet is an everyday occurrence. "It isn't as though I would be an imposition. I offer to critique his latest work. He offers to read mine. I think I'd like to stay with him."

"Do we have the time, Percy?" I ask, though I know the answer already. If Percy seeks reasons for going to Switzerland, I know we will go to Geneva. "Can your work delay?"

"The question is whether my creditors will delay."

Claire turns to me and smiles. Two things she seldom does these days. "And you, Mary, would you not enjoy seeing the mountains once again?"

Well, I would.

Percy says. "I think time with the man himself cannot but help." He sighs. "Send the letter, Claire. If he'll have us, we'll go."

"Anon," she answers with thespianic lassitude, but she posts her letter three hours later. The cause for even that much delay is at hand. Sliding her eyes toward Thomas, she bends forward over the low breakfast table, causing her wrapper to fall open as she breaks another scone.

Ah, she's in need of attention to pass the time until she's with Byron again.

She rises from where she sits, and stretches her arms above her head. "Thomas, I would a word with you if it pleases you." She leaves with her hips swaying like a ship on a downwind run. "Perhaps, in my room."

Thomas looks at Percy and quirks his eyebrow. "Sir Percival?"

Percy smiles at the man's manner. "She's a free woman to go when, where, and with whom she likes." He smiles at his friend. "She could do worse than you."

Thomas finishes his tea in one gulp, rises, and smoothing his rapier mustachios, breathes deep and says, "We'll talk later."

As I watch him leave I ask, "Percy, was that nice to put her on to him?"

"Nice or not, if he relieves but some of the pressure of Byron's defection from her, it will take much weight from me."

"It is your humility one loves."

I've startled him, then a slow smile creases his face. "Wise are those who are content with what they have."

Two weeks later, Claire receives a note from Byron and delivers it to us. Byron states his intention to be on the shores of Lake Geneva in mid-May. He lets us know he'll be near the village of Cologny in the Hotel D'Angleterre.

"'…after which, I shall retire to a most congenial villa,' he writes. 'Small but suitable. Do you come to the lake, I suggest you take lodgings near Villa Diodotai, and we shall converse.'"

"A separate place? It sounds as though he wants it easier to be rid of us," I mutter.

"But he may also wish a place to work in peace. Or he may simply wish a private place to be with your sister," Percy adds, "or to avoid her. The gossip about the two of them does not imply over-fondness on his part."

"She wants so much to be with him." *And I want her away from you, my love.*

We took ship for France, intending to travel overland from there. Always a miserable experience for me. Our time in Paris caused Percy to expand. Everything inspired him. Rhapsodies he wrote of what he saw and thought and of the people he met. He delved the works of the philosophers to frame his poems and worked as nearly incessantly as ever I knew him to do.

Chapter Twenty-Five

Arrival

O, France! What a difference between when last I was there! The scars of war were healing. Buildings that were rubble were cleared away, masons upon scaffolds were at work to replace broken stones. Percy's name was enough for us to visit scholars in their universities and libraries. The jewels of wisdom we reaped provided discussion for more than several evenings by a fire. A thousand ideas exploding like suns would not compass the thoughts we shared.

And as we traveled, I thrilled to a feeling as though the very fabric of what was possible was shifting.

"Hush now, my dear." Percy strokes my forehead and runs his fingers down my cheek. "'Tis sea-sickness, no more. The coast is in sight. We'll be off the water soon."

I lie prostrate in our ship, looking up at him with my arms hugging my waist, and groan. "That feeling of prescience has come upon me again, as though were I to turn a moment earlier, I might see a great thing."

"'Tis the strain of travel and nothing more."

"I'm certain I feel a current pulling me toward, something as though I might see more and know more and understand...something."

May gilds the fields south of Paris in splendor. The light that fascinated Renaissance masters lacks warmth, but the cool dryness of the air lends crispness to vision, letting us see for miles over the rolling landscape of repaired villages and restored fields. If the temperature is less than congenial, the magnificent sunsets cast rosy hues through glassed casements for us to marvel at where we sit by the fire in the evenings.

"I'm bored." Claire's refrain for the past week causes me to smile. Her beauty, a loveliness I so wish was my own, blossoms as we draw closer to Switzerland. *Byron might take an interest, if the man has not found comfort elsewhere. Please let him take my sister from us.* But charity toward her still dwells in my heart so I add, *and be good to her.*

"Why can we not travel faster?"

Percy's been thinking on our future as well. That night in bed as I rest my head upon his chest, he says, "Mary, I want to discuss something with you."

I lift on an elbow to look at him. "Diffidence? Is what you have to say so delicate."

"It may be." He shrugs. "But I hope it may be welcome to you." I lift my head and wait. "Hear me. Byron lives in exile because of London gossip, though he affects not to let those reports alter his actions overmuch. The man follows his reviews in the *Times* with a religious fervor he'd be the first to deny. But, it was rumors that drove him from England, and society abroad feasts upon being the first to send word back to London of the doings of their countrymen who live in their vicinity. Byron calls them 'jackals sensing blood,' but for a man gone from Britain to flee contempt, he is, rightfully, sensitive of condemnation. What I mean is, we ought to be aware the three of us are subject to gossip as well. There are many lascivious minds of prurient interest who salivate over our little family."

"Oh, Percy!" I start up. "Have I ever said anything against your loving my sister?"

"Shhh, my love. You've not. Again and again you've affirmed our right to love as we will in accord with the philosophy of free and intelligent humans, but..."

I lift an eyebrow. "But?"

"But, Lord Byron might not welcome us so much if we appear to the expatriate English as a *ménage à trois*."

Well, that is unexpected.

I lie back with my cheek on his chest. "Yes. It could very well be. I remember me of the time we were here years ago. The Swiss wish to be seen as pure and as white as the aprons the women wear. Londoners, especially those who have lived for a time here, cannot help but imitate a Christian moral stance, the better to get along with these neighbors, even if unconsciously."

"More inclination than imitation." Percy drawls, "That being so, I see a way for us to ease Byron's mind about hosting us."

I nod my head. "How then may we help?"

"The man might be saved any further embarrassment on our account, and the residents find no fault in us, if they saw your sister as but a companion traveling with a couple who are..." He pauses so long I look up to meet his eyes. "Married."

He continues to speak but I confess I do not hear a word he says.

We cross the Swiss border in early May. My heart sings as I look at the register of the Hotel D'Angleterre and see Percy has written, "Mr. and Mrs. Percy Shelley."

Not until the next week does the great man appear. That he may not attract attention, he has made his way, slowly, through France in a great shining gold coach, the very image of a famous diligence that belonged to Napoleon. So large is this conveyance his entire retinue, a doctor, one peacock, one dog, one monkey, and several servants, can ride inside with him; an additional number of footmen cling to steps and seats outside.

"For a man seeking to escape his reputation," Percy opined to me privately as we viewed the coach in the stable yard the day after the poet arrived, "he certainly knows how to be noticed."

The concierge sends a boy to us with the information that his lordship had gone for a sail this day.

"Come!" Claire pulls our hands to get us out of the chairs where we were reading in the wan sunlight. "George is out on the waters. We can appear to meet him by chance if we walk upon the shore."

Up and down we trudge along a shoreline path until, at last, we see Byron and one other approaching in a small boat.

"Ooooo! Oooooooooo!" Claire calls waving her handkerchief. "George! Geeeoooorrrge!"

"Shelley?" Byron calls from his seat at the tiller as he sweeps by. "Well met! Come you to my rooms!"

Once we find his door, our knocking produces a thin young man, pale of complexion and dark of hair, whose demeanor is less than welcoming. "It took you long enough," the man sighs down his nose.

Thinking I detect a trace of an Italian accent, I say, "Are you the doctor?"

Even in this day and age of equality and enlightenment, it puts some men off to be formally addressed by a woman. John Polidori is one of those. He turns to me and blinks in confusion.

"I assume you are Mary Godwin?"

"Mary Godwin Shelley."

He chews on the words. "If you say so." He allows us to enter, saying, "His Lordship is in the sitting room."

In a silence broken only by our echoing heels on the parquet floors, we trail the man through the suite to a room streaming with light. We see Lord Byron in profile sitting near a window as he reads a book.

My breath catches as the late daylight illuminates him. Adonis or Apollo could not be more handsome. A Grecian statue as Pygmalion crafted could not be more beautiful.

His high, unlined forehead supports brunette ringlets worn in the style of Caesar Augustus. Dark eyes, wide set and serious of purpose, rest upon either side of a face proportioned according to an Aristotelian mean. His nose is narrow, his mouth is sensually full, the dimple in his firm chin catches a shadow of light.

Byron turns to face us with an actor's grace, his movements studied as though every motion holds a story. Seeing our admiration, his smile slowly grows showing teeth that have never known tobacco. "Shelley!" A breathy, hearty inflection. "There you are, at last! Welcome to Lake Geneva."

So I learn my first lessons of the man. The ease with which he asserts his importance lets me know superiority is part of his character.

"Hello, George," Claire squeaks, tripping to his side, and he rises to place a kiss upon her brow. They stand a moment together, framed by the large window. Not until now do I understand the basis of their relation: *That is how she attracts him.* She holds a mirror to his masculinity.

We three and the doctor are seated on divans placed opposite each other, but the Poet sits in a winged chair at their head. Claire perches stiffly on the couch to his right, for a wonder, silent, with a trembling smile.

Byron's idea of tea includes several bottles of claret, which he presses upon us though it is still hours before supper.

He nods to the young man who brought us here. *Oh,* I think, *Polidori can smile. This one owns one face for strangers and another when in the presence of his Lord.*

"Y've met my doctor?"

Claire says, "Only in that he escorted us from your door to you. We'd not completed our introductions." She turns to face Polidori. "Doctor, I am Claire Clairmont and these are at once my friends and my relatives. I beg you to receive Mary, my sister, and Percy Shelley, a poet of some worth."

Polidori nods to us. "Your, ah, reputations, precede you."

Byron hastens to say, "John, here, accompanies me at my request to look after my health and to write of our adventures. He's published, I might add. At least one house thinks well enough of him that they offered him an advance, sight unseen, against his account of our travels. I've had occasion to edit him as we journeyed together. His notes should result in a little book that may amuse my followers." He tips Percy a wink. "Through critique we may create some improvement in his writing." He swings back to the doctor. "Eh, John? What say you to having Shelley and I review you? Ha, ha."

The look on his face is answer enough.

If Byron thinks he would fain be a source of gossip to the rest of the denizens of the hotel, he is far from correct. Although he affects to disdain the attention, he complains about English tourists with remarkable frequency, saying, "Those staring boobies with their mouths hanging open follow me incessantly."

But the stare I notice most is the one Byron turns on me. When he thinks no one but me sees, his eyes travel up and down me like a new land to be conquered.

On a clear morning, Percy rides to the far end of the lake. Late that night when he returns, he says, "I've taken a small cottage adjacent to Byron's villa near Coligny. It's called the Maison Chapuis."

It takes no effort for us to find Byron's Villa Diodati, an impressive salmon-colored block of stone with many windows less than fifty yards from our door. Diodati rises from lawns that slope to the water's edge.

"Its magnitude is equal to his status." Claire's breath shakes.

"But he said he had a small place. How will he fill that with just his retinue?" I ask.

"He must have such an edifice for the visitors he is sure to receive." She claps her hands. "Perhaps there will be a ball."

"Protect me!" cries Percy. "My purse will not stand the cost of two gowns the like of which you would order."

"Look how the water is as blue as the sky it reflects!" I exclaim from where I stand near the shore. Then, remembering Claire's phrase of delight from when we three walked through France, I decide to gently tease her with it. "Oh! It is so beautiful! Let us live here and we shall be happy!"

But she is looking through the trees toward the salmon-pink walls of Diodoti. "I'm sorry. What?"

"Oh, love," I say, putting an arm around her shoulders. "He will be here soon, and you will see all is well."

When the great man arrives, we send word of our presence and, happily, are invited to tea the next day.

In less time than it takes to tell, Byron has Percy in front of a table loaded with manuscripts, explaining each of the pieces he upon which he is working. Percy's face lights with wonder, "I confess I am amazed at both your output and the quality. You've penned phrases to shake heaven."

He could not have found a better way to endear himself to our host, who says, "We've plenty to occupy ourselves. I'm sure you have much to show me, too."

Is that a challenge?

When it is time for us to leave, Byron lifts my hand to his lips. Goodness, a kiss on the hand from him is more erotic than kisses on the lips from other men. Not Percy, but still...he glances at Claire and murmurs, "Stay the night." She does nothing to disguise her triumph.

That night in our bed, Percy asks, "I would know your mind regarding the Lord Byron."

"I find him...deliberate is the word, I suppose." I think a moment. "He treats Claire as set dressing for a tableau."

"But, the man is *sans doute* brilliant."

"I know his writing is brilliant, dear. It is just that I remained blind to any evidence of luminous wit in our first meeting."

He shrugs beneath me. "That is often so when we greet those new to us."

"You are more talented."

He chuckles. "A prejudice in my favor, but of the two of us, he is more accomplished than I."

"Than me."

"Than I," he corrects me. "The construction includes with the understood, *I am*."

"You are correct when the construction is used formally." I lift the covers and look down. "I do not think of now as a 'formal' moment. Remember, love, my father had me at grammar lessons before I was twelve."

Sometime later, as I drift toward happy sleep, I think, *Perhaps I shall grow to like George for Percy's sake.*

It soon becomes apparent Percy and George Byron form two soul mates. Their friendship's blossom is immediate. Ideas and conversation flow continuous and energizing between them, although I see the relationship in Byron's mind is hardly between equals. Yet I think Percy enjoys playing the role of particularly bright student to Byron's world-wise mentor.

"Is your objection to my characters?" Percy asks.

A studied moment's hesitation. "They are, I suppose adequate is the word." Percy's eyes are intent on where Byron sits reading his pages with his pen in hand. "But where is the stress between them? Without that tension, there is nothing but dialog. D'y' not see it?"

Days become weeks spent hiking the mountains and glaciers. One day, I leave the baby with the nurse and accompany them to view a great and shifting mass of ice. Frozen blocks, crevasses, and fields all creep toward the warmth of the valley with a never ceasing groaning and cracking.

"Here is the very antithesis of creation," I say.

"Odd that you say so." Byron's breath steams into the cerulean sky. "Percy and I began a conversation just the other day, when we sailed the lake, about the origin of things, and here you speak of endings."

"Rather say destruction than endings, I think."

"Origins, ontology!" Percy inserts. "From the Greek for the study of beginnings."

Hours the two of them spend sailing the lake are richest. Sharing of thought produces nights of scribbling where the silver of ideas finds golden form on the page. One evening, as we sit in the firelight, Percy talks about crossing the lake with George in a small boat. As he recites the events of the day, his excitement grows, "Here is a man who thinks with a brain the twin of my own, though one grown mighty with experiences!"

Byron nods toward my poet and thumps the arm of his chair with his fist. "Hear him!" he cries, lifting his glass. "His is a formidable mind, though still awakening."

Percy bows to Byron, glowing to shame the fire with praise. "I'll allow a small boat is the most congenial mode of travel ever conceived; to feel the lift of the sail, to listen to the run of the water from beak to stern as it trills accompaniment to conversation always causes my heart to fly among the stars." His eyes alight, he says, "Imagine crossing the very breast of the lake with reflection of mountains and clouds and sky on the water, and the sparkle of sunlight spanking off the wavelets. I feel the experience a metaphor for what occurs between us! We refine, build, and then join thoughts one to another, and another." He takes my hands. "The ideas, Mary, the ideas flow with the waves." He releases me and strides about the room as he speaks. "We share concepts about the relationship between Man, the natural creature, and Man, the thinking being! We discussed the conceit that a natural man is superior to ourselves. Does a man when born and raised away from civilization and stripped from the veneer of culture become one with the balance of nature and so behave in a gracious disposition toward his fellows? Is nascent man imbued with a tendency toward right action? And through contact with culture, does he become corrupt?"

"A Noble Savage is nay-the-less a savage," sneers Polidori from where he glowers, wrapped in a deep-red wing chair. "Without the training and the careful nurturing of a mentor, a man is incapable of ascending the heights of intellect. I note you've appropriated the Lord's tutelage for yourself."

Byron stirs himself. "The supply of my teaching is undiminished, John. You ought remember you have supped at that table often and well." He dismisses the interruption with a wave of his hand.

"That peculiar American, Franklin, says in satire, 'those with different manners we call savage' and says the term refers to any of those alien to our way of thinking." Byron's smile holds an impious aspect. "Such as the Italians."

But he fails to notice his doctor's reaction. The man flinches as though he had been struck a blow. I suspect I know the answer to Polidori's rudeness. Even as the doctor struggles to place words together in such way to be sensible, he finds himself forced to witness the soaring flights of intellect between his lord and Percy. *Can a green and pleasant hillside equal the power and thrust of a mountain?*

As mountains and hillsides, so are men. There! A flash of insight. *That is why I have ever preferred mountains, be they stone or flesh.*

Byron looks deep into his glass. "But what is the essence of man? What sets a man above the beasts?"

Percy says with a yawn as he reaches for a glass of wine, "One more, but one, for I'm drunk from the font of the gods, and to leave off of a sudden would do me harm. I'll not continue this discussion." He pauses, holding the vintage to gaze through it to the light of a candle. He sips deeply from the rich, red liquid. "Ah, there's that good." With eyes dancing he toasts me. "And now, my beauty, my muse, my love, we must return to our cottage. I must be 'alone alone, all all alone' with but thee for company."

That night in our bed, Percy confides a nagging doubt to me. "It seems Byron and I have a disproportionate relationship." He pauses a moment to think. "This does not bother me overmuch, as he is five years older than me. And, as long as I am content to listen at his knee, the man will dispense jewels. I have no desire to alter our arrangement." He yawns, for slumber is close upon him. "Overall, I am richer for our conversation."

As I lie in his arms, I stroke his hair and think, *Rest, my love. There will come a day when you shall be the greater.*

Had I thought Percy wrote before? Had I thought the scratching of his pen a pleasant companion? I underestimated his reserves. Percy writes incessantly and Byron engages in paroxysms of creativity.

The night following a long hike into the mountains, Percy forms the basis of a tribute to nature, *Mont Blanc*. A paean, he says, to the majesty of nature so that men might appreciate the world.

"I believe I might set the piece within your notes of our six weeks' adventures." He looks toward me. "Was that but two years past?"

"Almost that long."

He strokes my hair. "This piece fits well with your emotions when first you beheld the Alps."

Oh, that our works might intertwine even as our hearts.

But then there are often times when they include me in their flying thoughts. Such was the mind of Byron that I, too, know what pulls Percy when he describes the thrill of speaking with the great man, and best of all, Byron consents to critique a piece or two of mine. One morning when we join him for breakfast, I see my pages at his elbow and hear him say to me, "You've a talent, raw and unformed, but far above what one might expect from a woman of your years. You present a message in your work, some thought you wish to share, and these are of some worth. Were I you, I would continue to write. But, tell me, why work in prose?"

"Prose suites me well, and my messages are crafted for an audience who prefer to read novels."

"Ah," he says; his cup stops half-way to his lips. "Not only the ability to craft a message, but an understanding of who you wish to reach." He sips. "Remarkable."

"Mary?" Percy rouses from contemplation. "D'y' understand why we two are poets?"

"You've said poetry is meat and bread to the intellectual."

Byron snorts. "Why write for those whose minds have neither the patience nor the scope to hear what I have to say?"

Percy straightens and looks with surprise upon his mentor. "I'll grant a message needs must be crafted for the ears you wish, but I believe poetry serves another function."

Byron beckons with his biscuit. "Say on."

"When the sounds of my words causes the hearts of men to soar or plunge, then what I say creeps unguarded into their hearts and weaves into the fabric of their thoughts."

Byron lifts his head, looking at Percy as though seeing his pupil rise higher than expected. "Truth. Mary, note it well. Even as the grain freezes when cast before spring can warm the earth, so, too, a new thought must invest itself. New ideas are often rejected should they conflict with familiar beliefs in unready minds. In no small part does skill in writing depend on simply presenting ideas in a way that averts objection. Coleridge is correct about the ability to create a suspension of disbelief in the audience as a necessary skill for a writer." He shakes himself back from his thoughts. "But as to the selection of an audience, the literati are the ones who will change the world, so I craft my poetry to fascinate their hearts that my message germinates within their minds."

"Do not the masses deserve to have thoughts delivered to them in a way they can understand?" I ask.

"The mass of men seek nothing more than to forget." Byron's scorn cuts. "It is how gin distillers make their profits."

"Write as you will, Mary," Percy says with a chuckle as he takes my hand. "But keep in mind the difficulty you'll have to reach incapable minds, or worse, those who will not read and educate themselves."

"Yet, those are the ones who will bear the weight of change," I say. "Look to America, look to France. Perhaps the intellectuals there thought of great themes, but it was the masses who fired the guns."

"We've a little insurgent, Percy!" cries Byron, lifting his glass to me. *How he remains steady in his cups escapes me.*

"Then write, my girl." Percy runs his thumb over the back of my hand. "And never fear, you will be read."

I think his poetry far forward of most men's understanding, though he refuses to alter his style, saying, "If I struggle for an audience today, I know someday my ideas will find fallow ground."

Weeks of thought and of dreams become a month, then two months, while we thrill to exist in such a time and place when dreams are enough. I've a dream of my own in my arms. Little Willmouse thrives! Eyes and fingers and toes work his way into my heart in spite of my reluctance to open myself to him for fear of another disappointment.

"There's a happy creature." Polidori makes me jump one day as I am feeding little Will. When I look up, he is gazing at the baby tugging upon my nipple.

"John, do you know where my husband went?"

"Where else? Sailing."

"What o' th' clock?"

"Does that matter?" He shrugs. "Can we sit and converse awhile?"

The man has made it clear he wishes me to incline toward him. "Unfortunately, no. Percy's output threatens to overwhelm my ability to copy, and this," I look down at William and smile, "does nothing to make more time for me." When I continue to care for my son, he leaves without a word, stiffly stepping out of the room, and I think there is more than one baby here.

Claire and Byron take up the relationship they had begun in England. She pursues him, relentlessly. He tolerates her presence because she provides a ready source of release for him. It puzzles me because of the disparity of thought between them. One day I chanced to be familiar with Byron.

"Forgive me, George, if I am overly candid, but, other than her beauty, what is it you see in my sister?"

If I think he might show some offense at my candor, I mistake. "Is that not reason enough?"

"For a night, sure, but beyond a dalliance...?"

Byron swirls the wine in his glass and thinks a moment. "Your forthrightness does you credit, and so I shall return it. Does Percy cleave to you alone?"

"We are advocates of free love. He may find ease where and when he will."

"And surely he does not lack for offers?"

I tilt my head. "There are offers in plenty. I have heard it said the man will bed whoever fails to outrun him."

Byron snorts into his glass, making the wine erupt, and laughs a sudden bark that rocks him and goes on until he weeps and gasps for air. "So it is said of me." He wipes his eye with his knuckle, and then becomes serious. "The boy does remind me of a looking glass. Like me, he writes because he must. I write that I may learn to say what I want and to say it in my way." He darts his eyes to mine. "It's my life I can't sculpt. I suppose I am a bit of a bastard. But people are always at me. I don't want to be alone in those black hours of the night when evil dreams leave me awake wondering at their source, or days when..." He shrugs. "People don't like me, eventually."

My sympathy touched, I continue softly, "But, with regard to my sister, she does not seem capable of appreciating you."

Byron considers me and I hear him murmur, "Though I cannot help but wonder, there are lines I shall not cross." *I know what he is thinking.* He says, "Indeed Claire cannot, but there are other things a man may value, convenience for one. Hark, the wont of many a maid, and of matron to be sure, is to put on an affected antic, a feigning of disinterest when she sets her sights on fornication. Or many are those females who simper and posture, indicating, 'If you want me, you may have me.'

"That is an evil game, for then the girl would say to her friends, 'That man wanted me, and I denied him.' Or, should the act not be to her liking, she can say, 'He failed to entertain me.' Either way, it is a poor affectation that allows a semblance of morality without any commitment on her part and forces all responsibility upon the suitor."

He sips from his glass. "But your sister is not one of those. She is one to trip a man and beat him to the bed saying, Hale and Welcome!" He smiles as though recalling a pleasant memory. "So, for a time, I enjoy being chased rather than chaste."

I note his lips move silently as he commits his *bon mot* to memory.

He turns his head to me and catches my eye with his. "In the main you are correct about her wit. Make certain she leaves with you when your time here is done." He sips at his glass again and murmurs, "There's a dear."

That night as we ready ourselves for bed, I speak with Percy. "Would you have me more like Claire?" I say, placing my shift over the back of a chair. "More flirtatious, more overt in my expression?"

He pauses with his hands upon the buttons of his shirt. "More might kill me, love. Your sister is vastly entertaining, but in the end, whenever I am with her, she pulls the life from me. You do not."

"How so?"

"Well, though you exhaust my body, you do not drain my heart. And, as for my mind, you inspire me."

"To what, dear?"

Percy stands as still as a marble statue. "I would be thought admirable by you."

I lean into him. "Like you, I wish to be greater than I am. You create in me a need to be the best person I can be. I would have you know me as much for being a woman as for an ability to produce great works." I stop a moment and lock his eyes with mine. "As much, no less."

Such was the character, or lack of it, of Lord Byron. How one so brilliant in his poetry could be so benighted in his personal habit I've never fathomed. There came a time when he was honest in his spite of my sister. Eventually he derided her to others, writing, "I never loved her nor pretended to love her, but a man is a man—& if a girl of eighteen comes prancing to you at all hours—there is but one way."

He treated so many others before and after Claire with the same rude distain but somehow he never found himself alone where none would have him.

Chapter Twenty-Six

Lessons

There is a corollary to being free to love whoever you want; people will disparage you as morally bereft. Byron assumed my desire of him, but Polidori believed that free love equated with sexual experience, thus he became enamored of me, which added to the tension building in Diodati.

Another hypocrisy became evident as the months passed in Switzerland. The local inhabitants and the English vacationers concocted lurid tales of us from scant bits of truth. They embroidered the fables that surrounded Byron and, truth be told, ourselves. One rumor of our licentious behavior had origin in our habit for cleanliness. Our rambles required us to wash our limited wardrobe of underclothing, shifts, and stockings that kept our perspiration from our dresses, which would require regular washing. Upon seeing our intimate clothing drying outside on a line shamelessly visible from the roadway, the residents of Cologny averred debauchery was the source of such a quantity of laundry. The same was true for the sheets we hung over the second floor windows to block intrusion by telescopes aimed at us. Such letters to English newspapers made it plain our little salon was a "league of incest."

At the time, however, we believed the weather to be our biggest enemy.

Rain, days of it made even colder by the frigid airs of the mountains, pours from a sky the color of steel. I sigh and return to my copying. *At least I have a chance to catch up.*

By late July, I conclude this will not be remembered as a convivial summer. Continuing rains force us indoors more often than out, and the cold follows us inside. After a late dinner, we retreat to a smaller and easier to warm room and dispose ourselves by the fire in comfortable chairs arranged in a semicircle in front of the flames. We pass the evenings entertaining each other with conversation.

"I do regret this most inclement weather, my guests," Byron says as he settles into a chair before the fire. "I especially miss my travels with you, Percy." He waves a hand toward where the rain beats upon the windows. "But, there it is."

Any of the five seats are well warmed, but Byron's chair, according to his right as host, occupies the center, with Claire to his left, followed by Polidori. Percy is on his right, and I occupy the seat complimentary to the doctor's. The arrangement suits me well as I can see each of our company the better to judge their reactions. From his throne, Byron summons a servant to bring brandy for each of us. Polidori's attitude of casual indifference to our party has not changed, but I recognize his incipient lust for me in both the frequency and intensity of his gaze in my direction.

Good food and wine this night loosens George's tongue. "I have had a thought, or two, on reputation. You have to get the public talking about your work if you would be read. And money does help one to stay alive long enough to think and work. For those lacking in mental aptitude to understand your message, the best way to get them to purchase your work is to make them talk about you." His gaze catches my eye. "I have, I admit, sought infamy to this end.

"By the time I was eighteen, I'd tupped more women than I can count; broke their hearts, minds, and kidneys without regret or remorse. I've caught the pox twice, attended several black masses, murdered men both in anger and cold blood, and got my sister with child.

"If you would pass the long hours of the dark, if you would be a poet of heroic stature, then let your greatest inspirations be opium, claret, the wriggling navel," he clasps his hand between his legs, "and the honorable member for Cockshire."

Lifting his head the better to catch the light from the fire, he assumes a thoughtful mien. "We have the wine, the women, and the cocks here with us this night. Fortunately, the fourth item may be at hand." Byron asks Polidori, "Did you bring it?"

The doctor rises, takes a bottle of slightly clouded liquid and a medicine dropper from his pocket and places them onto the table at Byron's elbow.

"Ah, thank you, John." Byron sighs with relish. "My guests, I present Godfrey's Cordial." He gives a nod to the bottle and measures a dose into his brandy. "There," he sighs. "John, present!" and Polidori places his glass on the tray. Byron drops an amount into the doctor's libation. "Claire?"

She squeeks. "Oh my, yes!" Her eyes slide to mine. "It has a most salubrious effect on me."

And then Byron nods to Percy. "Will you partake of it?"

Percy smiles and extends his glass. "I shall. Lay on."

Byron drips a smaller portion into it saying, "I have, through habituation, acquired a tolerance for laudanum. You begin with this and we shall see."

Percy, watching the administration of the liquid, says, "I have heard the poppy does make passing time interesting." He turns to me and says, "Would you try the experiment?"

A journey into the unknown? I hold out my glass. "I would."

My portion is smaller than Percy's for, as Byron says with a wink, "You are so very tiny a jewel."

A hearty sip. I notice a bitterness my brandy cannot cover; otherwise, I find nothing amiss.

Conversation resumes. A joke, a story, and then Percy says, "George, I wish you to know how very much I enjoyed it when we were in the boat the other morning and you began musing on your new poem."

"I think I may call it, 'The Prisoner.'"

Percy thinks a moment before he offers, "Say rather, 'Prisoner of Chillon' for the castle we visited. It has a ring."

Byron glowers at any suggestion his work can be improved. "I shall consider it."

"A trifling suggestion only. But as to the poem, your opening descriptions astound me in their completeness."

Now the great man smiles. "How so?"

"You manage to convey a sense of the weight of years that assault your hero in the first stanza. I find that profunce." Percy pauses, he stretches his mouth open wide as though to relieve a tightness of his lips. "Profound. I mean," he stretches again. "Pro Found."

Claire giggles, and in a voice meant to be sultry and low says, "Proooooffoooound!"

Byron smiles.

And then we are all laughing and one by one repeating the word in different ways and accents. "Profound." "Pro, pro, profound." "Profount!" "Proficcient."

And Claire says, "Poodle." Which I think is the most humorous thing she has ever uttered and collapse with hilarity.

In the hours before dawn, I find other amusements profound.

Lying where our passions have thrown us with our covers askew, our bodies slick and our hearts thundering, I say, "Did we do what I think we did?"

"Four times," he gasps.

But before I fall asleep clinging to his chest, I spare time for one last happy thought. *This Laudanum be a sovereign pastime for stormy days.*

Percy is gone when I rise. I find a note at my place at breakfast. It says he and George are climbing a peak today. He expects they will be back in time for a late supper. I bathe and dress and take a moment to play with my Willmouse, clever little bundle who opens a way into my heart in spite of my worries, then spend the afternoon by writing in my journal, copying Percy's work, and listening to the rain sheeting against the windows. The weather breaks near eight and I begin the short climb to Diodati.

My explorers are seated round the fire when I arrive. Percy is in his hiking gear, warm pants with suspenders such as the Swiss employ, a white long-sleeved shirt, and a dark blue sweater. Byron has changed his clothing as well for slippers, loose flannel pants, and a silk dressing gown; he is the very laird of the manor. Polidori is still in his day wear. Pants, shirt, jacket and even shoes are a shade of soft dove-grey.

Percy rises when he sees me enter; his dancing eyes let me know he cherishes the memory of last night as he tenderly kisses me and leads me to a seat next to his to begin a story with the wide-eyed aspect of an excited child.

"George and I had something of a discussion, this morning, while climbing the mountains above the rain clouds." Percy watches Byron measure a considerable amount of poppy into his glass. "We attempted to define Life."

He pauses. The depth of those two lines that form between his brows lets me know his puzzlement. "It were a far more difficult exercise than I imagined. Life's manifestations abound around us but life is, in itself, a great mystery."

Byron interrupts him. "A moment, Percy. Let her catch up. Mary, as you aspire to the pen as well," he graciously includes me into the company of writers as he cocks his head to me, offering the bottle of cordial. I nod, and he drips an amount which I welcome. He sits back and continues his thought.

"Our discussion traveled further than simple thoughts," he says, swirling the brandy in his glass to warm it and waving it under his nose to savor the fumes. "We began by cataloging the attributes of writers. Think, you, of the compendium of knowledge a poet must have to express his," a glance to me, "or her, philosophy, history, mythology, political acuteness, in addition to knowing the technique of the craft, all these are simply the basics. There is philosophy, natural and political, as well." He does not take his eyes off the play of the firelight through the liquid as he says, "And from the need to understand natural philosophy, we were led to consider awareness. Here, young Mary, have you thought how you might define Life?"

My thoughts race back to Father's library, but I veer from philosophy toward empathy. *What properties has life in its struggle to be born?* "Empedocles assigned a property of existence to an appropriate combination of the four elements…"

"Ah," Byron sighs after a heroic quaff of brandy. "The Greeks are where we begin tonight? As the Greeks did, will you then say earth, air, fire, and water, in the proper proportion, create life? And were we to know those noble measurements, could we," he pauses as though standing on a precipice, "by knowing these constituents, could we invent…life?"

What wonder would that be? "Life is more than ingredients. My tutor, Mr. Baxter, caused a deceased frog's muscles to twitch by applying Galvanni's electrical fluid to them. Imagine were we able to make a deceased human's heart respond. Could we not restore and so prolong a life?"

Byron leans forward. "Would the result be miraculous or diabolical?"

"Percy." My mind, growing acute under the influence of the drug, remembers a conversation with him from years ago. "Do you remember speaking with me of the Luddites?"

"Those," he snorts. "They sing of a time when man was innocent of machine, never imagining having to do the mechanism's work themselves."

I touch his sleeve. "Quite so, my dear, but do you not see how created life might be used for purposes now accomplished by machines? If we classified the created as un-human there might be little objection to treating them as slaves. Or, now that one thought chases another, why could not nations build up whole armies of such to war against each other. If such lives are created by men, would the church condemn the waste of souls?"

"You chill me, girl," Byron says, drinking his glass dry. "Hideous."

Percy raises his hand to his head. "I've been thinking we are not so far advanced from Paracelsus, Agrippa, and other alchemists, though we are separated by hundreds of years."

Polidori sneers as he says, "You've gone so far as to study alchemy? How little we progress."

Percy lifts his head. "Albert Magnus wrote of an elixir that would impart life to the dead. Paracelsus, while he was in the university at Ingolstadt, no far distance from here, used the term Homunculus to describe a creature animated from blood, bone, spermatozoa, hair, along with other components, a mixture of noxious elements, buried with a horse's seed for forty days and nights and left under the light of the full moon to spontaneously erupt as alive. His instructions say to knead these well and feed the admixture on human blood for forty weeks."

Polidori erupts, "Oh, I hardly think..."

"In that you are not so different from the masses," Byron says to his doctor, pouring another tot before returning to the subject. "The Jews name such a creature a Golem. Rabbi Loew is rumored to have devised such a creature, but that it grew out of control as it gained great size. A cautionary tale for any who would seek the power of creation."

Percy takes a deep drink and says, "I have undertaken such experiments."

Byron halts in mid-sip from his glass and turns his head to Percy. "And the result?"

"Others in my house objected to the smell. I was asked to remove from my apartments."

Tension shatters and we laugh as though we might never stop.

I shake my head. Were we that arrogant, that precocious to discuss such a topic? What I remember most was how good those times were. I was so young and in the company of two of the greatest poet-philosophers of the day.

And there was nothing to fear.

Chapter Twenty-Seven

The Uses of Horror

Thinking of Life as a proper noun led to three discussions that colored the rest of my life.

In the first, two great minds, and I suppose my own, thrashed out the essence of what it means to be alive.

In the second, we debated the merits and capabilities of bringing a being to life.

But there was one other debate that had far-reaching consequence. Since I heard Coleridge discourse on creating a bond between a writer and his audience, I wondered how to make the reader decide to believe a fiction. A lie, however entertaining, is still a lie.

We continued our arguments through breakfast...

"Oh, the soul," sneers Byron as we sit to break our fast. "Priests and minstrels know the soppy tune to get people who know no better to believe in the nonexistent." He raises his hand. "That's art, that is."

Our topic continues with several pauses for food until Claire, sitting on the arm of Byron's overstuffed chair, settles her feet in his lap, which occasions the two of them leaving our company for a time. Emerging from his chambers an hour later, George asks Percy to sail across the lake. Following a late supper, we pick up the thread of our earlier conversation.

"Where did we leave the soul? Is it not amazing how often philosophical questions, having no other solution, succumb to Biblical rationale as though to say, 'thus and such be in the Bible and therefore, the very word of God.' Frustrating."

"Many others have attempted methodologies aside from religion for answering great questions," I say. "Such as the one presently before the group: namely, What is life? Aristotle sought to find answers through the use of logic."

Percy adds, "The most refined abstractions of logic have been applied to a definition of life in an attempt to strip away superstition. I assert nothing exists 'less it is perceived by my senses. Therefore, as we can neither see, nor hear, nor taste, nor touch the essential spark, I reject the biblical explanation of soul."

"But you cannot deny it exists." I smile to myself, thinking of a time when, in the thrall of a family of mentors, I knew there was more to the world than I could define with my senses. "I am sure there are things outside our perceptions that are real. Is a dream not real? Yet, can your senses register it when you are awake? However as to the soul, the Greek describes the soul as a property of Life. He goes on to classify souls as vegetative, animal, and rational."

"Better," Polidori slyly asserts, "but still short of the mark. Though Aristotle names what forms the soul takes, he does not define what a soul is or how one operates."

"Definition then," I say. "By use of the word soul, I seek to indicate what we think of as consciousness. Or I might use 'soul' to describe a unity of all living things and so define life as recognition of this unity. Did not the pagans say as much by including all beings when they indicated any being? As example, in the vocabulary of the ancient Britons we find neither 'I,' nor 'you,' nor 'they,' nor 'us,' nor 'we.'"

Byron nods. "Those who practice atavistic rites use 'a' as the personal pronoun, saying, 'Do a (you) go down and fetch a (me) water.'" Byron passes the bottle around again and says, "So, Life is something we may perceive through immediate experience."

Percy hesitates with the liquid in his hand. "It is a cold walk to our cottage..." He lifts the bottle.

"Then stay. I have rooms enough. Let me call a girl and have her make ready." After he speaks to a maid, Byron shifts back to our topic. "Having asserted we may perceive 'life,' will you define 'Life' for us Mary?"

I have not wasted my years under the tutelage of a Natural Philosopher.

"I should think the very words animate versus inanimate would differentiate life from non-living. At its base, Life may be distinguished from inanimate objects by the tendency to move or grow."

Polidori says, "Water moves, but is not alive." Since I rejected his advances the man will let no opportunity to contradict me pass; a petty inconvenience.

I nod. "Then shall we say Life is associated with biological processes such as digestion, respiration, circulation?"

"What of cognition?" Percy asks. "The ability to think and reason?"

"In some instances," I say, looking the doctor in the eye, "though undoubtedly alive, I dispute a plant's ability to form a sentence. In this modern age, we associate thought with the nervous system as opposed to the ancients, who centered cognitive effects, including love, in the heart."

"And what is the difference between thought and reaction?" Byron asks.

"Volition? A reaction is a simple response to stimulus. I prick your finger with a needle and you react, but to move deliberately, with purpose—do you see it? That would be a key difference."

Polidori will not be contained. "Life is not merely a condition that distinguishes animals and plants from rocks. It includes the ability to reproduce..." He stares at my bosom. *As subtle as a hammer.* Perhaps being a man of medicine, he believes he should lead the discussion, but doctors are not known so much for their quality of thought as much as they are valued for healing.

Byron frowns. "I had hoped for better from a physician. You give us a negative and claim it as a proof. 'Life is' can be parsed logically. 'Life is not' is a null statement, and as such, impossible to reduce to logic."

"Communication," I try. "That is a prerogative of higher forms of life, a result of cognitive processes, and one that can be perceived by the senses."

"And we return to consciousness." Percy rejoins the fray. "What does it mean to be conscious? Is the condition of self-awareness necessary to consciousness?"

Polidori, though halted momentarily in his charge, re-engages. "Do we begin to define what it means to be human? As it is impossible to create organic matter from inorganic matter, so it is impossible to create humanity from animals."

I have heard this cant. "Are animals not self-aware?" I say. "A worm must be aware of its surround in relation to its body, if not to others, for it will generate as readily with itself as with another."

"What better way to define self-awareness than masturbation?" Claire smirks.

Byron chucks her under her chin. "You may demonstrate later, my cat." He smiles and, looking directly at her, says thoughtfully, "A cat may be the ultimate in self-absorption, a living testament to the notion that humans exist to serve it."

"A cat may be self-aware, if we define consciousness that way, but unlike a dog, it does not care whether you recognize it." I say slowly, "Yet, they both demonstrate love."

Byron leans in. "Are we to stipulate love as an attribute of consciousness?"

"I think we must. Love for another, love for self. Love may be the ultimate aspect of awareness."

"A dog is surely aware of self and others." Claire will not be still.

"And a man?"

"Some say men are capable of abstract thought," I say, meeting Percy's eyes with mine. He smiles at the touch.

"Abstraction?" Byron says, lifting an eyebrow in my direction.

I must be precise. "I think conceiving of the abstract is the ability to go beyond conceptualization, or the use of empirical evidence through observation of the world, and then to form a hypothesis from these facts, concrete or reasoned, and, from that, to form a defensible hypothesis. Abstraction is the reduction to what we think of as the essence of the thing."

"And to reason to the formation of a theory that will stand transference to other situations." Percy rallies to my side.

"Can we progress from that?" Byron is keen now.

"What else is there?" asks Polidori.

"Those concepts which are distinctly human in essence," I murmur.

Claire giggles, "How far we have come from Life to what it means to be Human?"

"Even a blind pig..." muses Byron, stroking her hair.

"Although we've named it before this, how about, well, Love?" Percy asks. "For though a cat may exhibit affection, we cannot call that love."

"Why not?" I ask. "We cannot be sure a cat does not feel emotion. If we *catalog* its actions and compare them to our own when we experience an emotion, then what may we call it?"

"Reduced to Punning." Polidori shakes his head. "Love, then. Others?"

"Duty, patience, courage..."

"Temperance," Claire says.

Byron barks a laugh. "God defend me from that one. We are too cognitive by far. Here is the cure for that." And he passes the bottle of poppy around.

But Polidori has not done. He clearly views his contributions have not been respected. "Piety, self-restraint?" He spits.

"More to strike from my list." Byron lifts his glass in salute. "Irony is my forte."

I say, "Discrimination may be a human trait. However, let us return to love. We use Agape and Eros to define different forms of the emotion."

"Agape, to love pure and chaste, or Eros, to love carnally with passion and desire." Byron sips his brandy, "Hear, hear for Eros!"

"Enough you rogue," says Claire with her eyes aglint. "Soon enough 'twill be, 'and damned be he who first cries enough.'"

Byron looks from her to us with a weary grin. "What's a man to do," he sighs, "when a beauty not yet eighteen throws herself in his path?"

"Ignore her?" I ask, though I think I am unnoticed.

But Byron hears me and lifts his head. "Was that an answer Mary?"

"Another criterion, a negative one. Rage. Is that not as much a human attribute?"

Percy yawns and stretches his arms. "Too much for weary wits. I'll forfeit the field though I've no wish to sleep yet. Shall I call for a new topic?"

"I've a favorite poem I would share." Byron reaches for a book. "Mary, I believe you know the author, Coleridge."

"I do." I'm happy to hear he appreciates a man who I much admire. "Which piece, m'lord?"

"M'lord? On your knees, wench! The poem is *Christabel*."

"A horror indeed!" I cry.

"You know it?" Percy's eyebrows rise to me. "Where did you hear it?"

"At home. Several times. Mr. Coleridge spoke it. This poem is about a witch who ensnares a beautiful girl in order to do evil upon her. Some thought it inappropriate for me to hear it, but Mr. Coleridge felt I could benefit from the lesson in analogy."

"Well, then." Percy looks to Byron. "Let's have it."

George clears his throat. "It runs through such descriptions as to fire imagination, and the plot weaves terror and sensuality—very instructive for those writers who wish to add vivid description and emotional cues. In it, a maid meets a witch in the forest who takes her home, makes her a bath and prepares to join her. The young woman is entranced with the beauty of the witch, and watches as the she undresses."

Byron's masterful command of his voice let the rhythm of the words roll over us, and soon the poem has our imaginations and our willful belief in its grasp.

> *Beyond the lamp the lady bowed,*
> *And slowly rolled her eyes around;*

Then drawing in her breath aloud

Like one that shuddered, she unbound

The cincture from beneath her breast;

Her silken robe, and inner vest

Dropt to her feet, and in full view,

Behold! Her bosom and half her side—

Hideous, deformed, and pale of hue...Percy drops his gaze to my bosom, but instead of lust, his eyes go wide and a rictus of terror spreads over his face. He rises with his hands outstretched toward me as though defending himself, and he bolts from the room shrieking.

Well that was...unexpected.

As a body we follow him, finding him with his arm draped over the mantle of the fireplace in the dining room. His body shudders and shakes, he glances to me and, spinning round to brace his back against the wall, he shrieks again and again with his hands thrust forward as though to ward off a great evil.

"Eyes! Do you not see them?"

Claire bends in front of me and inspects the front of my dress. "I find no difference here."

"Eyes. There are eyes!" Percy's fear is a slithering thing in the room.

"Fetch cold water!" shouts Byron to a servant. "Bathe his face! Rub his hands!"

When we are able to calm him, he tells us, "O, most hideous! I saw eyes in place of your nipples. They moved to me as though guided by a sentience. They could see, and their lids blinked."

"Shhh, my love." I reach out carefully. "It is but the poppy that produces these visions."

But I exhale in relief as a thought occurs to me.

"Hush, hush, my love. Do you not remember whence this image came? It came from me. I said to you, oh so long ago, that Coleridge confided in me a story about this very poem. Oh, hush, Percy. Do you not remember Coleridge told me he considered making the witch have eyes in place of nipples but then said it was too obscene an image to use?"

The Uses of Horror | 199

Percy rolls his head until his gaze meets mine and focuses on me. "Ohhh, I remember. But to have seen...oh, love!" He buries his head in my shoulder for a time while the others whisper their reassurances.

When he quiets we return to our former chamber and the warmth of the fire.

"As what we have witnessed bears upon our earlier discussion of the characteristics of Life, let us return to its thread," Byron says, attempting to sooth us. "To the list of human attributes, I think we may add Fear." Byron sips. "I've had occasion, once or twice, to think of fear as a story device used for entertainment. Here, think me Scheherazade and listen." Byron lifts a book from where it nestles between his hip and the chair.

"I've found a curious volume gaining popularity named *Fantasmagoriana,* a French translation of an anthology of German folktales published late in the last century. On such a night as this, when a fire is a friend and conversation rollicks 'tween the sublime and the banal, a ghost story might be just the thing to enlighten and entertain us. Here is one close to your question Polidori: *The Specter Barber.*"

"Do read it!" Claire claps her hands.

"Once upon a time..." Byron shrugs and mutters, "As stale a convention as there ever was."

Claire giggles. "Oh, go on."

"All right, all right. Anyway, hmm, Once, etc., etc., there was a man who, having fallen on mean times, lost all his wealth. He journeyed far and wide and at last came to a Gothic castle whose master treated him most kindly.

"'You are welcome the night,' said the castellan. 'But beware of what ghosts you may encounter...'"

When Byron finishes the story he frowns at the volume. "I hope I've written better."

But I realize another aspect. "Fear, engendered in the bosom of the readers, is the most important part of it."

George looks up. "You have it. More."

"Listen, as Coleridge has said, if we might distract readers from questioning the plot, they will read the piece to experience a thrill of fear as entertainment."

Byron leans forward. "As the weather precludes going about to view the lake in comfort, why not make a contest among ourselves as to who may write the best horror story?"

Percy pulls at his lip as though he is daunted by considering crossing pens with the Lord Byron, but says slowly, "You say this book is popular? A small contest, with no wager, might pass some time, and we may generate something publishable. I'll essay the game."

"All of us shall," Polidori says. "And may the best man win."

"Man?" I ask. "Why not woman?"

"Why not indeed?" Byron smiles and looks at Claire. "You say you can write better than your sister."

"I have other things to do tonight," Claire simpers.

"One may hope," says Byron.

The stage thus set, the actors in their places await only the curtain's rising.

Chapter Twenty-Eight

Polidori's Tale

I thought of nothing but our contest, and by that I mean, I thought nothing. Neither grand theme, nor transporting message, much less a viable plot visited my imagination. To make matters worse, Percy existed in a state of grace where his writing flourished, his conceptions expanded, and the volume of his work grew exponentially.

He was frankly open, at least with me, about his relationship with Byron.

"The man is brilliance personified. Our conversations yield insight and direction for both his work and my own. The only fly in the batter that I see is that at the very time my mind is fired by the flames of creation, the man wants to go sailing. He would have me accompany him for a 'quick' (he says) crossing to see another castle. And so I am left feeling like Balam's Ass caught between two piles of delicious hay and unable to choose upon which to feed. I am fortunate that sailing is conducive to great thoughts."

In truth, I was less than sympathetic toward him. Did he have to care for a child every few hours, destroying any thoughts that crossed a brain before they could reach his pen? Thanks for the nurse who kept the bairn's linen clean, but still, there were things to which only a mother could attend.

And if that were not enough to frustrate me, in the middle of the chaos building around us, Polidori produced a rare piece.

The morning room in Diodati faces east, the better to let glorious sunlight stream in and warm us as we sit to morning tea.

Byron seems in a jovial mood. Each day he asks, "What horrors have we invented?" almost as soon as we are seated. "Shelley?"

"I fear I've nothing for the good of the order." Percy reaches for the preserves. "It is curious how poorly a poet writes when crafting prose."

Byron turns to the pot of tea. "I've nothing either," he says. "Exhaustion, I fear."

Claire snickers into her cup that we might applaud her skills. "Aye, me." She lifts her eyebrows artistically. "Busy."

Byron, indulgent of her, finishes filling his cup and takes a sip when he catches sight of the doctor over the rim of his cup. "John, you look as the proverbial feather-chinned cat. So, you found a subject?"

"I believe I have," Polidori drawls, trying not to appear enthusiastic although his voice betrays him.

"All I have at this point is an outline. It lies thus: the hero of my tale is Aubrey. An orphan but one possessed of great wealth, of position, and of a sister of passing beauty. I've also supposed an English nobleman, Ruthven by name."

Sycophant. George told us one of his mistress called him by that name.

Polidori lowers his voice for theatric effect. "Ruthven is both the villain and the subject of my story."

Which draws a smile from Byron. *As long as he is the star of the story, a villain is more than acceptable.*

Polidori continues. "Aubrey and Ruthven are bound together as traveling companions on the road to Greece, although Aubrey does not know Ruthven possesses an evil secret.

"During their journey, Aubrey amuses himself watching his companion flirting with women in the taprooms of inns they occupy. He appears to have considerable skill in gaining the confidence of the women who leave with him for extended periods of time, often overnight. But there is much darkness in Ruthven's purpose.

"Aubrey discovers the secret as though by accident. His first intimation is that these conquests, these innocent young women, do not appear to wish his companion farewell in the mornings when they take to their carriage. He supposes exhaustion is to blame.

"A second insight comes one night when a sound alerts Aubrey. He hears a soft cry from the room next to his. Lighting a candle, goes to investigate. Opening the door he sees Ruthven at his lusts. Aubrey, wishing pardon of his friend, begins to close the door but holds at the sight of Ruthven as he lifts his head. By the light of a single candle, Aubrey sees blood on the man's chin."

Polidori looks to us to judge the effect his story is having. "Is this a private matter, a folly of lust? Will he tell others of what he has witnessed? No, for there is a secret known only to Aubrey. A vow.

"While in Greece, the two fellow travelers are beset by toughs. Aubrey falls, rises, and fights on, but fails when numbers go against him. Fighting his own unequal battle, Ruthven opens himself to hurt to save Aubrey and falls wounded. The toughs retreat with their spoils, leaving their prey there sprawled on the cobblestone roadway. When Aubrey raises his comrade's head, thinking to hear his friend's last words, Ruthven tells him not to fear, all will be well. He then swears Aubrey to silence for a year and a day. Aubrey consents but the tale he hears shrivels him. Ruthven reveals he cannot be killed as he is already one of the living dead. A Vampyre. Ruthven is one who, for sustenance, must feed upon the living. He is a hematophage. Ruthven first seduces women, then attacks and kills them through a diabolical method; he opens his victim's veins and drinks their blood.

"Aubrey is repelled by what he has learned and the two go their separate ways. Aubrey returns to England shaken by his experiences, yet he re-enters society. At a soiree, he finds Ruthven apparently well. Mindful of his vow and in respect for the friend he once knew, Aubrey keeps his silence.

"As events unfold, Ruthven meets Aubrey's beautiful sister. The damned being, upon seeing the lovely girl, fixes upon her as his next target. Through his powers, he impels her to fall in love with him and, by and by, the two are betrothed. And yet..."

"Yet, what?" Claire, with her hand to her throat and her eyes wide, is clearly captivated.

Polidori smiles as a carnival barker when he perceives his audience is entangled in the web of his words and returns to his tale.

"When Aubrey objects to Ruthven's designs upon the sister, the monster reminds Aubrey of his vow. As a gentleman, Aubrey acknowledges his responsibility to his word. However, the creature, too, is bound by a code. His victims must invite him to imbibe, and so they share in the responsibility for their deaths."

"Oh," Byron exclaims. "That *is* choice! Will we not know ourselves guilty in some wise of the follies that attend us?"

Polidori sits back in satisfaction and places his fingertips together.

"That is all I have for now. I expect the rest of my tale to center upon these questions: Can Aubrey find a way to warn his sister of the vampire's intent without breaking his vow? Can Aubrey thwart such a beast?"

"Can he?" Claire breathes.

I confess I too wish to know.

"I think," Polidori hesitates, "the answer will be, he cannot."

"Oh, no!" cries Claire.

Polidori addresses her. "The sister must die and Aubrey will be left with nothing but a quest for revenge upon an unnatural being."

"Marvelous, marvelous," Byron says. "A vampyre, at once noble and monstrous, but desirous for all that! Though I have read other accounts of the vampyre, to combine the legendary being with a romantic hero is original, I think. Capital and well done, John!"

However, George Gordon Byron knows a good thing when he hears it and swoops. "I'll help you finish it and we'll publish under my name that the public might buy it supposing me the author, but you, John, shall reap considerable reward, for we shall split the profit."

Polidori's face is a study in contradiction. Joy at being so received, happiness at such an offer of support, and chagrin to find he will never know the applause of the audience.

Byron looks at us around the table. "Let us hope the days to come will bring inspiration for the rest of us."

I think, *Oh, that I might.*

Days pass in that summer of cold and rain. With each morning, I have nothing to report but my frustration. But one night when my mind can think no more, inspiration occurs.

I lie awake late, late listening to another storm approach through the valleys and gradually know my mind at work on an idea so vivid and of such power it leaves me nearly frantic to scratch it down on paper. Throwing on a wrapper, I rise and seek the writing desk in the study downstairs and sit stroking my lips with the feather of my quill.

Hours pass and my vision does not fade but grows stronger the more I write, until at last, my ideas are spun out, and dawn silvers the snow upon the peaks. "Oh, let it be good." I breathe over my pages, and run back to our room.

"Percy," I cry. Sliding between the covers and shaking him. "Wake up!"

"Oy! You're frozen!" He jerks away. "What o'clock?"

"Nearing five, my love. The lark sings."

He sweeps back his hair. "Say it is the nightingale, love." He groans. "I thought I felt you rise but a moment ago."

"Hours, so many hours ago." I lift my hands to show him my pages. "I have been visited by an idea for my story. Light a candle, love." That done, he returns to the covers of our bed and I rest my head upon his shoulder. "There, better." My smile broadens. "What would you say to this?"

Words spill out as though I am still held captive in the rapture of creation. As my tale emerges, he wraps an arm around me and goes still.

When I finish, he says, "It is horrible."

I laugh, falling back upon the pillow and kicking my legs into the air. "I hardly dared hope you'd say that."

And so began the most momentous years of my life, fraught with hope and despair, with tragedy and joy. And though I worked and struggled as my story fought to be born, I never knew how those years would end.

Chapter Twenty-Nine

Creation Takes More Than Seven Days

Percy and I descended to the morning room together well before the rest rose. Was this the same place, and were these the same furnishings as yesterday and all the days before? Did the light slant through the panes of the window as it always had? As the light strengthened, did I sense a new day dawning for me?

———————◇———————

Despite the early hour, the servants make up a fire to warm us and soon the kettles, one for tea and one for coffee, sing upon the hearth. Tapping my foot and biting my lip, I wait for the others to rise.

"Oh, why don't people wake up?"

Percy touches my knee. "All things in their time, dear. Coffee or tea?"

"Tea. I'm awake enough."

First to arrive is the soon-to-be-bested Polidori, who nods to us. "A scone I think," he tells the maid. "Is there coffee? I am abysmal."

I lower my head and look out through my lashes at him. *Good. He has been insufferable since he told his story.*

"I don't doubt it, Doctor," Percy chuckles merrily. "You imbibed as Neptune last night."

"Surly not Neptune, though I had cause." He smirks as he moans, holding his head. His recent victory makes him almost cordial. "Not Neptune, yet as the Cyclops says, 'Someone pissed in mine eye.'"

Claire stumbles in, still in her night shift and wrapper. "Do I smell coffee? Give me the pot."

Byron can wake the day after the most heroic of bouts looking as gay as a box of kittens. "Morning all!" the most genial of hosts bids us. "Everyone served?" He sips his tea, sighs with satisfaction, and then comes the daily inquisition. "What news my authors? What abominations have we?"

Percy tips me a wink. "Mary has something for us," he says, smiling.

I pause. I clear my throat, and then, "Last night, my story came to me as I lay awake listening to the storm approach. I thought of the lightning and one thought blended into another until I knew I found the subject of my story." *At last.* "I've not slept since that time. My pen could scarce keep up with the images that flowed unleashed from my brain to my hand." I rise clutching my pages. "Hear what I have written."

"Think you of the sound of an approaching storm and count the seconds between the flash of lightning and the sound of thunder as their intervals shorten. 'One, two, three,...'" Dazzling light forces entry into our rooms, limning the bedposts and the furniture.

"But now, hear a growing noise as of machinery whirring within the house. Step by the light from the brilliant flashes, cross the floor, and open the door to exit our chamber.

"Slashing rain upon the hallway window draws attention. Look out through the panes of a great window silvered by near incessant lightning. Flinch. Raise hands to shield eyes.

"All the while that whirring of diabolical machinery increases. Foreboding grips frigid fingers about hearts.

"Let there be light!

"O, for eyes to pierce the darkness inside the house. Only the lightning answers. There! The landscape outside seen by the flashes. Look out upon a leafless tree and know this night part of a dreary and cold November. Glimpse the full moon as she rides a midnight sky through the tattered and lightning-rent clouds.

"Sounding machinery calls us still.

"Tread a hallway bare of any carpet. At its end a stairway lifts. Step slow up to another door slightly ajar. Come closer and push it open until the scene is thrown before our eyes. We cross the threshold to stand in a stone room.

"Inside see a doctor, robed in a long coat of white. A chemist possessed of an awesome formula, the key to engendering life.

"Now, the untried master of the secret stands erect and lifts his eyes to a shuttered window set into the wall of the room. Lightning strikes from cloud to cloud above us. Brightness blazes between the cracks of the wooden slats and where the shutters are set into the frame as thunder rocks the very floor where we stand unable to flee. The scientist lifts his hands, palms upward, open and questing.

"Power! Raw and limitless! For centuries upon centuries, now dust upon desert sands, mankind has known how to deal death, but he alone of all men has wrested from the very universe the method to convey life!

"Astonishment that he alone possesses the secret of this scheme pulses through him with each beat of his heart. Is it the nearness of the bolts of energy or is it the force of his secret that trembles potently within his fingertips?

"Confidence sits upon his shoulders and whispers his cause is just. He has paid a fearful price for such knowledge, but though he knew not the cost when he began, had he known it, still would he gladly pay.

"He thinks of the year past that rolled away in twin states of anticipation and humiliation. Friends and family are forgotten. His best friend, his own father, and his fiancé languish for word from him while he, single-minded, pursued a chimera. Knowing this time as a needful solitude where none might see another failure, he passes the year alone in his efforts, alone in his anguish. All, all alone and friendless.

"As winter snow melts to spring he searches musty tomes for clues to his quest. May, June, July, and August spend themselves in the discovery of the proper location for his experiment and in the selecting and manufacture of the needed machinery. September fades away in steaming, unclean dissecting houses, but he must have flesh for use as sculptor's material. How terrible that cold damp labor! The smells of the charnel house became familiar as he sought the bones to form a frame. What fresh, warm corpses did he probe with profane fingers to find each organ? How selective he needs must have been? Larger is better, for it is easier to connect the conduits of the body. And then, what sheets of skin has he sewn to clothe the clay?

"And, Lo! The needed resources were found: a laboratory, equipment, and body. All as ready as his mind to challenge the unbending will of the ages! No other could know what feelings sweep him onward as he toils ever forward, shackled as though to the wings of a hurricane that ravages the seas.

"Exultation thrills within him, for he shall bring light where all is now darkness! Where now fester the moist swamps of ignorance, he shall raise lands of reason until they are mountains of enlightenment! Mankind shall achieve ascendancy from what he does this night! Again, he raises his grasping hands to the skies. He shall engender a new species—a new Prometheus to throw down older gods.

"He looks down upon the still form resting on the surface of the table that occupies the center of the room. No father has felt such pride! No father will ever know such gratitude as he shall claim from his creation!

"He lifts his eyes and gazes into a distance beyond these walls of stone and wood. What else might he dare? If he could he create life from these insensate bits of flesh mayhap he could restore life to the dead. So might mankind conquer time itself!

"But though he stands at the summit of his quest, he remembers times when he thought himself with his hand upon the very door of accomplishment only to suffer failure—the demolition of all his dreams and work, an hundred failures and another hundred more.

"Placing his wrist to his forehead, he feels a fever, his eyes burn, his skin is dry, his throat is raw, and his breath rasps hoarse. *I am unwell,* he thinks. In his labor, he has forgotten to care for his body. Yet even when he should be abed, thoughts of triumph bear him onward.

"His candle burns low. Another flash of lightning, another crash of thunder, and rain begins to fall, pounding against the slates outside the windows. With what hesitation does he place his hands upon the table made of rough wood that lies in the center of the room? He leans against it exhausted, worn from the expense of effort, but hopeful, eagerly anticipating success, yet fearing failure. The lines of his face are etched deep as the crevasses that rive a glacier. He bends his head over the table, inhaling the fetid odor fouling the room.

"It is time.

"He straightens.

"The noise of a powerful engine driving disks of glass between their electrical contacts surges. He attaches silvered electrodes to either side of his creation's chest and head. Another flair of lightning, another crash of thunder, the ultimate climax of the storm drives the machinery beyond its limits. With a jerk, he closes a switch and Galvanni's fluid imparts the spark to what lies beneath a sheet!

"A crackling. The form beneath the sheet convulses and arches, heel and head alone touching the wooden table. He stops.

"Nothing.

"Again the electricity pulses! In rising panic, he sends the impulse into the unaware flesh. Again! And once more, until at last the body beneath the sheet falls and lies still and unmoving. Until he despairs and slumps to the floor.

"Silence broken by the storm alone fills the room, but then...

"With a sibilant, 'ohhhh, unhhhhh,' the creature draws breath and, see! It stirs! Not the feeble and random jerks of the electrical trickster in the theater, not the wracked senseless thrashings of that stimulation. This is the purposeful movement of knowing itself.

"The scientist lifts his head. 'Life!' he whispers.

"He stands. 'LIFE!'"

———————————————⧓———————————————

Mouths agape and cups forgotten, they sat in silence, until, and at last, they applauded.

Chapter Thirty

First Draft

Byron was predictable. Once he declared the work had both merit and originality, he suggested that as provider of the impetus that engendered the work, he would be my editor and the resulting book should bear our names, his first, as co-authors.

Percy proved a lion, telling the man that he too had some small skill with a pen, therefore he would be the one to edit the material, "Not that Mary has much need of my help. As for ensuring publication, the inclusion of my name ought to be helpful. Her name, however, will stand alone as author."

Byron was courteous, but I could tell he was cheeked. "As you will, boy. I suppose, as this will be prose and not poetry, you should prove an adequate editor."

July brings no relief from the weather. We began to make jokes. "You may have any weather you wish," Percy says, standing on the front balcony with his afternoon cup of tea in hand. "As long as you wish for a cold rain."

Sunlight, such as it is, sweeps the room and warms a patch of floor so my toes revel in the unaccustomed sensation of heat. Willmouse clings to my fingers as I hold him so he may practice walking until we fall together on the Persian rug, and I hold him.

"Mary and the Christ child." I look up to see Claire sneering. "Is there a more perfect picture of motherhood?"

I am in far too good a mood to put up with her sniping. "If there is, I doubt she resides in this house."

She turns her attention to Will, holding out her hands to him. "There, Popkin. D'y' want to come to me?"

"Gubbr."

"Oh! Did y' hear? He said my name!"

She always has possessed the ability to see herself in a starring role no matter the situation. I decide not to fight with her. "As clear as could be. And 'Aunty Claire' at that."

Claire, sensing a truce in the air, sits next to us and puts her hand over Will's eyes. "Where's a baby? POP!"

Oh good for Will. He gurgles a laugh, and can anyone resist a baby's laugh? We sit and play with him for a time and that is enough.

"D'y' have nothing better to do?" She lifts her chin toward my desk.

"Nothing pressing. With the men off to the mountains for a second day, there is little to copy. I've been working on my story."

She straightens. "How is that coming?"

"Some days are better than others." I hand Will to her and recline to look up at the carved wood ceilings.

"With this story, I think the creature must become a man in all senses." I pause. "Oh, but he has so much to learn. Like Willmouse, he must learn to speak, and to read and converse. So much and yet, I have only so few pages finished. And I keep thinking of the rest of the plot."

She does not glance up from making faces at the baby. "And how does it go today?"

"Well." I pause to put my thoughts together, which in truth are never far from this project. "I think he is unjustly rejected by all men. They see a monster; however, the creature is a paragon in thought, strength, and endurance. His body, riven by scars and discolored, is yet vastly superior to normal men."

"A noble savage?"

"I did think of that, but more. The creature possesses the ability to endure the effects of weather, thirst does not ravage him, hunger does not assail him, he can run faster and farther than a normal man." Claire's attention is gone from me as she waggles her fingers at Will. "The scientist, having given life to the creature, must now be surprised at an unintended result. Think of the chamber where he imparts life to the creature. His purpose attained, he shouts to the very heavens, 'HE LIVES!' Our scientist scrabbles to the head of the board and pulls the sheet away. There lies his creation but now he screams, 'Oh horrible! Oh horrible! Oh most horrible!'

"The experiment has changed the flesh. He sees perfection of form he sought. The creature is gigantic in stature! Its limbs and torso lie in perfect proportion to his massive size, his hair, long, flowing, and black, his teeth, pearls of white.

"Now our scientist confronts another truth: each piece of this being serves in terrible contrast to the whole! The skin that he sought to cover the creature in rosy splendor has turned a jaundiced yellow and, stretched beyond its natural elasticity, the veins and arteries may be seen as they pulse below the sheath. The lips, rather than full and red, are straight and black as they frame its mouth. Eyes flicker open to show irises of animal gold.

"All his effort, his labor, bent to the pinnacle of perfection are thrown down from the heights in this monstrous parody of man."

Claire watches me with her mouth agape. "Yes. That is a true horror. Well then, what does he do with this parody?"

"I think he abandons him to whatever mercies the world may show."

She raises her eyebrows. "Good luck with that. Now, Willie, Phoo, Phoo, da baby!"

I labor as though I never wrote before in the days to come. A thousand questions and stray thoughts assail me. By August, my work begins to take shape.

I ask Percy, "Do you have time to review my pages?"

"I wondered if you had stayed with it."

"Stayed with it? I cannot put it down. Here."

For a time, he perches upon the settee, sipping from his cup and absently nibbling a biscuit, but as I watch, his motions slow, the cup in his hand rises half the way to his lips and no more. He sets nosh and drink aside and uses both hands to hold the pages. He stands and seeks a window where he might read in the light. Until, at last, he swivels to me and says, "Abandon this story."

"What?" I cry.

"Abandon the story if it is still your intention to produce a short work. This must be a novel in its own right. You've a depth here. If you've not grown too weary of the writing you must develop it."

I wake, if lying abed and not sleeping for hours can be said to wake. I turn to the laudanum more often to get sleep these days. "Percy?"

"Hmmf?" A murmur from beneath his pillow as he sleeps on his side facing away from me. I place my hand on his hip and, gently, shake him.

"Are you awake?"

"No."

"None of that. I've had an idea."

"Good for you. Write it down and go back to sleep."

He rolls onto his back and stretches his arm behind my back. I sigh laying my head upon his shoulder. "Just listen..."

When at last I wind down, he mutters, "Hear me, love. Write it down lest you lose it."

But my vision spent, I am too drowsy to get up. "That is too much trouble, and there's no need. The thought is so profound I doubt I shall be able to forget it."

He was right. By breakfast, the thoughts have flown.

"Fie! Such waste!"

"Do what I do, Mary. When I have an idea in the night and cannot remember it in the morning," his smile is tender, "pretend it was no good."

Small pieces of paper with scribbled hieroglyphics litter our bed chamber from then on.

Days pass while I sit by the desk in our little cottage, thinking and composing. One morning, my body goes rigid with the shock of discovery. *I have found it. A shift no one will see coming.*

My surprise to readers who expect the Creator Myth is this: instead of the Pygmalion falling in love with Galatea, here the sculptor rejects his creation. Percy seeks a hero, but My creature becomes a metaphor for the pain of rejection and it bends its will toward revenge. I must change the point of view to that of the man who engendered a monster.

When my notes are committed to paper to keep them from escaping, I rush through the cottage seeking someone to show my pages to. Claire is sitting before the fire playing with Willmouse.

"Claire," I thrust the pages at her. "Read this."

"Again?" But she sighs. "Hold the baby."

She lifts her eyes to mine when she finishes reading. "If the creature must learn to survive and to communicate, perhaps he might find a family who could take him in."

"No, that won't work. I want him to be too hideous for anyone to aid him."

"Give me William." She holds her hands out for my boy and places him over her shoulder while she thinks. "Could he hide in a nearby cave or a disused outbuilding where he might overhear and watch a family? That way they would be unaware of him."

"Perhaps he might abide in a wood shed attached to the home." I stroke my thumb over my lower lip. "In this wise does he learn to speak, and perhaps to read. Then, when he is discovered, their reaction must be the most extreme. They must drive him away with fire and stones!"

"Why?"

"No man must tolerate him, no woman love him. In all he finds, there will be no acceptance. Once the monster learns to speak and read, he turns the knowledge gained to attack his creator."

"Oh, you use the Lucifer story of knowledge and desire to become greater than his maker."

"I seek to echo it, sure. In seeking vengeance, the monster devises a plan to kill all those Victor loves before taking his life."

"That is the scientist's name?"

I nod while I think. "Yes, Victor. Reflective for triumph, is it not?"

"Heavy handed though. What shall be the monster's name?"

"I have a notion never to name it."

William fusses and Claire picks him up. "Don't stop." She cradles him and rocks him against her body to keep him quiet. "I'm listening. The monster is an abomination, this being of mismatched parts, intended to be beautiful, but hideous to behold, and beloved by none. Can you carry it off?"

Rising, I step to my desk and take up the pages where I wrote the scene of creation. I read aloud. "It was on a dreary night in November that I beheld my man completed…" I stop and close my eyes, seeing the chamber at the top of the house. "I am consumed by this story. Even now it unleashes a thrill of fear in me. Can I carry it off?" I shake my head. "I cannot stop." I look out the window where it has begun to rain, again. "But I do not know the ending any more than I know my own."

In mid-July, Percy finds me in my usual spot sitting at my desk by the window and, stepping quietly behind, he bends over and says softly in my ear, "You have grown pale, Mary. I fear your tale is wagging you."

"I cannot sleep lest I have my drops."

He straightens and says, "Byron goes to Geneva for a few days. What would you say if I could show you a sight that will take your mind off monsters? I propose a trip to Chamounix to ascend the mountain there far enough to view the Mer de Glace." He rolls the words out like a barker at a fair in hopes of finding an easy mark.

He's judged me aright. I lift my face to his and smile. "I am for you."

"Good. It's settled."

"When do we leave?" Claire calls from the doorway.

We stand upon the outcrop of rock where our guide leads us. I take the final steps toward its edge like a dreamer. There before me, like a white ribbon that has sliced into a darkened rock, lies the River of Ice winding from the heights.

Jean, our French guide, says, "Three glaciers flow and meet to form thees mighty revere. So far above us, the confluence ees lost in the clouds zeese day, though they may be seen on a clear morning." He sweeps his hand across the horizon. "Zere are at least seven glaciers near Chamounix, but ze Ice River eez ze greatest of all. Behold, zee source of Viking legends regarding the end of ze world."

"Poetic license," murmurs Percy.

Claire and I are swathed in layers of clothes. Huge boots laced over wool stockings are drowned in wide woolen pantaloons that are, in turn, covered by our long tweed skirts. A freezing wind blows from the highlands toward the base of the mountain and drifts up to where we stand, making our skirts press against our legs and flap behind us. Thick shirts worn under thicker jackets warm our shoulders. Hats pinned to our hair are tied with scarves under our chins to hold them on against the strong valley winds. We are become mountaineers with coils of rope looped over one of our shoulders and hanging down below our hips.

"They're heavy," Claire complains.

"You weel need zem latair." Jean arranges the coil where it falls between Clair's breasts with much care. She ignores him, leaning toward the ice as though intent on seeing a wonder.

As we climb we see riven, frozen blocks and smooth clean sections. I know I have found one of those places of the world the common people call, "spirit-touched." During a rest, I stand stock-still, letting the ice fill my imagination. I turn to Percy, who brings up the rear of our little roped-together party to where I stand atop a large block of ice. "You glow," Percy says, looking down at me.

My chest heaves as my lungs struggle to compensate for my excitement in the thin air. "Do you see? Here, or some place very like this, the end of the world, is where I shall set my story."

His head comes up and he looks around. He nods, and slits his eyes against the glare of the sun coming off the glacier. "Stark. Dramatic. Ice and snow, blocks and field." He nods. "'Twill serve."

We make it back to our little cottage barely before the end of July. All I am ready for is a bath and bed, but shortly after Claire skips out of the door to run up to Diodati, Polidori arrives. Byron wishes a report. We have little choice but to attend to his lordship. Accordingly, I swipe myself with a damp cloth, dress, and trudge to the villa for a late supper.

The food, despite my intention to hold to the vegetables, is heavy. All I can think of is how I am so tired, the skin beneath my eyes pulls downward. I leave it to Percy and Claire to speak of the journey. There is barely time for the draft George pours for me before my eyes close. I swear only a moment flies by, but I am rudely shaken. I open my eyes to see our host peering down at me. "Get this one to bed, Percy." He chuckles as he smiles at me. "And I'll do the same with the other."

Throughout August, I work on my first draft, extending the story and making improvements as I go.

"Percy, I've named my hero."

"I thought his name was Victor; it fits him."

"I mean his surname. Can you call to mind the castles we passed on our voyage home?"

"Our six weeks adventure?" He looks up at the candle on the table next to him. "D'y' mean the rock with the ruined castle, Drachenfels?"

"Another. There was one at some remove; we could not see it, though you spoke its name. Frankenstein. I'll call the scientist Victor Frankenstein. Most appropriate."

"Why is that fitting?"

"The Jew man created the Gollum, and so I shall have a Jew give life to my creature." I am sure there will be those who understand, but the name is only a drop in the well of my imagination this day. "I left off telling you of the creature forces Victor to create for him a mate who would not be aghast at his visage. When Victor refuses his demand, the creature vows to wreak havoc on his creator's life by killing all those Victor loves."

Percy nods from where he sits with his journal on his lap. "A ghastly fate."

"The trick is for the monster to destroy these victims before the scientist can kill him." I brush my lips with the feathered end of my quill. "Now begins a reversal of roles for my characters, the hunted turns hunter. I think once the creature accomplishes his destructive goal, Frankenstein will swear revenge on the monster. He chases his creation with the intent to kill, and the monster flees with the intent to draw Victor to such extremes of exhaustion he too will die."

"You manage one horror only to find a worse." Percy's eyes are wells of blackness in the candlelight. "Mary, are you well?"

"I hardly sleep, but whether with residual terror of what I can conceive or from wonder, I know not. I find distractions to lighten my mind. I play with the baby, I talk with Byron, he has me review his new poem, the one he calls *Manfred*," I spare a smile for Percy, "And I copy and comment upon your masterpieces, *Mont Blanc* and *Prometheus Unbound*, but I cannot cease this story, Percy."

There is plenty of time to write. I soar as I seek an end for my story. I despair at how crude my words seem a day after I write them.

"It's little more than an outline, love." Percy rubs my shoulders after I fling yet another page into the fire. "Not even a full first draft. You'll get it if you just do not quit."

"Percy, can you bring to mind where I would place the climax?"

"I thought you said a glacier?"

"That has changed. Once I heard story from a whaler of Dundee. He spoke of the ice fields of the far north. Were I to set my story there amid the shifting floes, it would give more of a feeling of separation than even the glaciers of Switzerland."

"Indeed, and thus strengthen the notion of extreme pursuit."

"But there is more. I've in mind a device. Once I learned how to create a frame for my work, reflecting as though between two mirrors the opening setting and the end. And I might have a dialog, such as the ones you use in your work, between a whaler and the monster that begins and ends the piece and so places the reader aboard a vessel trapped in the ice."

"I believe you ought to try it. See how it goes."

My heart beats. My breath comes fast. "Oh, but this is exciting."

A mirror, a frame, bookends, what have you, a device by which one can bind the beginning and the end of a tale. As though saying two girls enter the woods to start a story and ending with the girls as they exit the forest. Easy when you know how, and a trick that lets the audience breathe and sigh with the satisfaction of entering the world after passing through a time of troubles. Baxter taught me that device, how long ago? Four or five years, was it? Beneath the pines that bordered the view of the Tay as I sat upon a carpet of needles dressed in the stiff twill skirt of a naturalist. I'll say it now. Despite their betrayal, which was not far wrong, I miss them, Christian and Isobel, and their father. There is where my fancies first took flight.

Oh, and I remember how my heart beat so hard when I wrote. It does not fade: The thrill of creation remains sharp no matter how many times I feel it.

Chapter Thirty-One

We Fall from Grace

An excellent analogy for life: a series of mountains and valleys.

I climb rocky heights that touch the sky, only to fall into the darkness of vales unseen. Do others feel the rush of rising ambition and breathless falls from overachievement as do I?

I think it was at Geneva that I began to recognize the signs that presage humiliation. On a morning when the interminable cold rains again slash the windows, Claire made an announcement, but hardly the one for which she had hoped.

Percy and I are alone in our bed when a small knock sounds on our door. He rises and strides across the carpet. "Yes?"

"Percy?" Claire's voice trembles. "May I enter?"

My sister has never been so polite. More likely are the times when, without knocking, she bursts into our chamber no matter how we are engaged. I nod for him to open the door.

She comes to us clothed in only a shift. "Came you from Diodati so?" She nods and takes hesitant steps toward our bed. Her eyes are red and pouched. *She's been crying,* I think, *and for some time. What has occurred?*

I throw back the covers. "Come sister. Be warm between us. Percy? Get in." We fit against each other though there is little room. As we hold her, she begins crying in earnest. *Is this another of her hysterics?* An uncharitable thought, as it turns out. The matter emerges amid sobbing hiccoughs.

"I am with child."

Byron's response when Percy and Claire go to him with the news is less than paternal. An hour goes by before they return to our cottage.

"She's gone to another room." He's trembling and short of speech as he paces the floor. And then it bursts, "I could scarce credit an educated man, and a poet of his renown, able to spew the invective he unleashed upon," he looks to me, "us."

I shrug. "He does have a command of the language."

He stops and turns a frown to me, his eyes like cold glass. "He began his abuse by asking, 'Is the brat mine?' I straightened, ready to give as well as he gave. "'The brat" can be no other's, George.'

"'What proof?'

"'She was not pregnant when we left England, and well before that time, she honed herself for you alone. Since we arrived you have been her only partner. How do you propose to care for your child?' I asked him."

"A worthy riposte." I smile.

"But no *touché*. He changed the subject in order to insult us this time, d'you believe it? He had the infernal gall to declare he did not want the baby to be raised in the bohemian house of Shelley."

"No! The man is no more pure than London snow. Did he offer anything other than calumny?"

I've seldom seen Percy sputter with rage, but he cannot speak until he crosses the room to pick up a decanter of whiskey and fill a glass. He downs the great draft in one long drink and tosses his head as he shudders. "George said, 'My sister will care for the child.'"

"O sweet sanctimonious pretender. How is his lifestyle superior to yours? Though you have not lain with your sister, you've had mine."

One eyebrow lifts, as he quirks his mouth into a rueful smile. "I mentioned something quite like that, though with a different emphasis. His response was to purple and swell. Claire ran from the room in tears at this, but I continued to fight him. 'Fear not the expense, your lordship. I shall settle money on both your publicly known mistress and your child.'"

'Tis woman's bane. Though men might swear love for us in the night, we bear the responsibility alone during the day. That thought causes me to swallow hard. My flow is overdue, but now is hardly the time to mention it.

Had Percy not been so taken aback by the great lord, he might have spoken with more care in trying to gain Byron's support for Claire. As it was, Byron assumed the role of the injured party, blaming Claire, and me, and Percy, and the sky, and the lake, and...as things lie, Byron is sure to sulk and Percy is angry. You'd have thought they had gotten each other pregnant.

George avoids our party, sending a note to us that, "This day is not conducive to company." But he also sends pages from his poem, *Manfred*, to me along with a curt request for review and comment.

About a week later, we are summoned to join the lord for dinner. The servant, a model of reticence, shows us in saying only, "Milord is already in the dining area awaiting you. Please, follow me."

Dinner conversation is stilted. "How have you been?" addressed to me.

"Well. Busy with my book."

"Do you have my pages? Pass the fish."

An interminable time later, we retire to the sitting room. *The chairs before the fire have been rearranged,* I think as we enter. A semicircle still, but the chairs reflect a new reality. Mine is now next to Byron, separating Percy from him. And my sister? Her status reflects her place, which could not be farther from her lord.

What passes is Byron has thought of a plan regarding his incipient fatherhood. He begins by addressing Percy as though my sister and I do not exist.

"I'll make arrangements for the child's care though I have no wish to see it."

An improvement on the whole, I think. But if I hoped for maturity, I was mistaken.

"You and Mary must accept your sister's bastard into your home, should it live. In three or four years' time, you may bring it to Naples. I shall have someone deliver it to me." He raises his head and all the arrogance the man possesses goes into his next statement. "I wish no more of you."

And Percy says, "As I hold the lease upon our cottage, we shall leave at our pleasure, not yours."

Two days later, Percy, Claire, and I meet with his lordship to further negotiate the paternity. Byron manages to communicate with us how he is the wronged party. Did he not agree to be our host? Has he not been free with his time and skill with Percy? Will I not acknowledge the debt I owe for his tutelage? He says the least Percy and I can do is to review his pages in a timely manner when requested. It is late August, and my nineteenth birthday passes unmarked.

Despite what he has already done to her, the humiliation Byron heaps on my sister is only begun. Percy returns from a meeting with George with a list of requirements.

"He says, 'That girl is to provide care for her baby and maintain her silence as to the brat's parentage. She will tell people she is the baby's aunt.'" Percy shakes his head. "The man had the effrontery to try to enlist me by saying this way Claire might save two reputations, his and mine.

"When I insisted Byron eventually take over care for the child, the man turned it back upon us as though we would steal the child from its lawful father. Another wrinkle, he says we must agree to surrender the child whenever we are asked.

"He never gave a damn for the other children he fathered, but let someone stand for the babe and the man wills himself to become the paragon of fathers, saying he would come to the aid of the poor child as soon as it is no longer in need of essential mothering by my 'concubines.'"

In mid-September, there is no more to hold us on the shores of Lake Geneva. Claire occupies her days by weeping and composing long, agonized letters to the Lord of Diodati. Byron, to his credit, visits us on the day we leave to bid us farewell, but if he is cold to us, he is frozen to Claire. Turning to me he says, "Do you keep writing, Mary. You may have a talent, and I'd not like for my efforts with you to be wasted."

I occupy the days with my little book. The pages of my story go with us to London. Although I had envisioned but a short story like the ones we read round the fire at Diodati, my work has so progressed I determine to follow Percy's advice and make a novel of it.

I'm considering other settings as the story unfolds; my notebooks show how often I change the line of the plot. I've need of some structure to help me order my scattered scenes. Sudden revelation claims me.

And that night after supper I cry, "Oh Percy, I have it!" in joy and dance toward him with pages in my inky hand. "Look you, love. I'll set my tale aboard a ship all frozen in the ice! And have a race between the creator and the created in dog sleds of the Esquimeaux. It is a race of deadly earnest."

He thinks a moment and says, "Also you present a battle of nature and man with the reader left to contemplate which shall prevail. Excellent, Mary."

Though safe in London, far from the turmoil of Geneva, finding the quiet to write proves elusive.

A pounding on the door wakes us yet another morning.

"Must they begin at dawn?" groans Percy, getting out of bed. He touches aside the lace from our window and peers out at the street below. "And must the maid always allow them to stand upon our doorstep? A new record, Mary. I believe three men have arrived at once this day." He lets them stay outdoors as we dress.

"I have a plan," he says as we sit to table and sip coffee and tea while the sun climbs over the trees of the park opposite our house. "I'll walk abroad in town to show the creditors I do not fear either them or their tactics."

"But, dear, that is not our solitary care. There is one worse, Claire."

"Claire." He looks down. "As she swells she adds fuel to fires that are the gossips, and we've not the finances to send her to the country again."

Another pounding on our door causes him to turn his head toward the entry. "The ire of the righteous. I've yet to tell you of recent incidents. Twice, as I walked the streets, someone has called an insult within my hearing, and once a woman spat upon my shadow. I fear the gossips from Geneva have transmitted their filth to London. I suppose we shall have to remove, though I do love this house."

"You are not alone in that."

"Though I still do not care for their approval or censure, I must admit, these attempts to shame us have found the mark. Oh Mary, I would that we might display the innocent children who are but the result of love," he glances at my waist, "however, one pregnant odalisque results in more than sufficient gossip, and two? Two would produce an alp of approbation. I fear we must house Claire elsewhere than with us."

I sigh as I reach to touch his hand. "What has happened to not caring what the world may think of us as long as our love is true?"

"The world turned while we ignored it." He straightens and smiles down on me. "Fear not. All will be well."

But our situation is far from well. That very day, the Bailiffs arrive to evict 'Shelley, et al.' and to seize our possessions. We are forced to watch as our treasures are thrown into wagons and carted away.

"Oh, not the little china figurines," moans Claire. "Not my silver-framed miniature."

It requires but two hours to empty the house and put us on the street in the clothes we are wearing. We are without so much as a roof to cover us from the rain and must seek friends to house us.

Another week passes and Percy returns. "We'll remove to Bath," he says. "The tourist season is over and the elite will have vacated the town: no one goes there at this time of year! Rents are negligible. No dunning for bills, no fears of the tipstaff, no gossips following us about to scandalize us. I've found two homes in the center of town so though you keep separate quarters, you two may still be close to the theaters, the lecture halls, and the library, thus you can entertain yourselves while I carry on the fight here."

"I fear we cannot do otherwise."

And so we remove to two homes in Bath in a good section of town and well appointed. I am to reside across the street from the Abbey Churchyard. Wide walks and the shops in town are most convenient. From the second floor, I see the ladies of Bath passing to and fro visiting one another. Claire enters and steps to the window with me. "Mary, look at this fabric." She's been to the dressmaker's again. "Silk, no less, the color of a summer forest."

"It is beautiful, sister, but can we afford it?"

"How can we not?" She lifts her chin toward the window. "I'll not give the Biddies of Bath the satisfaction of looking like a tramp."

An odd thing is occurring. We no longer resent each other. Perhaps it is because Claire, to all appearances, has given over her quest for Percy, preferring to spend all her efforts to win back Byron. She composes long letters filled with her misery at being separated from him. *Yes. That is the way to win a man. Beg him with tales of woe.* But I encourage her nay-the-less. What else does she have?

Percy returns to us as often as he may between sessions with his solicitors and appearances at court. His new editor, Leigh Hunt, and his editor's wife keep him.

"Have a care for your sister, Mary," he tells me in a letter. "She needs help with the coming baby."

With some heat I think, *And I do not?* I am tired and there are things I'll have him know. I write, "Honestly, you simply refuse to see what is in front of you. I am as alone as she. I am as pregnant as she. I am as in need of comfort as she."

His return admonishes me. "But Claire does not have the security we two share. She is worried that she will be abandoned. That the baby is not mine is beyond doubt. The dates do not match. Should I throw her over, as Byron has done, though she will not admit it, she will be without any resource."

She is hardly alone in that, too. I sit up straight and take up my pen. "You have a habit of finding women in distress and forgetting the ones you have rescued. Did you not save Harriet, and, once she was away from her father, did you not pay court to me? Look where that led. Harriet alone, and pregnant with your child, and me far away from you." My eyes fill. "I lade my days with work rather than write foolish letters to an absent love, but do not think my yearning for you is less. Yes, I have my work, the first draft is done. I am polishing my Latin that I may read the philosophy of those ancients in the original, but...I think of you each day. Do you think of the times we had in Switzerland? Do you see in your memory the shining peaks and the wooded vales? Where are those bright discussions we knew in Diodati when ideas rocketed toward the sky, or even..." I pause before I finish my thought. "Or even as I miss your touch. An imagination and an empty bed is still an empty bed."

By the next post he writes, "I swear, it will be well."

When? I would not be pitiful, but I want so much to cling to him, my spite erupts. "Attend Claire. I have my story to finish."

I write incessantly in our little home in Bath. In spite of dealing with solicitors, Percy publishes two works during the time I toil. *The work. The work is all. The work.* Percy takes my pages with him to review them, making suggestion after suggestion. He rewrites what I have done and substitutes his own. Where I write, "hot," he writes, "inflamed." Where I set down, "it was a long time," he says, "a considerable period elapsed." Saying, "It's just that you're a little bald here, my love. A touch of style, similar to what I've written for you, ah just, here I think, and your audience will thrill all the more."

His corrections shift the tone of my work the way a path in the wood diverges. But I comfort myself that though one route visits the depths of the glades and meadows and the other the banks of a stream, their tracks still wend through the same forest. I know he means well, and I do not mind his input, as his words have a polish mine lack. I see no reason to omit his additions and so leave them.

He is Shelley, after all, but I fear my manuscript resembles the pieced-together being who is my subject.

Through it all, I learn and learn from the experience of an author of long works greater than any I had undertaken heretofore. How will it end? With death, as all good horror stories ought.

Claire writes as well. She shows me her impassioned letters to Byron.

> *I shall do whatever you desire, loving you all the while for the*
> *rest of my life.*

Though sisterly love has rekindled between us, I think of Claire as a morality play where a woman can be impregnated and left at the convenience of men. Father cast me away because I rejected him for Percy. But where I turned away from him fearing where our love might lead and for no other reason, his rebuff was personal.

Thinking of Father, I remember him saying, "All authors must have a purpose, all works a message, lest the results be mere entertainment." I lift my quill and run the feather over my lips. I'll show my audience the consequences of discarding human beings. Let me write the havoc, the chaos, of a world without mothers.

October comes, and with it, a blow falls like a sword into my heart.

Time and again sister Fanny writes to me. How difficult it is to resist her pleading and my selfish refusal to allow her sanctuary. In her letters, she tells me that far from becoming gentle with age or wisdom, Stepmother grows ever uglier, ever worse. Fan writes,

> *There are nearly no servants now, and Mother says I must take*
> *up their work as well as my own. Oh Mary, there is so little food.*
> *Mother commands me not to eat so much, saying I am much*
> *to blame.*
>
> *Our Aunts in Ireland say I may not reside with them no matter*
> *what I tell them of the condition of our home. They say I am*
> *tainted by you and Shelley and my being there would occasion*
> *speculation of their morality. If you and Shelley do not let me*
> *reside with you...I will be away at any cost.*

Father makes it worse by putting her in the middle of the fight between him and me.

Father says to remind you of Percy's promise of support. He says
he may not write philosophy while the menial tasks of publishing
other writers' work occupies him.

Percy hears from her, too.

I chanced (at least it was chance on my part) upon your sister
Fanny. She begged me with tears in her eyes and a quaver in her
voice that she might live with us.

I do not want her here, selfish harpy that I am; I think one sister to vie for Percy's affections is enough, and I do not wish to repeat my mistakes by giving Fanny the chance to take Claire's place. I write a plausible excuse to Percy.

Claire's pregnancy must be secret and you know how Fanny talks.

Then comes a letter from Fanny posted from Bristol saying she has run off.

There appears no road for me, no home, no love. I know not
what I shall do.

A premonition strikes. Desperation will make her mad. I send a note to Percy by the next post telling him to come to me as soon as he may. He must catch some of my concern from my words, as he arrives faster than I can credit the next morning. I give him the letter along with my thoughts.

"What's to do?" I ask.

"Remain here while I look into this as best as I might."

"I ought to go."

"No, love. You must care for Willmouse and the new baby. I shall journey rough and fast, for I intend to take the post-chaise to Bristol to learn what I may. It leaves in an hour."

A day later, I receive Percy's hastily scrawled note.

I inquired at several inns and learned a young woman was there,
but she left for Swansea. They said I was not the only one to inquire
after her. From their descriptions, I think your father arrived in
Bristol before me. Perhaps she sent a note to him as well.

That's likely. I could see her imitating me by putting a note on the mantle before she left.

Two days later, I receive a letter from Father.

Breaking the seal, I learn of Fanny's death with my foot frozen upon the first step to my house. My legs give way and I sit on the stoop, heedless of passersby.

Go not to Swansea, disturb not the silent dead; do nothing to destroy the obscurity she so much desired.

How shocking it is to open a door to see tragedy in the form of a loved one.

Percy's shoulders slump as he stands on the threshold. "I discovered her." His voice croaks and deep etched lines cover his face. Travel-rumpled clothes, stains of hasty meals, and the smell of someone too long on the road without care surround him. I get him into the front room, tenderly ensconce him in the big chair, and ring for the maid.

"A pitcher of water as quickly as you can bring it," I tell her.

"Brandy." A weak gasp.

I wait in silence, stroking his temples until she returns and he can fortify himself. At last, he tells me the story.

"As we thought, your father found her first. The inn-keep told me the story without my having to give my name.

"He said, 'It's been a circus 'ere, gov'ner, I'll tell you 'at. A right seven-day wonder, y'moigt say. Not ever' day a woman dies in the Mackworth Arms, it ain't. But custom near overflows, so some good come of it.

"'She come on 'er own past sunset tellin' th' missus she din't want nothing but the room. Missus says there was a look about 'er.

"'Th' next day, she don't show for brekky, nor dinner neither, so I goes to 'er room and knocks, cause I runs a decent establishment, only I don't 'ear nothin'. I goes in and stops cold.

"'She's layin' cross the bed sideways and startin' ter smell. I looked around and sees naught but the girl, a medcin' bottle on the floor, and a note, but I don't touch nothin'. I closes the door and locks it and calls the law, but y'knows what happin's afore the law comes? A gent arrives askin' the question you done. I shows him up and lets 'im in thinkin', *here be the cause of 'er fearin',* and I'd best not anger the bloke. 'E gives me a sixpence, and shuts the door. I leaves 'im be and goes to fetch the constable, but when I get back, there's none but the dead.'"

"Oh, my sister. What an end."

"Only a little more," Percy's voice is near a whisper now. "The talk of the town said the law could not deduce her name, but that she was wearing an old corset with the initials M.W. stitched on it."

"Oh!" I put my knuckles to my mouth.

"What? Does that mean something to you?"

I nod. "It was Mother's. It's true then, Fan is dead."

"I believe your father carried away anything that might have identified her. The coroner wrote, in lack of evidence to the contrary, her death is ruled accidental rather than a suicide."

"I see Stepmother's hand in that. She must have instructed father before he left to eschew knowledge of Fanny should the worst have occurred." I think a moment. "Yes. That way the family Godwin is spared the shame should her death be ruled a suicide. But should we not inform the law?"

He takes my hand. "Mary, think. There is too much calumny heaped upon our names. No, we cannot be part of this."

What no one knows is that I was the one who told her Laudanum had great beneficial effects for sleep. She must have needed sleep so very badly to escape a life she could not stand.

My sister, who I loved, lies for all time in Potter's Field with no stone to mark her. My only solace: at least it was a quiet death.

One more stick in the fire. Harriet's solicitors are now importuning Percy for additional money.

He peers into my face. "Are you well, my love?"

"Has it ever occurred to you that, like a muscle o're-strained through unaccustomed exercise, one's brain may feel most heartily abused? I cannot write. My thoughts are thick, yet my desire to continue to compose does not diminish."

"Are you sleeping well? I felt you rise twice in the night."

"I'm experiencing a repeating nightmare. I walk through a castle, at least I conceive the building to be so. As I walk I'm searching, searching for something I wanted but cannot find. Up long staircases, weary unto collapse but no closer to my goal. On and on until I discover I am in a place where I cannot continue, some precipitous height." I fall silent. "And then I jump."

"It is the writer's curse. I have friends who say something like this. You seek the triumph of publication." He hugs my shoulders. "It will pass when you find yourself in print."

November slides away. That is almost all that can be said for so cold and lonely a month. My worry and despair continue and color my letters to him in London.

I Love you Percy, and not only because you are all that keeps me
from Fanny's fate. Take this copy and make suggestions, that I
might delve all the deeper.

December comes and with it come Percy's comments on the book. There are so many. He's rewritten some passages, added some paragraphs of his own making. *Will these words so different from my own distract readers?* When I say, "I beheld my man completed," he writes, "I beheld the accomplishments of my toils." And that is far, far from the only change he makes.

Then there are ideas he inserts.

"Mary, I sense a lack in your fourth chapter. Can you call to mind my stories of Paracelsus and Agrippa? They have great influence on science, and, as your work has as much to do with science as it does with philosophy they ought, therefore, to be mentioned."

Does he wish to create himself in me?

Throughout early December as I try to write, distractions continue: before I can find my balance from Fanny's loss, another stroke falls.

One mid-December day, I work in a back room of the second floor—I favor for the ivory-colored walls that reflect a soft indirect sun. I glance up when Percy enters with the mail. I see him peal the seal, open the page, and grow silent and still. *Something untoward, then.*

"Oh, ye Gods! What more can you do to me?" He drops the paper and covers his eyes. I cross the room to retrieve the note. It is from Percy's bookseller, Thomas Hookham, a trusted friend.

I'm sorry to say your wife is dead, and dead apparently by her
own hand. She was found floating in the Serpentine...

I call to mind that pleasant curved channel in Hyde Park and Kensington Gardens fed by the Westbourne, where courting couples boat between the dim tree-lined banks as they pass beneath ornamented bridges.

There is no doubt this is a suicide. She was found with a note to
her father. An investigation of her body is to be performed soon.

Autopsy he means, that peculiar indignity inflicted to discover causes for the untimely death upon those unfortunates who end their own lives.

"I'll have your boxes packed," I say. You'll return to London as soon as you wish."

He's in shock. Though we noted a lack of correspondence from Harriet this fall, what there was concerned few words of his children and more of her need for money. There was gossip about the men in her life being people of no consequence.

Percy leaves that very afternoon. "I'll write, Mary. And I'll return as soon as I can."

The autopsy is finished; the ghouls put up their knives. Her suitor,
a lowborn person of no estate, threw her over when he learned
Harriet was pregnant with his child.

Already unsure of my situation, I am undone by her death. Pregnant and cast off? My brains conjure fantasies. Did she suffer at the end, as she must have all the days before her walk toward the bridge? Was she, as Ophelia, borne up by her skirts, mermaid-like, before her garments, heavy with their drink, pull the poor wretch into the mud? How close is this to me? How many women, seeing no other resort, kill themselves rather than suffer the despair of love lost or the slings and arrows of the righteous who would shame them? Even my own dear mother attempted to end her life one time. *Ah, Father, in loving her, you earned my love no matter what came later.*

When I read what Percy has sent, I shudder and write to Claire:

Unfair world that makes outcasts of children because of an accident
of birth. You deserve not to be ostracized for loving Byron any
more than I for loving Percy. Sister, I would not have you end
as Fanny or Harriet.

Claire responds by the next post.

Fear not for me. While I believe suicide is the only logical solution
to a situation where life becomes intolerable, I'll not tread that
particular road to hell.

My response is immediate.

Should life be but a continual accumulation of anguish, it is still
dear to me and I shall defend it.

Call it a pact between us with no force other than our will, but I feel better for it.

Almost the moment Percy returns to Bath, a letter from his solicitor informs him Harriet's parents, the Westbrooks, are suing for custody of his children. When Percy rushes to London to claim his children, he is as roughly rebuffed by her parents. Harriet's father tells him he is, "…a lunatic to think we would allow someone like you and the slut who seduced you away from our daughter to take our grandchildren?" He is further abused by the courts who deny the natural father his right to his children.

We learn such a finding requires ironclad proof of his failings as a father. The judges' ruling tells us much about how damaged is his reputation.

A parallel can be found in these two deaths. Both Fanny and Harriet died thinking there was no succor. Fanny poisoned herself of despair. Harriet threw herself into the Serpentine and drowned, past caring that she took her unborn child below the waters.

So, in the late months of that long ago year, one death lay at my feet and another at Percy's. Such a thing to share.

There was a time when unforeseen consequences, those calamities of life, nearly made me quit writing. But when I searched some unknowable place within me, I discovered a passion that would not be ruled.

Over the past twenty years, I've seen promising writers fall time and time again. From that I learned when people are pushed to exchange their passion for the false solace of lowering their expectations, we all lose.

Chapter Thirty-Two

Perseverance

All that winter, the world would not stop even a moment that I might rest. I wrote knowing if I were not able to find my own way in the world, there were none who would suffer my care; there was a frenzy upon me combined with the thrill of composition. So I found my purpose that winter. If my writing could help just one person refuse to accept limits imposed by life, I'd have made my contribution to history. If my words caused the world to give women an education they need to reach their goals, I'll have made a difference. And if I might help erase the traditions and policies that push women to insist on less, I shall have achieved my goal. Percy, Father, Mother, even Byron settled for no less.

But then it was tedious to express concepts but dimly glimpsed. My work proceeded but slowly.

If Bath denies me companionship, I'll employ a strategy that served me to keep away *ennui* before. I will learn something of value. Through inquiry I find a tutor, one able to ignore my reputation, and begin a course in advanced Latin. For comparative reading, I choose Robert Southbey's translation of Amadis of Gaul. And music, and discussions. The good citizens of Bath cannot bar me from attending such concerts and lectures that are open to the public, though they tried. I grow accustomed to the whispering that attends my entrance.

But when I ignore them, the Biddies of Bath step up their efforts to make me uncomfortable. Their gossip is vicious.

"Shelley is frequently in the company of two women." "They live as in a bohemian commune." "Impossible to tell who belongs with whom." "We are forced to tolerate a public display of the potentate and his harem."

As the child of my Mary Wollstonecraft and William Godwin, I assumed my life would inevitably lead to greatness. I expected to be a philosopher, but expectation depends on persistent and generous support to create a place where soaring greatness can occur. Now, such support has left me. My Father, Baxter, Percy—none of them are near me in this dark winter.

Gentle England says women must be the property of men who have the responsibility for their care and must be compensated by their subjugation. That I reject, and I know this rejection colors my writing. And so, as I write away the troubled hours working on my little book, I conceive my creature as bounded by others' perceptions, others' expectations even as women are.

Percy returns from his solicitor with a thoughtful mien. "Remember the story we invented for our time in Switzerland with Byron?"

"That we share your name?"

"That is it. I think we need not continue to pretend we are married, my love. That fiction has outlived any purpose."

My heart falls.

He steps forward and holds me. "Think, how if it were real?"

"Percy?" My throat is so tight.

"I am asking you to be my wife in the eyes of the law, Mary. Will you?"

My eyes are overflowing. "Tomorrow, or any time you will," I stammer.

"Good. The wedding will be just a formality, but it will help me in court more than I can say."

"A formality?" I lift my eyes to his. "Do you propose we speak false vows? While I'll have no government, secular or sacred, tell me when, who, or how to love, I shall not accept a sham marriage."

He misunderstands. "I mean, do not think of marriage as violating your belief that you are still independent. My solicitors tell me it improves my chances to gain custody of my children should I be settled as a married man."

"Well and good, but I'll not commit a fraud for the courts. I warn you, do not take vows if you have no intent of keeping them."

We are wed at the end of December, in St. Mildred's.

When I send around to our friends and family the news, to my joy, Father responds saying he will attend the wedding. On the day, I look up to see him walking through the doors of the church toward us. Father has grown older. His cares have turned him gray in the two years since I last saw him.

"Great good luck to the two of you," he says to Percy, shaking his hand. He looks at me. "I hope she is no longer as rebellious of family authority as she once was." When he walks me through the kirkyard before the ceremony he says, "You appear somewhat more mature, but appearances are oft deceiving."

"Believe what you will, Father. I know those who have forsaken me from those who have not."

He snorts in derision. "As I remember it, you abandoned me. Still, I urge you to remember your obligations. Invite to your husband to attend a salon later in the month. I wish to make his renewed financial support known."

Ah, now I know why someone with so jaundiced a view of marriage came. He cares about the money and luster Percy will add to him.

Thomas Peacock steps up to give us congratulations. I think he means to be comforting when he says, "Marriage may often be a stormy lake, but celibacy is almost always a muddy horse pond."

"...and forsaking all others, cleave only to you," and Percy says, "I do."

He did say it.

On the subject of hypocrisy, upon learning of our marriage, Byron writes to Percy accusing him of forsaking his philosophy.

"It matters little," Percy says, showing me George's letter. "I shall tell him our marriage is but a matter of convenience and my principals as to free love remain untouched."

"Claire will be glad to hear it."

He turns and gazes intently at me, but I school my face and so betray nothing of my thoughts. "I must also reassure Claire of my love, lest she feel the urge to act upon being entirely abandoned."

I nod curtly. "We do not need another suicide laid at our feet."

"Does she still write to George?"

"Often and with passion, but he does not answer her letters."

"I wish he would at least give her hope."

"She has hope," I gaze out the window, "because that is all she has."

Percy is in London more and more often. He presents himself to the courts as a married, settled poet of renown well prepared to take care of his children. "Bring those darlings to our home soon," I write.

Claire does not help me feel gentle toward her. Whenever she sees William she teases him, saying when his father brings home his children, William will lose his status as eldest son. "You must learn to sit quietly when they speak. You shall lose your preeminence and be helped third at the table." She slides her eyes to mine and says, "I remember when your mother had to learn that lesson."

Two can playact. My eyes open wide, my mouth as well, in the very semblance of astonishment. "I never learned that lesson, Sister. I only let Stepmother think I had been properly schooled."

Claire delivers a child on 12 January, fortunate for me as it gives her something to do other than irritate me. She calls her daughter Clara Alba, but the name lasts no longer than it takes for letters to be exchanged with Geneva.

> *I wish my daughter be named for my sister. You may retain the name Clara, if you wish. As Percy is adamant about declaring me the father, on whatever papers you deem necessary, you must write the name, Clara Allegra Gordon in honor of my sister.*

There can be no question of her parentage to any who know Byron. With her high, round forehead and small, straight nose she is the very image of her father. She resembles him even in the way she gazes at the world as though she is a creature of higher state than those who change her swaddling clothes.

Chapter Thirty-Three

The World Turns Again

That was the winter Percy wrote to me saying, "I have found friends with whom I may stay…"

———————————◇———————————

Hours of writing do not tire me enough to sleep. Through long nights, I wonder whether Percy would leave me? I determine to be of value to Percy though he is away. He has found lodgings with a friend and editor, Leigh Hunt, and his wife, in Hampstead, outside of London. I felt I might inquire if I could alleviate some of the burden of his care from them.

> *Dear Mrs. Hunt:*
>
> *Dare I say, Marianne? I feel you and your husband are so kind*
> *to my Percy; I would eschew formality.*
>
> *I do hope this finds you and your household well. Knowing Percy's*
> *habits as I do, I wanted you to know I would be most pleased to*
> *assist with the care of my husband.*
>
> *I am so sorry for my husband's thoughtlessness at the skills of*
> *being a guest. If you wish to send his dirty laundry by return*
> *post, I shall launder it and send it back…*

January proves difficult for me. My little book grows into its second draft. I read voraciously, but every day I wish for Percy's voice, and each night I ache for his touch. I would my letters held more cheer for Percy and less my own worry.

In mid-month, even though he is wrapped in law, there arrives a gift: I am sent for.

> *Your letters are so sad, my love. The way you dwell on Fanny*
> *and Harriet weighs upon my heart. I am living now with my*
> *new editor, Leigh, his wife Marianne, and her sister north of the*
> *city. They say there is more than enough room for you here, so*
> *do you come and stay by my side.*

Unfortunately I leave his letter in my room, in the drawer of my night stand, under a book, where anyone could find it. One day when she visits, Claire stumbles on it.

"Oh, I am more than willing to leave," she exclaims. "Let us leave as soon as our luggage may be packed."

"Sister!" I'm aghast. "And what would George say if his child became ill on the rough roads."

She slumps in defeat. "Write to me as often."

"I shall my dear. I shall."

And so in the waning week of the two-faced month I sojourn to Hampstead where the Hunts have a cottage, cottage being a most humble term for what awaits me.

From the seat of my carriage, I see their cottage as built in two stories of light brown stone and surmounted by at least five chimneys. A wide building standing in defiance of the Window Tax, it must be bright with sun inside. When the road leads me around the front, I see a red door set into an ornate sill with neat grounds, surrounded by a stout fence of vertical posts.

But if the house is firm and substantial, I cannot say the same for the slim, tiny woman with glinting dark eyes and hair in black ringlets who leaves off tending her winter garden to meet my carriage. Marianne Kent Hunt holds out her arms to me as I descend. In addition to owning a wisp of a figure she has a voice that caresses.

"Most welcome. I hear you write more than letters about laundry."

"I do." I shrug. "Little published, but perhaps one day, soon."

"Here you may find all the quiet and all the peace a writer could desire." A shrill shriek shatters the air. She shrugs and smiles. "Whatever peace that is left by the children."

That quickly, I am enchanted with her.

"I think they are in Leigh's study." she leads me past her four rollicking children toward a room in the back of the cottage. Percy and Leigh sit together in the sparse room decorated with many tables and two overstuffed green-and-white striped chairs near a window. They are speaking in earnest about some piece that wants critique as we enter, but the moment he sees me, Percy rises and comes to me, kissing me. I blink once, but if this is a home where convention could be thus flouted, who am I to demur? I open to him, thrilling in feeling myself once more in his arms.

"When you are quite through," comes a soft but curiously deep voice, "please allow me to meet this exquisite creature."

Leigh Hunt, handsome as a man may be and dark enough to call exotic, stands slightly taller than my husband. Ducking his head with his face tilted slightly to the side, he uses his most penetrating eyes to full advantage, looking directly into mine. I notice he is wearing a silk dressing robe and slippers though it is past noon. I think this is a home where ideas reign and convention is put to flight. *Yes, here I shall find the stimulus to write.*

He smiles thoughtfully as he leans back in his chair. "Could you but know the poetry with which your husband describes you, your learning, your ability not just to follow his thought, but to range far afield from his and," he tilts his head, "the way he describes your beauty and passion."

"Percy is given to hyperbole."

"Do I exaggerate?" Percy protests from his seat next to Marianne. "I did but compare you to the dawn above the Alps."

Marianne stops to examine my face. "If anything, you are more beautiful than he told." But then turning to her plate again, she says, "I simply have to do something about my jealousy."

I chuckle. "I promise to give you no cause."

"Pish. I have a sister who gives me cause a-plenty." She sighs. "I understand we have a similar problem. My younger sister is in love with Leigh, and he with her, so what can I do?" she says with a naughty grin, inviting me to join in a conspiracy.

Oh my. Are these like minds regarding love and propriety? Her encouragement to be indiscrete is irresistible. "Only one? I have two who would gladly take my place." I pause and my lips tighten. "Had."

She reaches for my hand and gently enfolds my fingers in hers. "Percy told us of Fanny. I'm so sorry for your loss."

Leigh tries to recapture our former mood. "Percy's description of your commitment to your parents' philosophies is rare in a day when children seek to cast off the teaching of the hearth."

One day, I set aside my pen and blow out a long breath. *How the words leap from the page, and how trenchant their meaning!*

"Percy, listen to me a moment, I've a thought about my story. Suppose I erase all the history of Elizabeth being Victor's sister? I've so many lines showing their love, the problem of incest becomes insurmountable. But should I insert only a few lines, I can create her anew as an orphan raised in the home with Victor and only called 'Sister' as a courtesy. This way I may retain their intimacy and allow them to marry without causing even the Biddies of Bath to blush."

Percy thinks a moment, and he slowly smiles. "What a device! 'Twill serve."

I sit back and breathe in contentment, stroking my lips with the feathered end of my quill. "I can scarce credit there could be a world that holds such joy as writing. Here, here is art! Is this what you experience when you put ink to paper?"

"There are times when my pen draws fire from the stars." He smiles gently upon me. "I give you joy at finding such a moment."

The next day when I read over the manuscript, I wail, "It is trash! Oh, Percy, what made me think I could write?"

There is that same gentle smile. "Just needs more thought. Persevere. All will be well." He kisses my head.

I blow my lips like a horse, reach for another sheet and sharpen yet another quill. "Can we not afford one of those new pens like Leigh showed us, one with a steel nib?"

"Do you think your words deserve it?"

"Beast!

Spring arrives with its rain one day and warming sun the next. I continue to write toward my goal. Within this work, I find more than I ever sought. I put up my quill, rise from my desk, and stop to look at the ink stains on my fingers in a kind of wonder. The sound of the fire snaps softly through the house, and I follow it. By the light of an early morning in summer, soft and cerulean, seeping into the room, I see Percy reading my pages by the light of the flames. He looks up, sensing me standing watching him.

"Do you have any idea how exciting this is?" I squeak.

He nods. "I believe I do." His smile sends a rush of sentiment that builds upon what I feel at this moment, and so I say, "Everything I have seen and done and the people I have known are present for me when I write."

"It will ever be thus," he says tenderly. "I've not known a writer who lived in the shallows. We tend to swim in the deeps."

"Then listen to what I'm writing today. You know, much like Coleridge's Rime, I've set my tale upon a boat in distress." I take a breath.

"Ship. It must be large if it is capable of so long a voyage."

"No matter. *The ship* is trapped in the ice of the far north. But here is something new. I conceive of another character who will lend stability to my story. Instead of the reader jumping between the point of view of Victor Frankenstein and that of his monster, I shall have a polar explorer..." I go quiet a moment, thinking of a teacher I once knew. "A natural philosopher, I think, narrate the piece, d'ye see it? I'll name him Robert Walton. But the genius is in this. Having Robert for a narrator allows me to construct a frame for my story with the location aboard his ship in the far north at both the beginning and the end."

"You ought to break his narration into sections, lest the reader become bored with only a single voice and a single response."

"I have thought of that." My voice holds a note of triumph. "As a device to give my audience another view, I shall insert a series of letters to Robert Walton from his sister."

"Elizabeth?"

"Not her, that's Victor's supposed sister. Robert's sister. I'll name her Margaret. He keeps her letters when he sails and reads them from time to time during his voyage. This has the additional benefit of lengthening my narrative. She will make Robert aware of his own o're-reaching ambition to explore. It is she who will help him understand that the quest of life is neither for glory, nor justice, nor knowledge, but the love of those we love."

Percy thinks for so long a time, I wonder if his mind has gone from me to wherever his own imagination creates poetry. At last he shakes himself and says, "And echo Victor's ambitions as well. Are you sure you are but nineteen? I've known writers with many years and many publications who cannot think in such depth."

What he says pleases me, and I offer a small smile in recognition of the pretty compliment. But I am not done; in the fore of my brains are ideas that will out. "Thus do I layer my story through several people in such a way that allows the reader see what others think of the events they relate. I'll have it be a story within a story.

"This man, Robert, the master of the ship, is also the leader of a scientific expedition when he witnesses a race. First, a giant in a sled pulled by dogs passes the ship. That man is followed by Victor. But the scientist is *in extremis* and throws himself upon Robert and pours out his tale of horror as his final act."

"Very like my own dialogs."

"Do you think? This will give me scope in the telling to use another device, a journal. It ought to enhance the anticipation for the audience to hear someone reading of horrific acts."

"Lay on. Let me know if I can help."

I kiss him and, skipping out, I call over my shoulder, "Much to do, love!" I throw a cape over my shoulders. "I'm going for a walk and a bit of thinking."

Chaos greets me when I return. Marianne's sister has returned.

"Elizabeth! How can you be so foolish?" I hear Marianne bellow. The children standing or sitting in attitudes of huddled retreat speak volumes about how long such arguments have ruled in this house. I glance toward the shut door of Leigh's study where Leigh is standing, listening.

"Look in a mirror!" Elizabeth screams.

"Leigh?" I whisper.

Leigh looks up, his mouth clenched and his eyes turned down at the corners. *Here is profound unhappiness.* "She arrived while you were gone and it took only a moment for the flames to burst. Take little notice, Mary. It's but a storm that will pass as always." Hours later, Elizabeth slams through the house and out. Marianne emerges a few moments later. "I fear dinner will be delayed. Cook says she can put together something cold now if we are hungry."

That night alone in our room, I tremble as I hold Percy.

"That was like when Claire and I fought."

"Very like." I feel him nod. "I remember."

"Oh Percy, please find us a house away from here."

"I dislike the idea of leaving a place where we find people who do not despise us." He puts his chin on top of my head. "If I do, shall Claire come with us?"

"I think our wrath is spent. There should no occasions for strife. Especially as she is fixated upon Byron."

It is worth a note in history that eight months later, when Marianne delivers her next child, a boy, she names him Percy Bysshe Shelley Leigh Hunt.

Chapter Thirty-Four

Pyrrhic Victory

Was it no more than persistence that I finished my story? Did I need something to do and my little book was at hand? Did I supplant the terror my life had become with a horror of my imagining?

Did it matter?

I am delivered of a child in May, a daughter, and in a sign of how much my relationship with my sister has improved, I name her Clara Everina. A beautiful daughter but, colicky from the first, she is not a delight. She does not eat enough, but I think she heals that place in my heart of the little girl I lost.

Through the autumn, I read sections of my book at salon after salon to gauge my audience's responses. I see their shudders. There are comments. They should have reviewed the work rather than condemned me for writing it. I see their abuse as the reluctance to accept a young girl as author of so gruesome a tale. "A woman writer ought tell of affairs of the heart and the hearth, not a story of such horrible imaginings that will incite nightmares."

"I'm thinking, if we wish to avoid the condemnation people have when they learn a woman can have such dark thoughts, we must create a fiction." Percy is looking out our front window as he thinks of a solution. "One time-tested solution: were we to say the idea came in a dream, people might more readily accept it."

"Because women are given to nightly terrors as a natural consequence of their gender?"

He misses my sarcasm.

"Just so." He smiles, thinking we are in agreement.

"I'll say it was one of your waking dreams then, but that is as far as I shall go to mollify them."

"Perhaps we might request author anonymity as well."

I clamp my mouth shut until I can bear the loss of another dream. "As you will." I let out a shaking breath.

He gazes at me judging my sorrows. "That will have to do."

My book will still be published, my words and ideas read.

Comes the day when I send my hideous progeny to publishers. "Go forth and prosper," I breathe over the pages. As Percy has written the foreword, people assume he is the author.

One passes on it.

> *We regret this work is less than acceptable for a house of our repute. We find it flawed in subject and mechanics; however, should you care to present us one of your new poems, we shall review that with pleasure.*

Another returns the work with nothing more than a note.

> *Rejected.*

Then, what joy. A publisher accepts the work. I hold the letter and turn to where Percy sits in the front room. "Lackington's wants it!"

They take the piece, agreeing to a small run of 500 copies using the cheapest paper and cover stock. As for pay, although I am denied an advance I am to have a share in the profits.

"It is your first work, Mary. They are a poor house and cannot spend much money on an unknown author," he murmurs in my ear.

I spin around and throw my arms around his neck. "Published! And be damned who does it! Look at the letter, I retain copyright." I look up at him with tears spilling over. "That ought to be of some use should there be another edition, shouldn't it?"

"Surely there will be." He kisses me.

A publisher's proof finds its way to our door in late September. I review it again, and again, making notes between the lines. Perhaps one more draft might have been a good idea. I meet with publisher to go over suggestions and emendations. Father accompanies me, "In order that the family name be upheld to the highest standards."

As we leave, he says, "I feel the book will reflect well on me, Mary." High praise indeed. I return to the house determined to dedicate the book to him.

Lackington's projects December as a target. From conception to publication takes a year and a half, more or less, of writing, edits, revisions and copying. As the wheel of time spins slowly through the end of autumn, I wonder if my pages will find favor with anyone.

Shortly after Christmas, Percy and I walk arm in arm to the booksellers' stall and see where my book is displayed in the front window. I watch a young man pick up a copy, but before I can speak, I overhear him say, "Perhaps if Percy Shelley wrote it, it might be worth a few evenings."

And then I hear the shop owner laugh with derision. "Shelley would not claim the work. His concubine wrote it."

"Wife," I say.

"And what would you know?" he snarls.

"I am Mary Godwin Shelley."

"And I," says Percy, "Am her husband."

The shopkeeper has the temerity to ask me to sign some copies.

I read the reviews: The Monthly Review calls it, "Uncouth and entirely amoral. Unrealistic."

George Gordon Lord Byron, I scarce believe it, secretly writes the most damning critique in the most-read magazine of literary critical review in all of England, *The Quarterly Review.*

a tissue of horrible and disgusting absurdity.

"Gads, Mary!" Percy says, reading the libel. "He's not forgiven you for keeping his name from it!"

"Petty man. More like for refusing his bed."

"It could be he's still upset about Claire."

I touch his arm. "Remember how you coerced his promise to support the baby? It could be that, and no more."

But Byron's criticism rebounds. As George himself says, "Infamy is still fame." There are those who buy a copy to see for themselves the source of the great man's defamation. Criticism aside, a thing is happening as more and more people read it.

Bad reviews are the lot of a writer, but there is the sweet with the sour. Sir Walter Scott, old friend of Family Godwin, likes it and writes a positive review, although he assumes Percy is responsible. I write a letter to him. "I had not wanted to reveal my identity out of respect for those who love me. There are few who's opinion means so much."

But most importantly of all, the people like it and buy all 500 copies, though I find publication fees equal sales profits. I do not see so much as tuppence for my work.

As to controversy, that sister of fame, my reputation grew and is still embroidered these many years later. Our little ménage à trois fuels as much speculation today as it did then. Foolish, but we were so very young and in love. There's a much-used excuse.

While the first printing looked to be the last, demand fueled need and, miraculum dei, *as if demand stimulated the printer like a jolt of Galvani's fluide* électrique, *a second printing was requested.*

And now a third.

I am resolved to take this chance in this edition to rein in the runaway editors who savaged my text, with Percy and my father foremost among those have added, or subtracted, or corrected my text.

And interpretation? Where are those who see the meaning behind my story? It is a simple enough message.

I know my father's rejection formed the crucible of my story. It was he who molded me, he who formed my mind, and he who cast me away, but it is a facile argument to say my book is about my father and me. There is far more to what shaped my words than petty writer's revenge. After all, I am the daughter of two of the greatest philosophers of our time and have lived with one of the greatest poets and learned from many others.

So this: my book is about the castigation by the ignorant, who refuse to listen to new and original ideas and seek to shame new thoughts by disparagement.

The fire mesmerizes me. I see myself, a very young and terribly serious girl, there in the flames. I breathe out as I stretch my hands toward the warmth. My skin grows tight and thin with age. Spots brown my knuckles and veins bulge on my wrists. I had such beautiful long, tapered fingers. I laugh at my ability to dissemble. Then, as now, my fingers were smeared black and crusted with ink underneath my nails.

I seek the flames again. Sure, there are those dear black smudges on her chin and nose, but something's amiss. She slumps and she places her hands over her face. I see her shoulders heaving as she cries.

I wish I could say all will be well. With every fiber in my being do I ache to tell her, you will be famous, and wealthy, and independent at last, and people will read your words and grow. Women shall be as free of the consequences from loving as are men, and men will be as aware of the responsibilities of creating life as women.

And, oh, with all my heart, I wish I could tell her her work will make a difference, for I know that is what she wants more than breath itself.

I so wish I could.

Author Bio

M. R. Arnold holds degrees in science, professional writing, journalism and communication. While a master's student at the the University of Missouri school of Journalism during the mid' 80s, a fascination with literary non-fiction led to using the techniques of Wolfe, Capote, and Thompson in feature assignments which led to selection as one of the top ten student science writers in the nation, and publication of non-fiction in several magazines.

Electing to study for a Ph.D. at the same university Timothy Leary attended, The University of Alabama in Tuscaloosa provided a wonderful chance to learn as much about research and the effects of communication as it taught about the human condition.

After more than a decade of teaching feature writing at the college and university level, the lure of writing fiction prompted early retirement. Today, once a month critiques for a west coast writing club, NightWriters in San Luis Obispo offers a way to give back to the local writing community. Twice recognized by Writers of the Future for novella length science fiction gave the confidence to begin this book. Monster, the story a Mary Shelley's early life represents five years of applying the skills of research, magazine feature story journalism and fiction writing.

Often citing that the best ideas occur during daily beach walks makes living on California's Central Coast a valued aspect of life.

CPSIA information can be obtained
at www.ICGtesting.com
Printed in the USA
BVOW08s1919090917
494433BV00001B/1/P